CREEPING

CREE

PING ™

story
MIKE RICHARDSON

script
ZACK KELLER

cover & line art
DOUG WHEATLEY

colors
RAIN BEREDO

letters
FRANK CVETKOVIC

DARK HORSE BOOKS

president & publisher
MIKE RICHARDSON

editor
MEGAN WALKER

collection designer
SKYLER WEISSENFLUH

digital art technician
ADAM PRUETT

Published by Dark Horse Books
A division of Dark Horse Comics LLC
10956 SE Main Street, Milwaukie, OR 97222

DarkHorse.com

Facebook.com/DarkHorseComics
Twitter.com/DarkHorseComics

To find a comics shop in your area, visit comicshoplocator.com

First edition: June 2022
Ebook ISBN 978-1-50672-489-8
Hardcover ISBN 978-1-50672-488-1

1 3 5 7 9 10 8 6 4 2
Printed in China

FSC www.fsc.org MIX Paper from responsible sources FSC® C169962

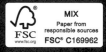

Library of Congress Cataloging-in-Publication Data

Names: Richardson, Mike, 1950- author. | Keller, Zack, author. | Wheatley, Doug, artist | Beredo, Rainier, colourist.
Title: Creeping / story, Mike Richardson ; script, Zack Keller ; art, Doug Wheatley ; colors, Rainier Beredo.
Description: Milwaukie, OR : Dark Horse Books, 2021.
Identifiers: LCCN 2021015119 | ISBN 9781506724881 (hardcover) | ISBN 9781506724898 (ebook)
Subjects: LCSH: Graphic novels.
Classification: LCC PN6727.R518 C75 2021 | DDC 741.5/973--dc23
LC record available at https://lccn.loc.gov/2021015119

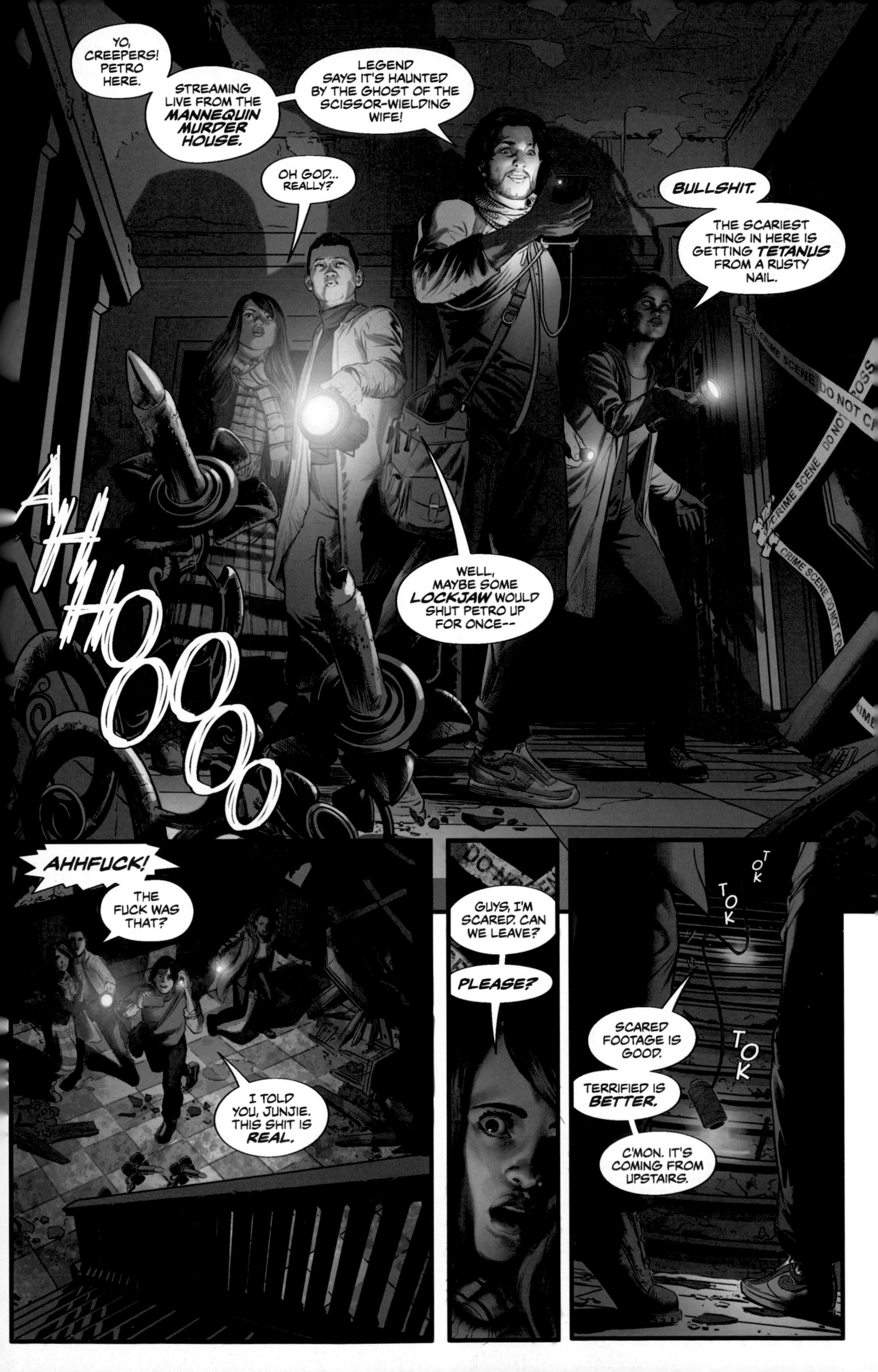
YO, CREEPERS! PETRO HERE.
STREAMING LIVE FROM THE ***MANNEQUIN MURDER HOUSE.***
LEGEND SAYS IT'S HAUNTED BY THE GHOST OF THE SCISSOR-WIELDING WIFE!
OH GOD... REALLY?
BULLSHIT.
THE SCARIEST THING IN HERE IS GETTING ***TETANUS*** FROM A RUSTY NAIL.
WELL, MAYBE SOME ***LOCKJAW*** WOULD SHUT PETRO UP FOR ONCE--
AHHOOOOO
AHHFUCK!
THE FUCK WAS THAT?
I TOLD YOU, JUNJIE. THIS SHIT IS ***REAL.***
GUYS, I'M SCARED. CAN WE LEAVE?
PLEASE?
TOK
TOK
SCARED FOOTAGE IS GOOD.
TERRIFIED IS ***BETTER.***
C'MON. IT'S COMING FROM UPSTAIRS.
TOK

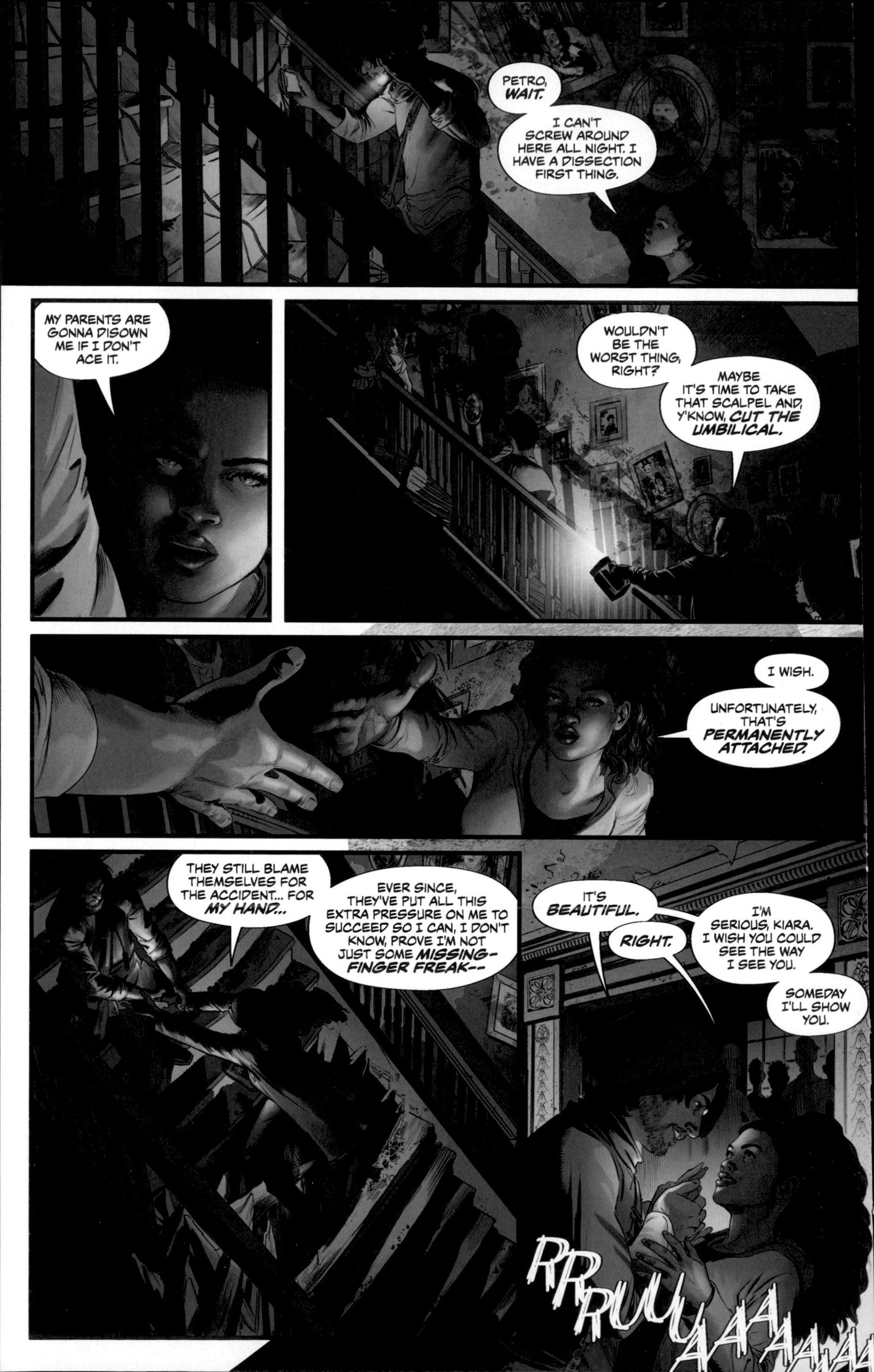

PETRO, **WAIT.**
I CAN'T SCREW AROUND HERE ALL NIGHT. I HAVE A DISSECTION FIRST THING.
MY PARENTS ARE GONNA DISOWN ME IF I DON'T ACE IT.
WOULDN'T BE THE WORST THING, RIGHT?
MAYBE IT'S TIME TO TAKE THAT SCALPEL AND, Y'KNOW, **CUT THE UMBILICAL.**
I WISH.
UNFORTUNATELY, THAT'S **PERMANENTLY ATTACHED.**
THEY STILL BLAME THEMSELVES FOR THE ACCIDENT... FOR **MY HAND...**
EVER SINCE, THEY'VE PUT ALL THIS EXTRA PRESSURE ON ME TO SUCCEED SO I CAN, I DON'T KNOW, PROVE I'M NOT JUST SOME **MISSING-FINGER FREAK--**
IT'S **BEAUTIFUL.**
RIGHT.
I'M SERIOUS, KIARA. I WISH YOU COULD SEE THE WAY I SEE YOU.
SOMEDAY I'LL SHOW YOU.
RRRUUAAAAAAA

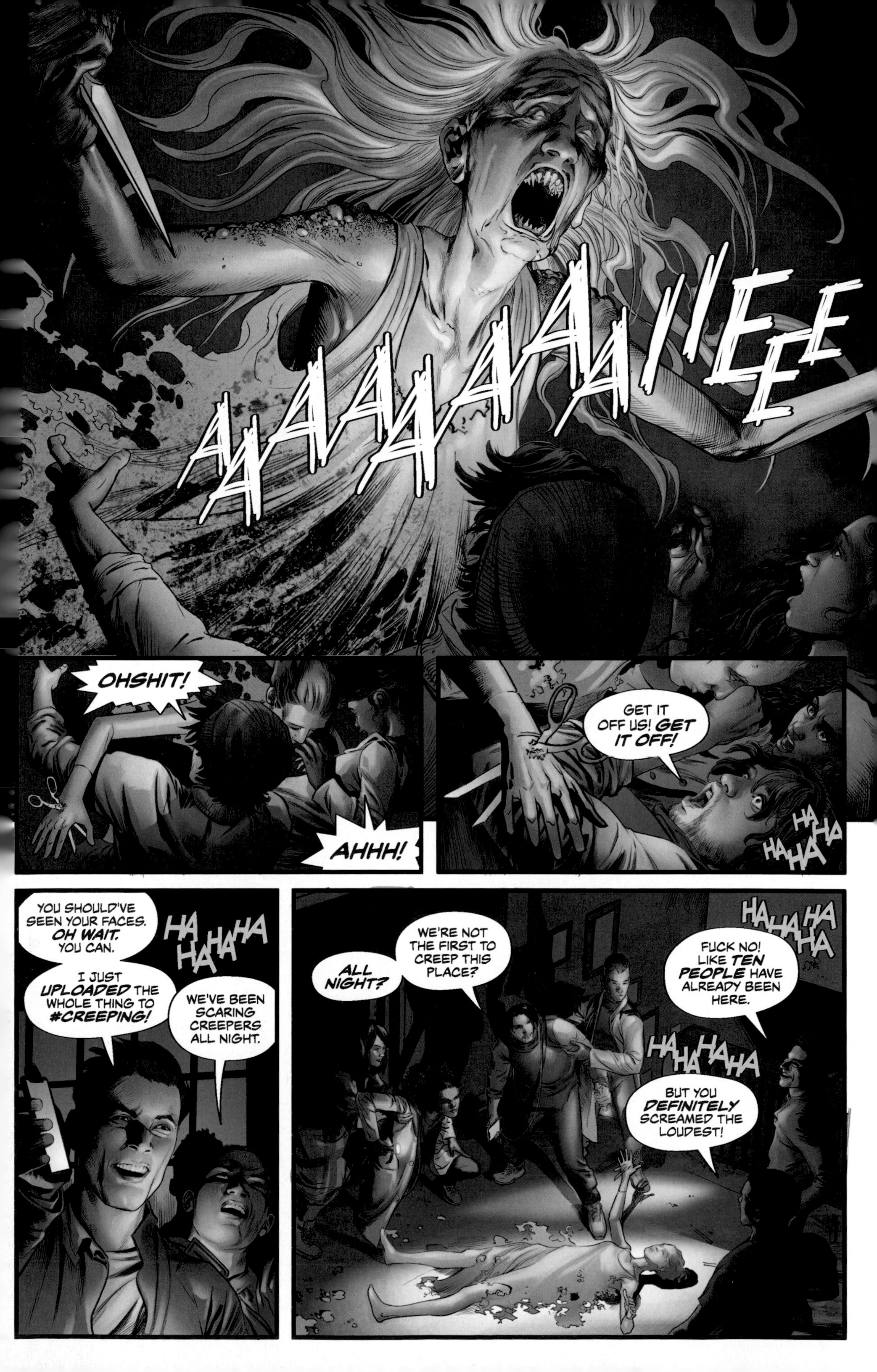
AAAAAAAAAIIEEE
OHSHIT!
AHHH!
GET IT OFF US! GET IT OFF!
HAHA HAHA
YOU SHOULD'VE SEEN YOUR FACES. OH WAIT. YOU CAN.
HA HAHAHA HA
I JUST UPLOADED THE WHOLE THING TO #CREEPING!
WE'VE BEEN SCARING CREEPERS ALL NIGHT.
ALL NIGHT?
WE'RE NOT THE FIRST TO CREEP THIS PLACE?
HAHAHA HA
FUCK NO! LIKE TEN PEOPLE HAVE ALREADY BEEN HERE.
HAHAHAHA
BUT YOU DEFINITELY SCREAMED THE LOUDEST!

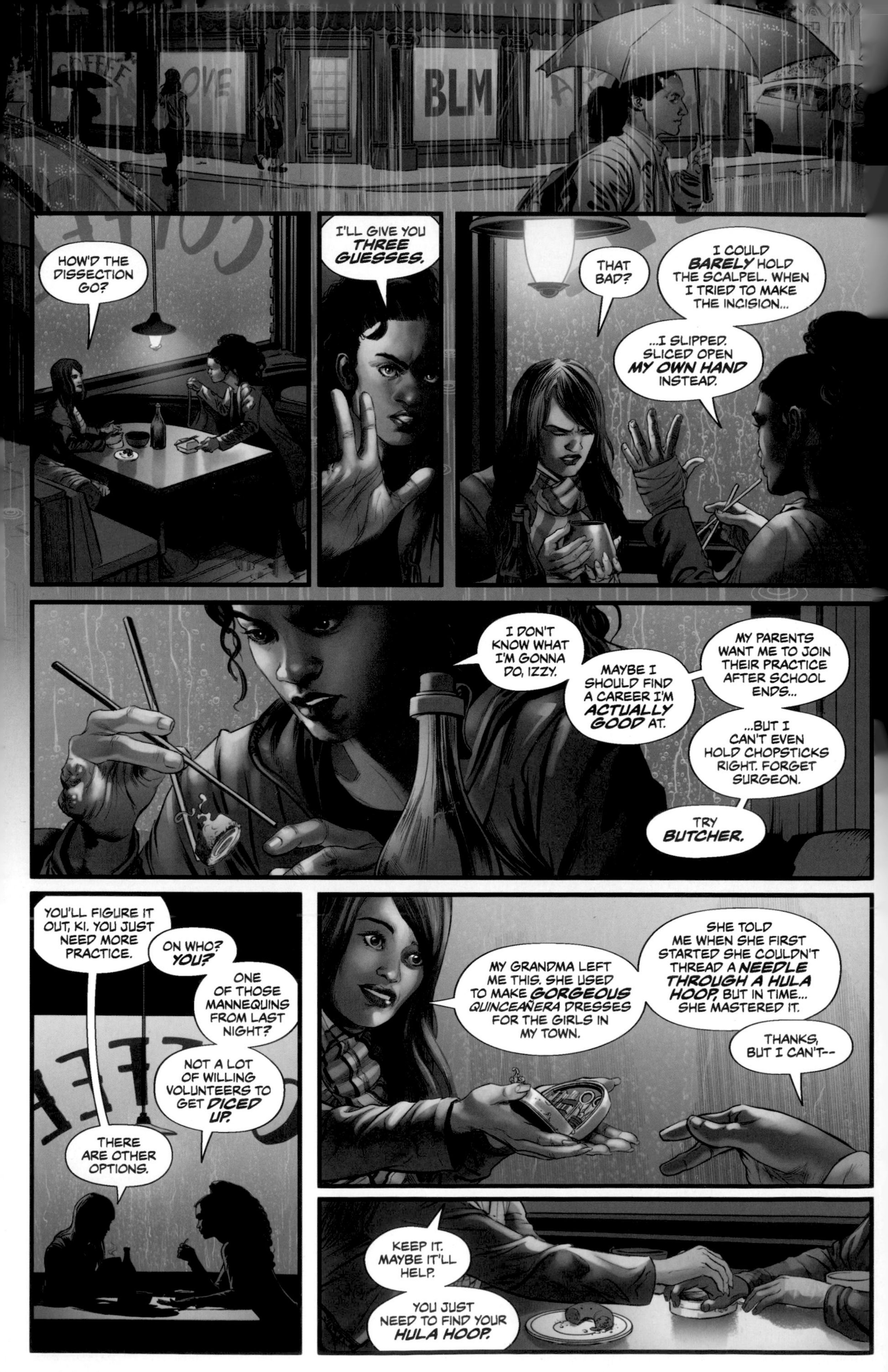
COFFEE
LOVE
BLM
HOW'D THE DISSECTION GO?
I'LL GIVE YOU THREE GUESSES.
THAT BAD?
I COULD BARELY HOLD THE SCALPEL. WHEN I TRIED TO MAKE THE INCISION...
...I SLIPPED. SLICED OPEN MY OWN HAND INSTEAD.
I DON'T KNOW WHAT I'M GONNA DO, IZZY.
MAYBE I SHOULD FIND A CAREER I'M ACTUALLY GOOD AT.
MY PARENTS WANT ME TO JOIN THEIR PRACTICE AFTER SCHOOL ENDS...
...BUT I CAN'T EVEN HOLD CHOPSTICKS RIGHT. FORGET SURGEON.
TRY BUTCHER.
YOU'LL FIGURE IT OUT, KI. YOU JUST NEED MORE PRACTICE.
ON WHO? YOU?
ONE OF THOSE MANNEQUINS FROM LAST NIGHT?
NOT A LOT OF WILLING VOLUNTEERS TO GET DICED UP.
THERE ARE OTHER OPTIONS.
MY GRANDMA LEFT ME THIS. SHE USED TO MAKE GORGEOUS QUINCEAÑERA DRESSES FOR THE GIRLS IN MY TOWN.
SHE TOLD ME WHEN SHE FIRST STARTED SHE COULDN'T THREAD A NEEDLE THROUGH A HULA HOOP, BUT IN TIME... SHE MASTERED IT.
THANKS, BUT I CAN'T--
KEEP IT. MAYBE IT'LL HELP.
YOU JUST NEED TO FIND YOUR HULA HOOP.

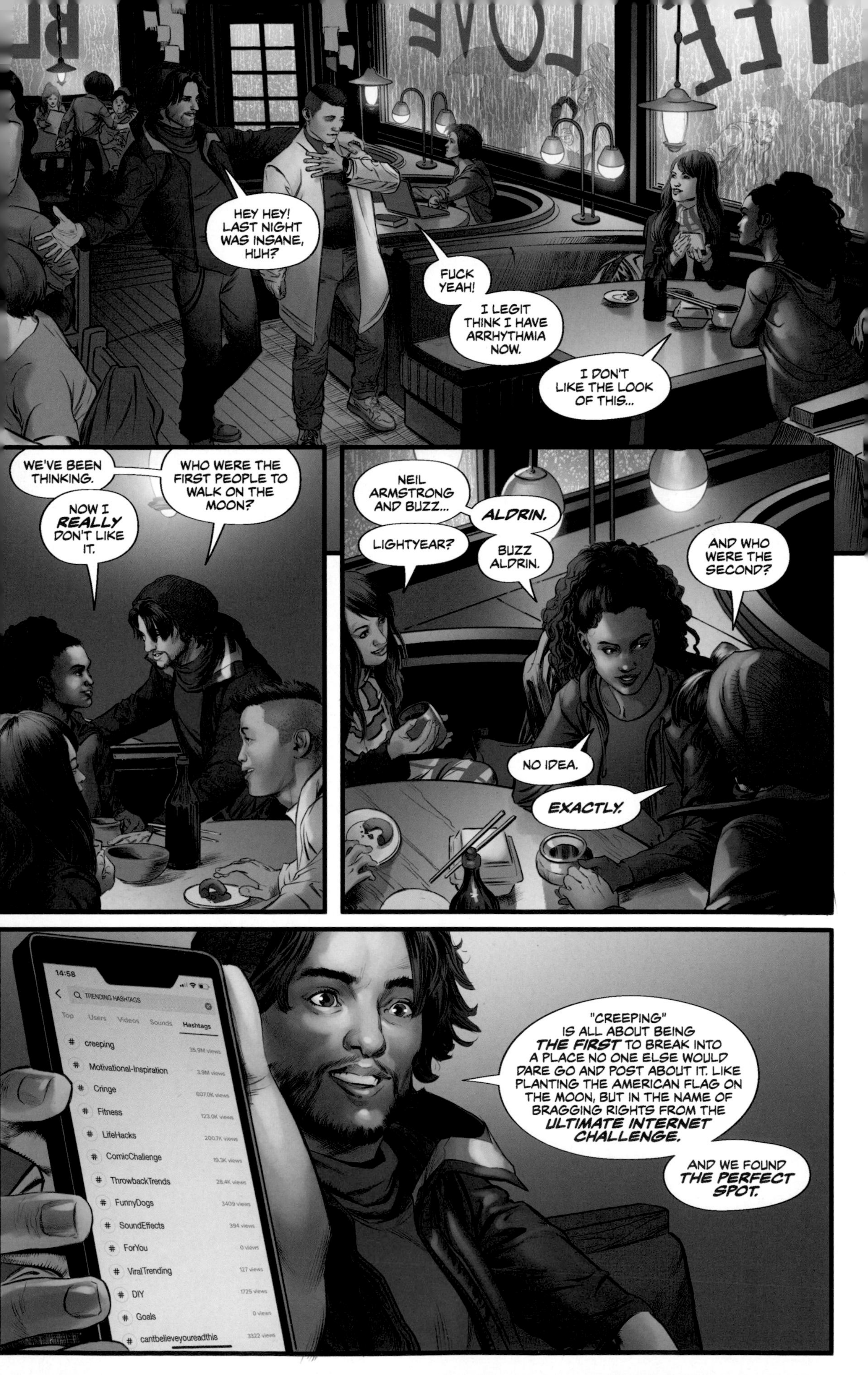
HEY HEY! LAST NIGHT WAS INSANE, HUH?
FUCK YEAH!
I LEGIT THINK I HAVE ARRHYTHMIA NOW.
I DON'T LIKE THE LOOK OF THIS...
WE'VE BEEN THINKING.
WHO WERE THE FIRST PEOPLE TO WALK ON THE MOON?
NOW I *REALLY* DON'T LIKE IT.
NEIL ARMSTRONG AND BUZZ...
ALDRIN.
LIGHTYEAR?
BUZZ ALDRIN.
AND WHO WERE THE SECOND?
NO IDEA.
EXACTLY.
14:58
TRENDING HASHTAGS
Top Users Videos Sounds Hashtags
creeping 35.9M views
Motivational-Inspiration 3.9M views
Cringe 607.0K views
Fitness 123.0K views
LifeHacks 200.7K views
ComicChallenge 19.3K views
ThrowbackTrends 28.4K views
FunnyDogs 3409 views
SoundEffects 394 views
ForYou 0 views
ViralTrending 127 views
DIY 1725 views
Goals 0 views
cantbelieveyoureadthis 3322 views
"CREEPING" IS ALL ABOUT BEING *THE FIRST* TO BREAK INTO A PLACE NO ONE ELSE WOULD DARE GO AND POST ABOUT IT. LIKE PLANTING THE AMERICAN FLAG ON THE MOON, BUT IN THE NAME OF BRAGGING RIGHTS FROM THE *ULTIMATE INTERNET CHALLENGE.*
AND WE FOUND *THE PERFECT SPOT.*

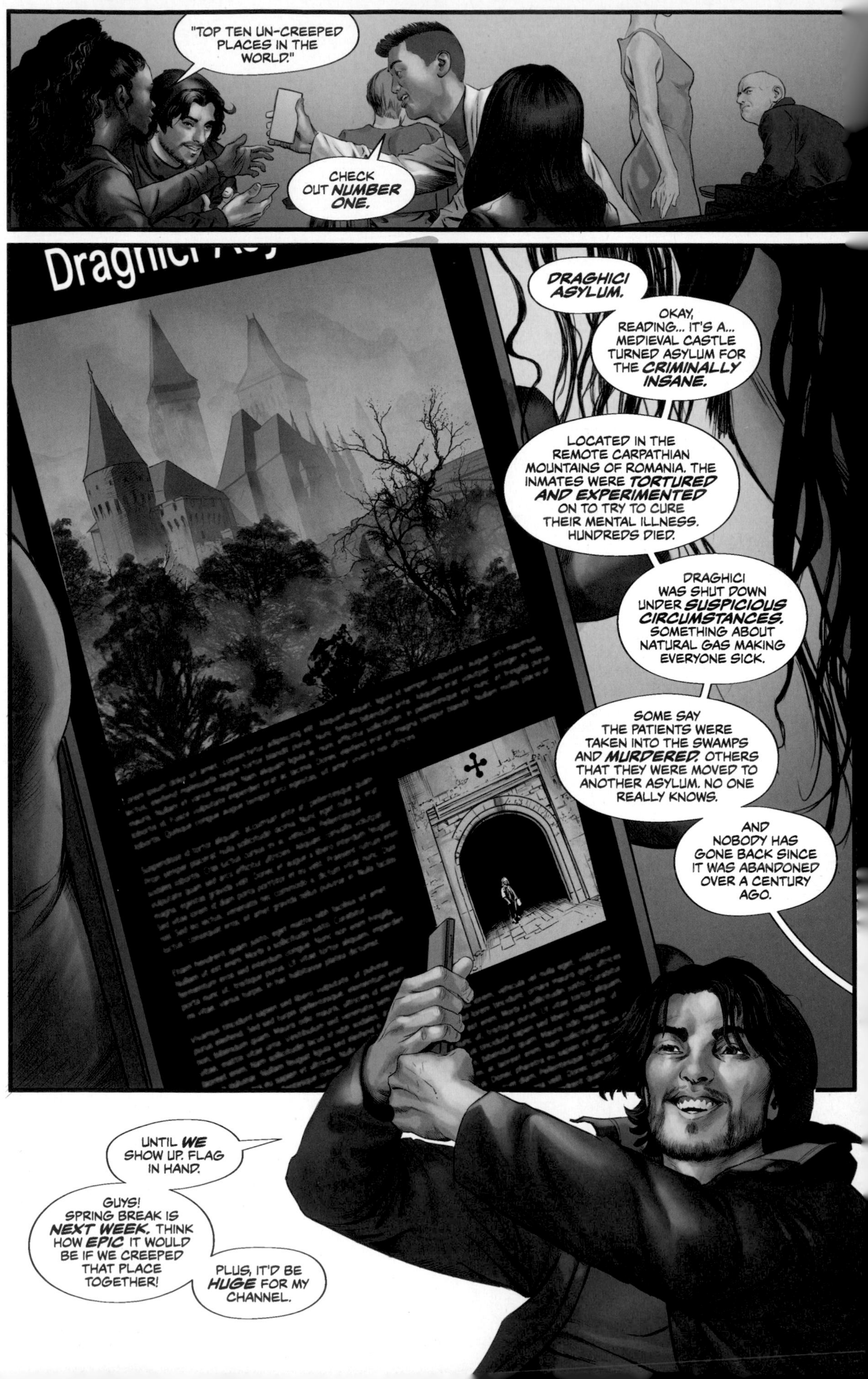

"TOP TEN UN-CREEPED PLACES IN THE WORLD."
CHECK OUT NUMBER ONE.
Draghici Asy
DRAGHICI ASYLUM.
OKAY, READING... IT'S A... MEDIEVAL CASTLE TURNED ASYLUM FOR THE CRIMINALLY INSANE.
LOCATED IN THE REMOTE CARPATHIAN MOUNTAINS OF ROMANIA. THE INMATES WERE TORTURED AND EXPERIMENTED ON TO TRY TO CURE THEIR MENTAL ILLNESS. HUNDREDS DIED.
DRAGHICI WAS SHUT DOWN UNDER SUSPICIOUS CIRCUMSTANCES. SOMETHING ABOUT NATURAL GAS MAKING EVERYONE SICK.
SOME SAY THE PATIENTS WERE TAKEN INTO THE SWAMPS AND MURDERED. OTHERS THAT THEY WERE MOVED TO ANOTHER ASYLUM. NO ONE REALLY KNOWS.
AND NOBODY HAS GONE BACK SINCE IT WAS ABANDONED OVER A CENTURY AGO.
UNTIL WE SHOW UP. FLAG IN HAND.
GUYS! SPRING BREAK IS NEXT WEEK. THINK HOW EPIC IT WOULD BE IF WE CREEPED THAT PLACE TOGETHER!
PLUS, IT'D BE HUGE FOR MY CHANNEL.

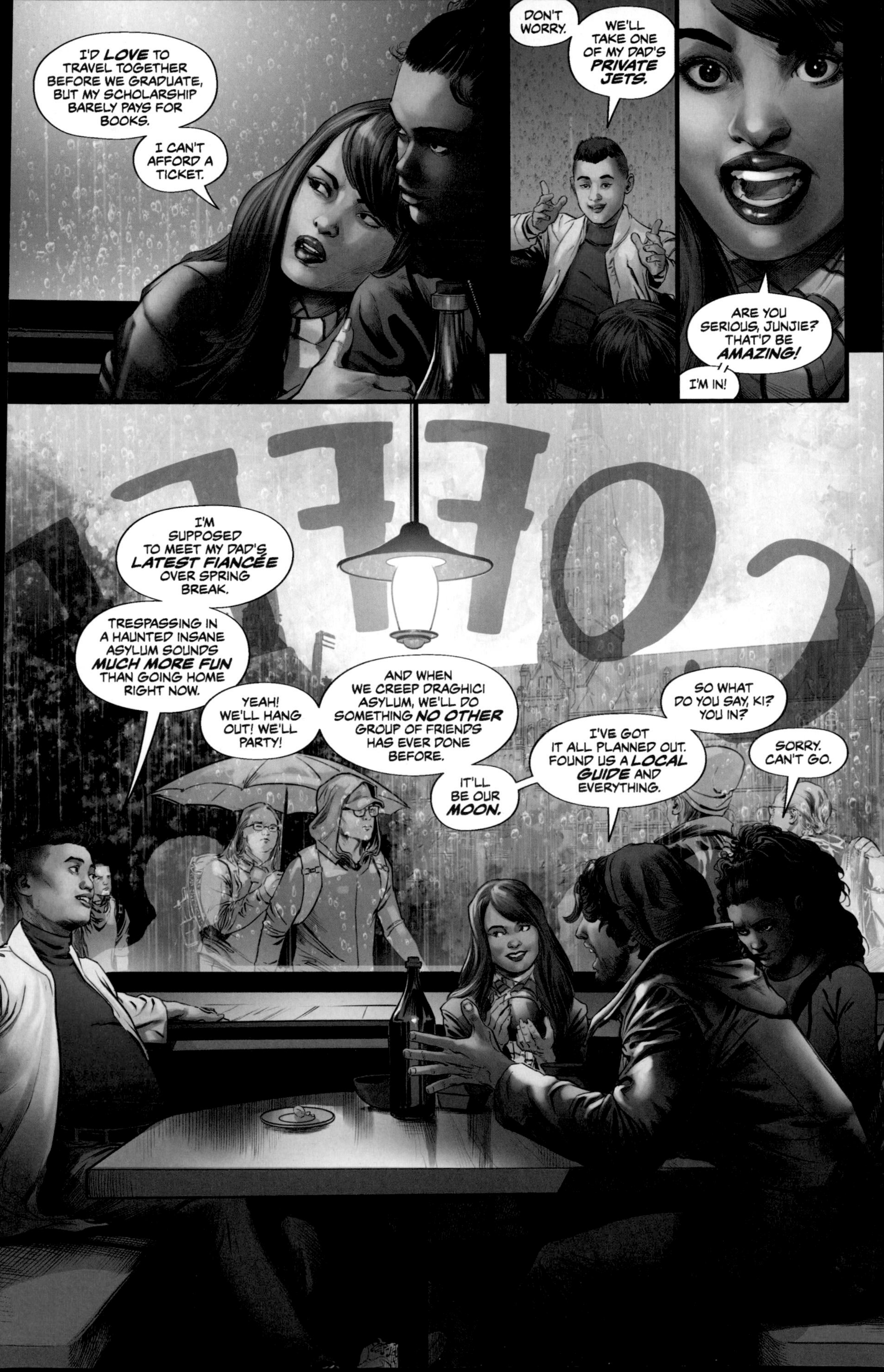
I'D LOVE TO TRAVEL TOGETHER BEFORE WE GRADUATE, BUT MY SCHOLARSHIP BARELY PAYS FOR BOOKS.
I CAN'T AFFORD A TICKET.
DON'T WORRY.
WE'LL TAKE ONE OF MY DAD'S PRIVATE JETS.
ARE YOU SERIOUS, JUNJIE? THAT'D BE AMAZING!
I'M IN!
I'M SUPPOSED TO MEET MY DAD'S LATEST FIANCÉE OVER SPRING BREAK.
TRESPASSING IN A HAUNTED INSANE ASYLUM SOUNDS MUCH MORE FUN THAN GOING HOME RIGHT NOW.
YEAH! WE'LL HANG OUT! WE'LL PARTY!
AND WHEN WE CREEP DRAGHICI ASYLUM, WE'LL DO SOMETHING NO OTHER GROUP OF FRIENDS HAS EVER DONE BEFORE.
IT'LL BE OUR MOON.
I'VE GOT IT ALL PLANNED OUT. FOUND US A LOCAL GUIDE AND EVERYTHING.
SO WHAT DO YOU SAY, KI? YOU IN?
SORRY. CAN'T GO.

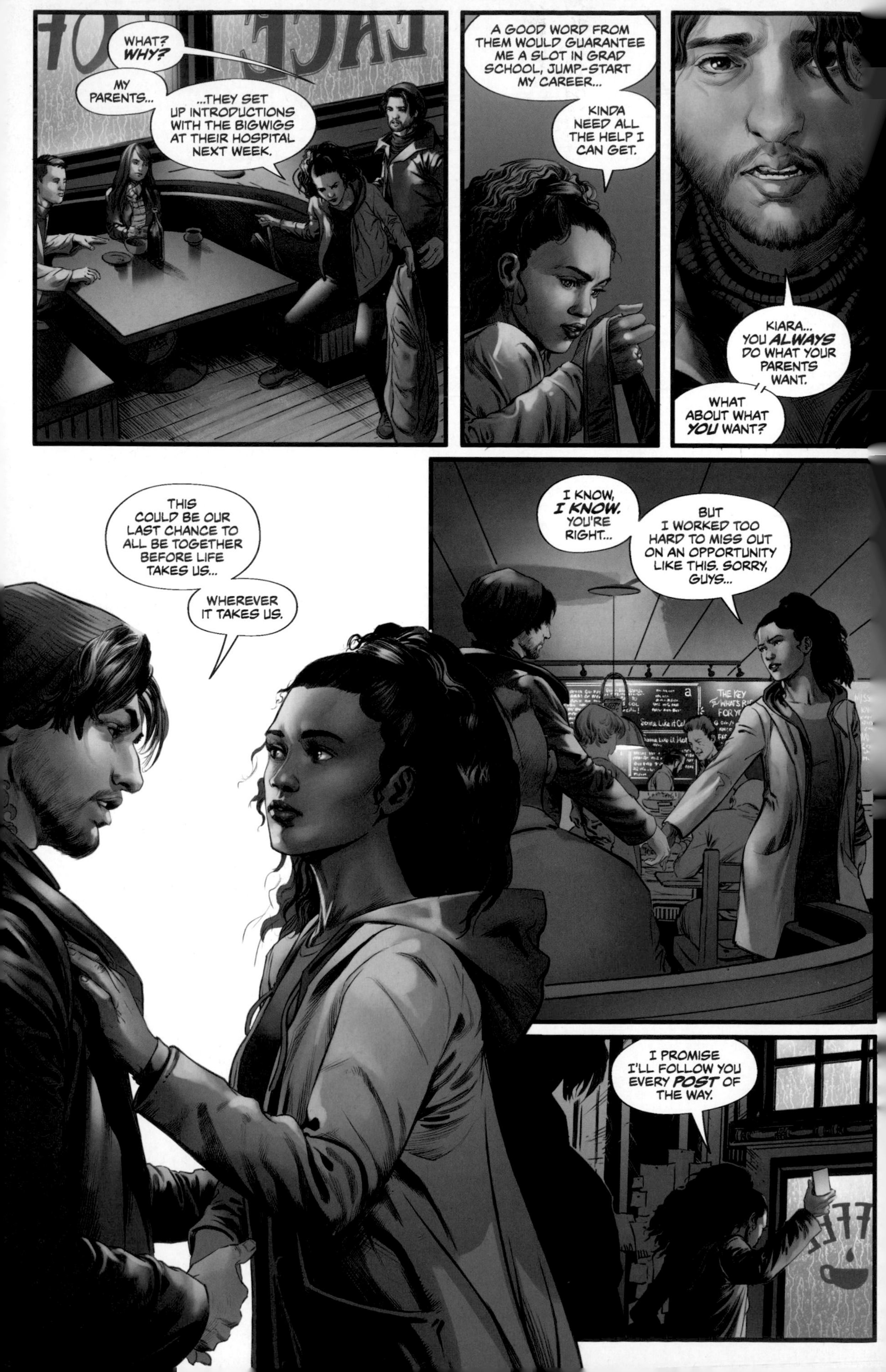
WHAT? WHY?
MY PARENTS...
...THEY SET UP INTRODUCTIONS WITH THE BIGWIGS AT THEIR HOSPITAL NEXT WEEK.
A GOOD WORD FROM THEM WOULD GUARANTEE ME A SLOT IN GRAD SCHOOL, JUMP-START MY CAREER...
KINDA NEED ALL THE HELP I CAN GET.
KIARA... YOU ALWAYS DO WHAT YOUR PARENTS WANT.
WHAT ABOUT WHAT YOU WANT?
THIS COULD BE OUR LAST CHANCE TO ALL BE TOGETHER BEFORE LIFE TAKES US...
WHEREVER IT TAKES US.
I KNOW, I KNOW. YOU'RE RIGHT...
BUT I WORKED TOO HARD TO MISS OUT ON AN OPPORTUNITY LIKE THIS. SORRY, GUYS...
I PROMISE I'LL FOLLOW YOU EVERY POST OF THE WAY.

THE NEXT DAY

BZZZ
BZZZ

Petro>

Today 03:00 PM

gonna be a long flight without you

BZZZ
BZZZ
BZZZ

Petro>

Today 03:00 PM

gonna be a long flight without you

gonna be a long week without you.

Kiara. Saw your flight was delayed. Too late for us to pick you up. Take Uber. Don't wake us.

Tomorrow's itinerary: Breakfast with Stanford Medical Center surgeons. Lunch with alumni donors. Dinner with hospital CEO.

M
Mom

hospital CEO.

Don't forget to wear your glove. We'll explain what happened AFTER they hear your accolades. Mom.

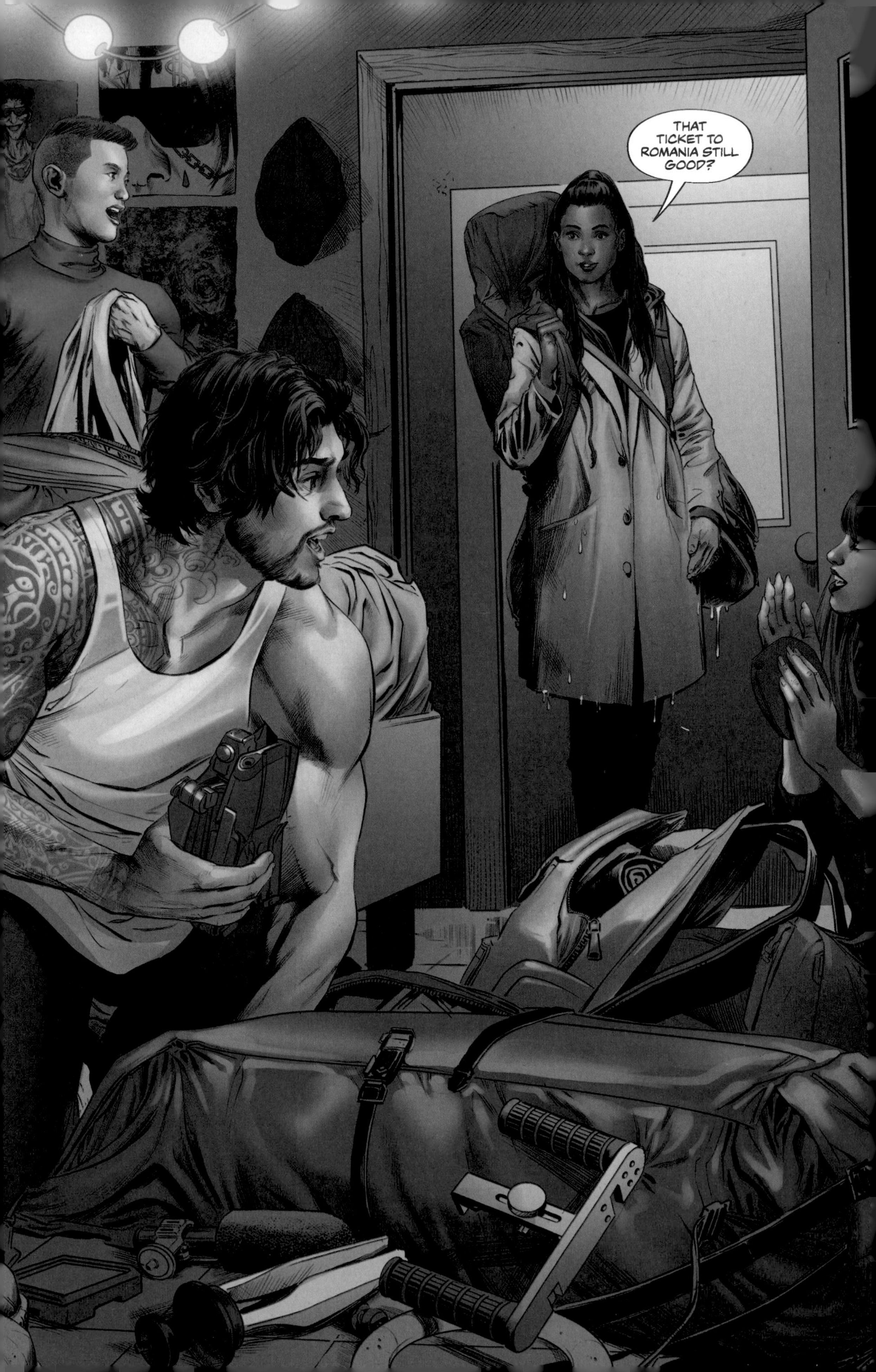
THAT TICKET TO ROMANIA STILL GOOD?

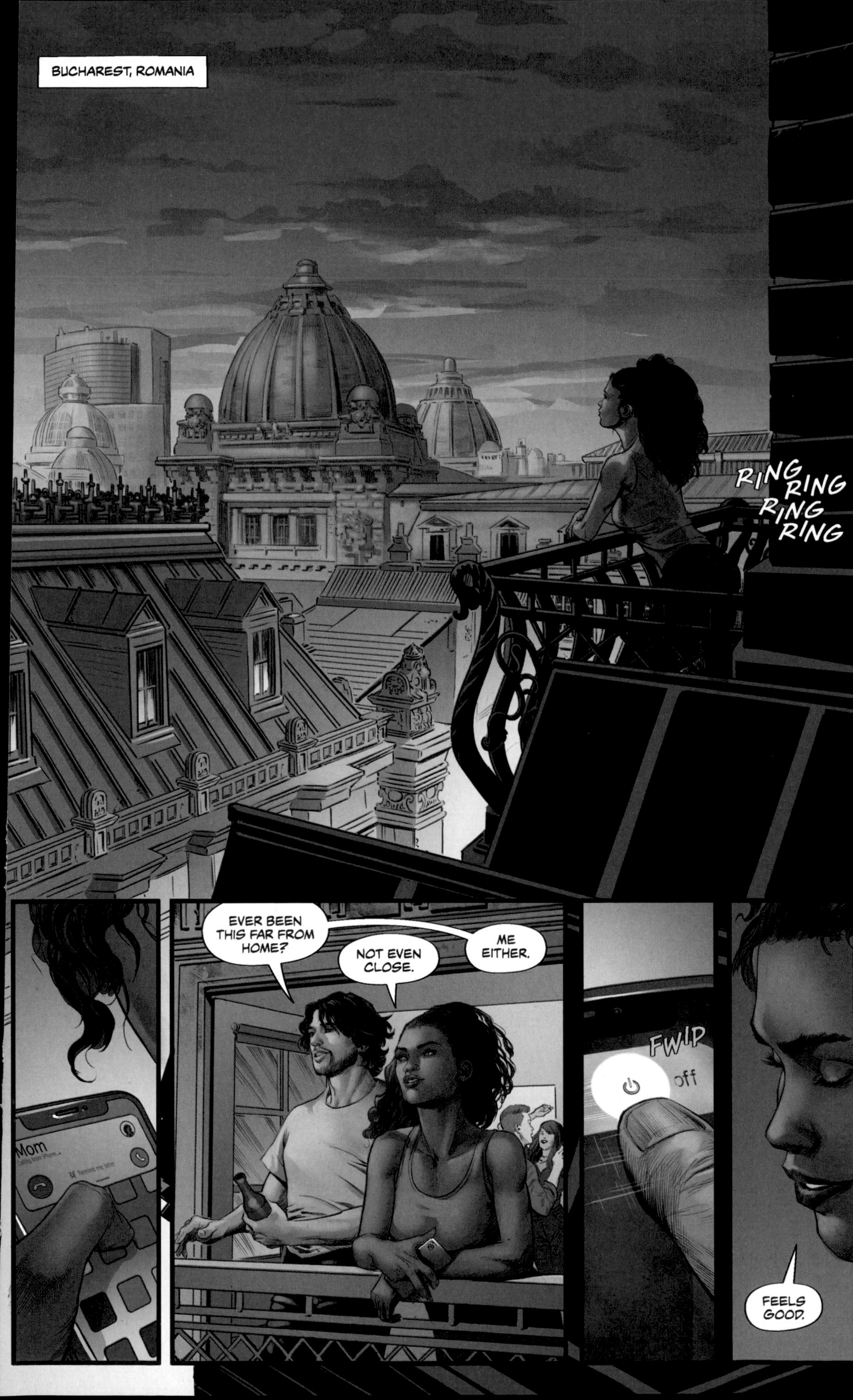
BUCHAREST, ROMANIA
RING RING RING RING
Mom
EVER BEEN THIS FAR FROM HOME?
NOT EVEN CLOSE.
ME EITHER.
FWIP
off
FEELS GOOD.

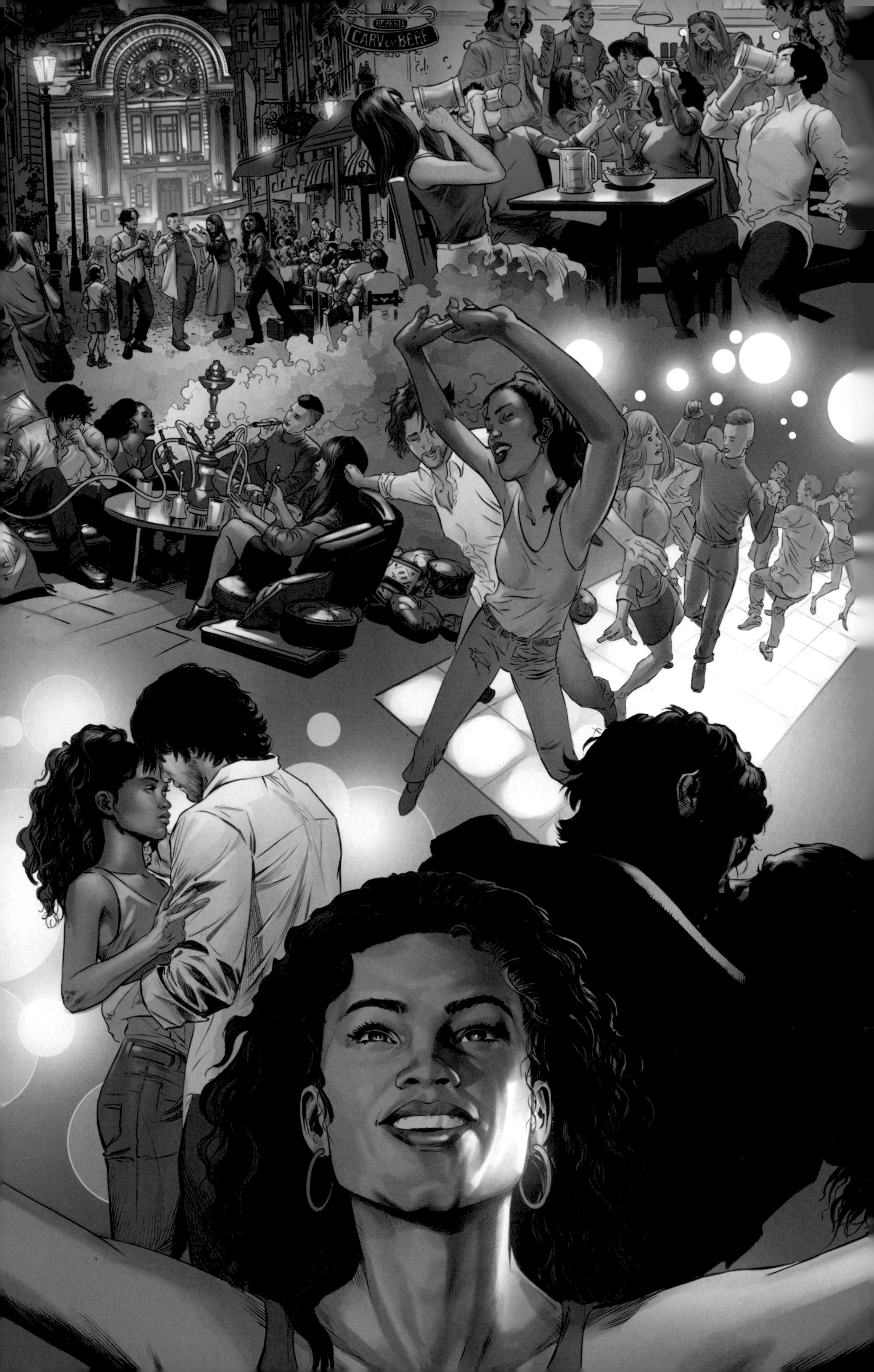
CARV CV BERE

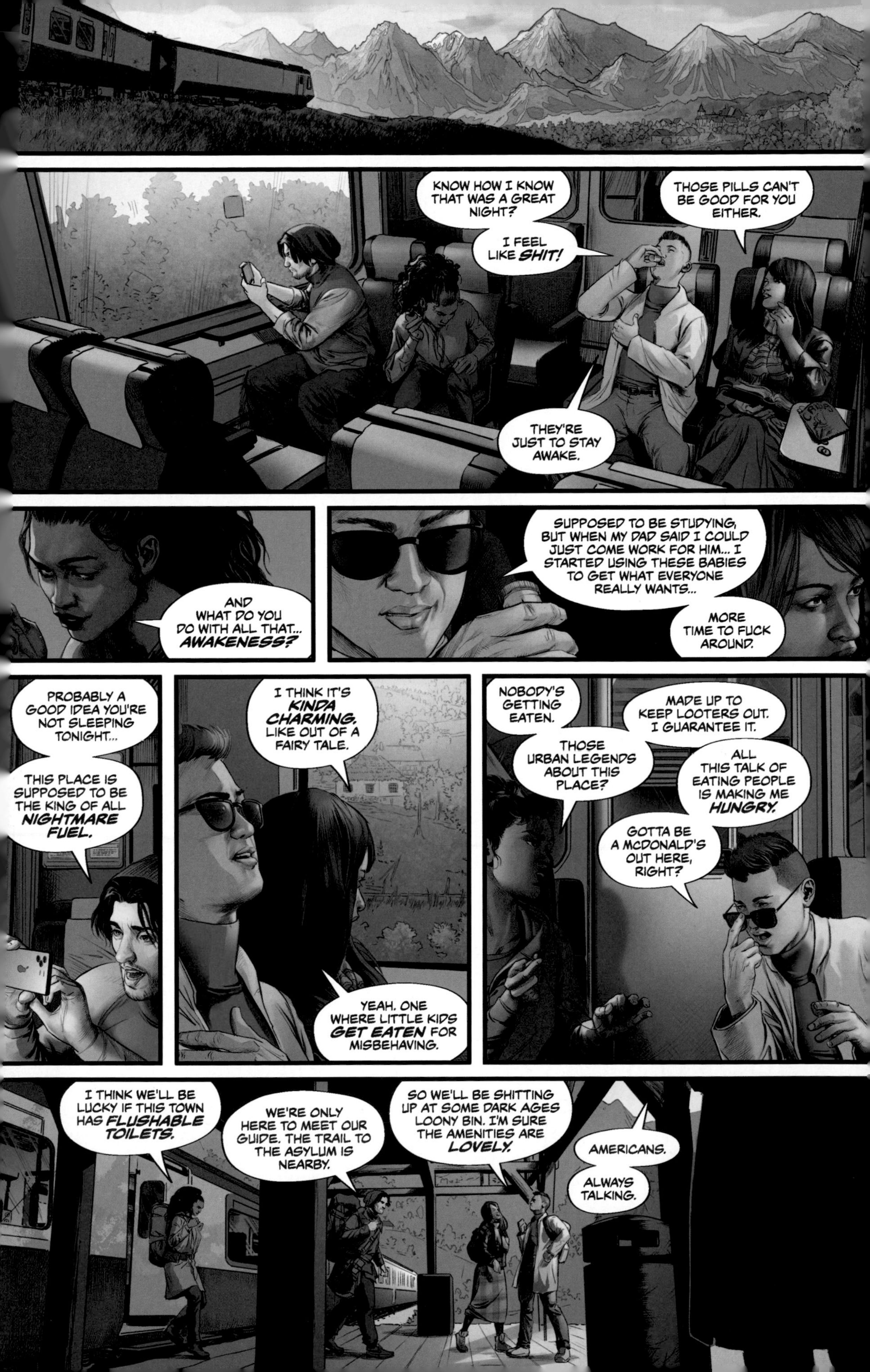
KNOW HOW I KNOW THAT WAS A GREAT NIGHT?
I FEEL LIKE SHIT!
THOSE PILLS CAN'T BE GOOD FOR YOU EITHER.
THEY'RE JUST TO STAY AWAKE.
AND WHAT DO YOU DO WITH ALL THAT... AWAKENESS?
SUPPOSED TO BE STUDYING, BUT WHEN MY DAD SAID I COULD JUST COME WORK FOR HIM... I STARTED USING THESE BABIES TO GET WHAT EVERYONE REALLY WANTS...
MORE TIME TO FUCK AROUND.
PROBABLY A GOOD IDEA YOU'RE NOT SLEEPING TONIGHT...
THIS PLACE IS SUPPOSED TO BE THE KING OF ALL NIGHTMARE FUEL.
I THINK IT'S KINDA CHARMING. LIKE OUT OF A FAIRY TALE.
YEAH. ONE WHERE LITTLE KIDS GET EATEN FOR MISBEHAVING.
NOBODY'S GETTING EATEN.
THOSE URBAN LEGENDS ABOUT THIS PLACE?
MADE UP TO KEEP LOOTERS OUT. I GUARANTEE IT.
ALL THIS TALK OF EATING PEOPLE IS MAKING ME HUNGRY.
GOTTA BE A MCDONALD'S OUT HERE, RIGHT?
I THINK WE'LL BE LUCKY IF THIS TOWN HAS FLUSHABLE TOILETS.
WE'RE ONLY HERE TO MEET OUR GUIDE. THE TRAIL TO THE ASYLUM IS NEARBY.
SO WE'LL BE SHITTING UP AT SOME DARK AGES LOONY BIN. I'M SURE THE AMENITIES ARE LOVELY.
AMERICANS.
ALWAYS TALKING.

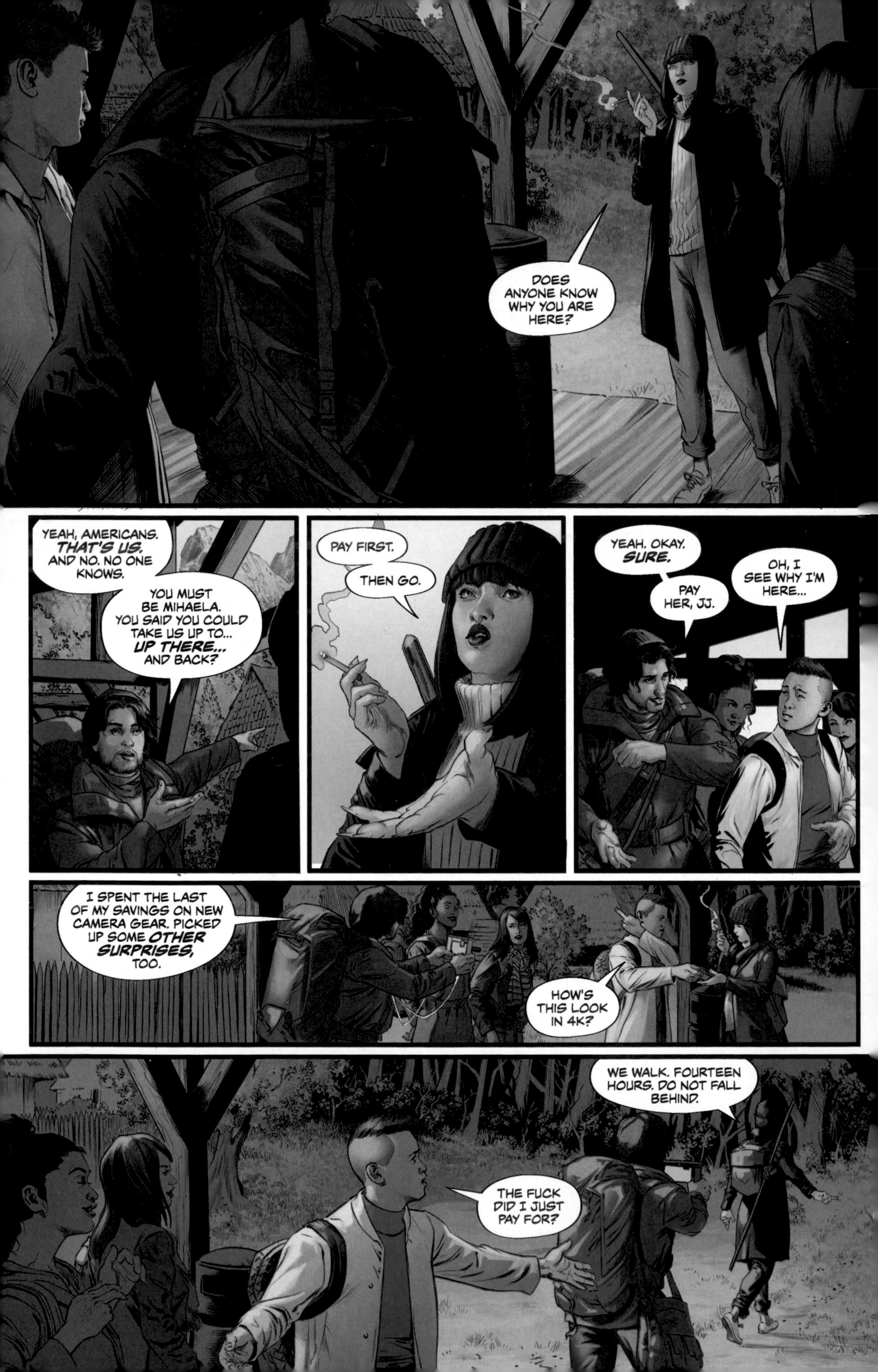
DOES ANYONE KNOW WHY YOU ARE HERE?
YEAH, AMERICANS. THAT'S US. AND NO. NO ONE KNOWS.
YOU MUST BE MIHAELA. YOU SAID YOU COULD TAKE US UP TO... UP THERE... AND BACK?
PAY FIRST.
THEN GO.
YEAH. OKAY. SURE.
PAY HER, JJ.
OH, I SEE WHY I'M HERE...
I SPENT THE LAST OF MY SAVINGS ON NEW CAMERA GEAR. PICKED UP SOME OTHER SURPRISES, TOO.
HOW'S THIS LOOK IN 4K?
WE WALK. FOURTEEN HOURS. DO NOT FALL BEHIND.
THE FUCK DID I JUST PAY FOR?

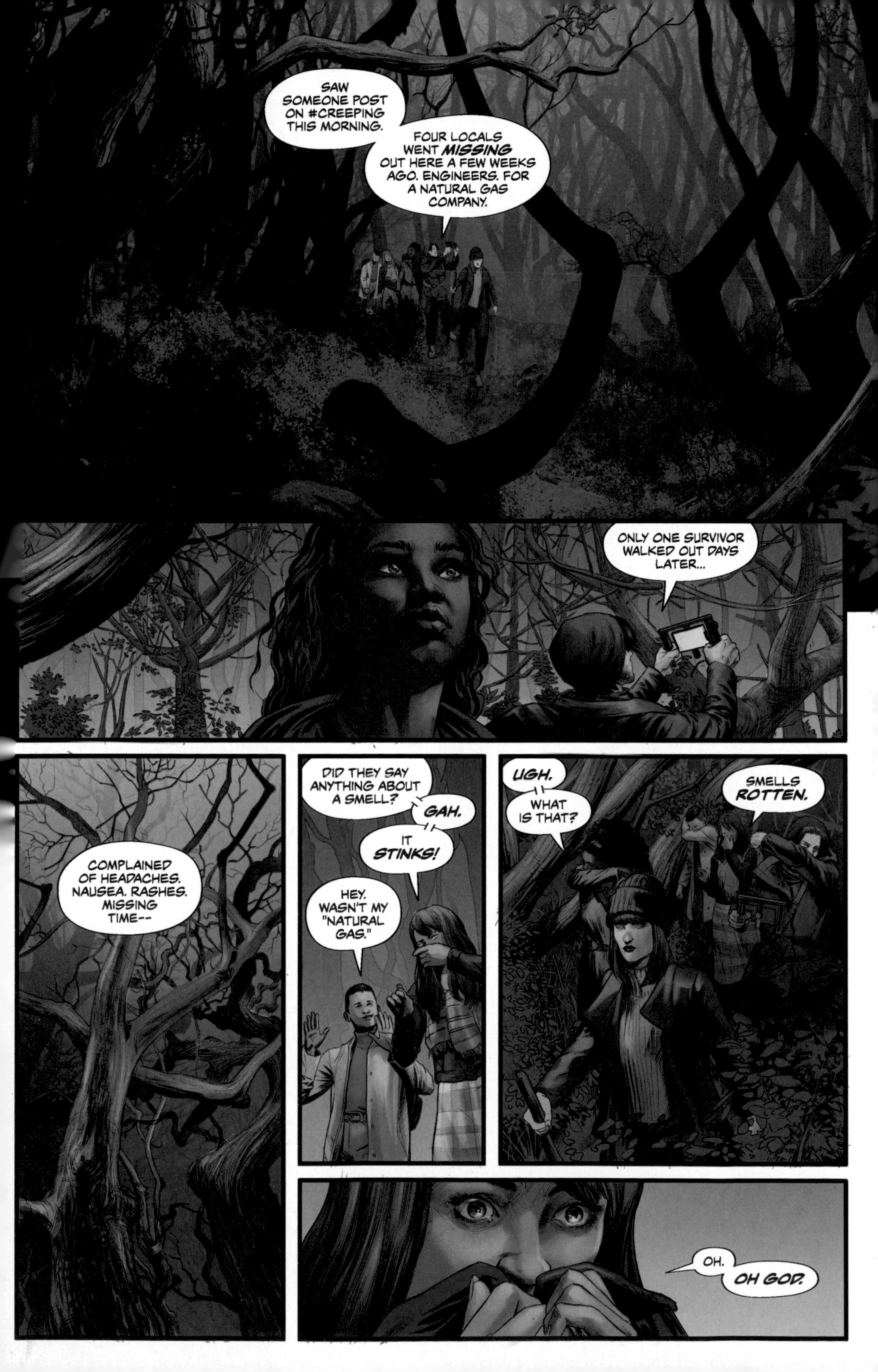
SAW SOMEONE POST ON #CREEPING THIS MORNING.
FOUR LOCALS WENT MISSING OUT HERE A FEW WEEKS AGO. ENGINEERS. FOR A NATURAL GAS COMPANY.
ONLY ONE SURVIVOR WALKED OUT DAYS LATER...
COMPLAINED OF HEADACHES. NAUSEA. RASHES. MISSING TIME--
DID THEY SAY ANYTHING ABOUT A SMELL?
GAH.
IT STINKS!
HEY. WASN'T MY "NATURAL GAS."
UGH.
WHAT IS THAT?
SMELLS ROTTEN.
OH.
OH GOD.

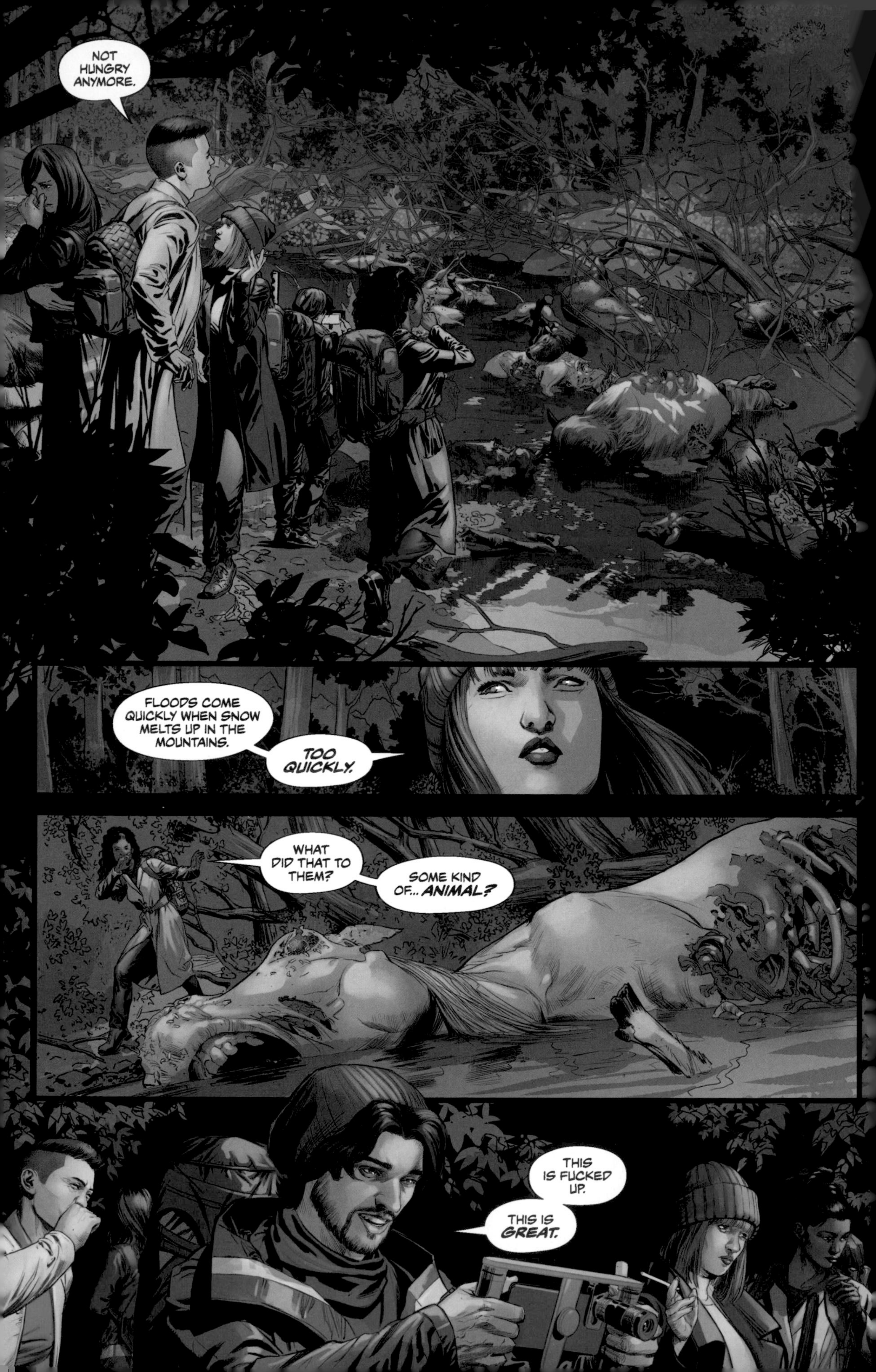
NOT HUNGRY ANYMORE.
FLOODS COME QUICKLY WHEN SNOW MELTS UP IN THE MOUNTAINS.
TOO QUICKLY.
WHAT DID THAT TO THEM?
SOME KIND OF... ANIMAL?
THIS IS FUCKED UP.
THIS IS GREAT.

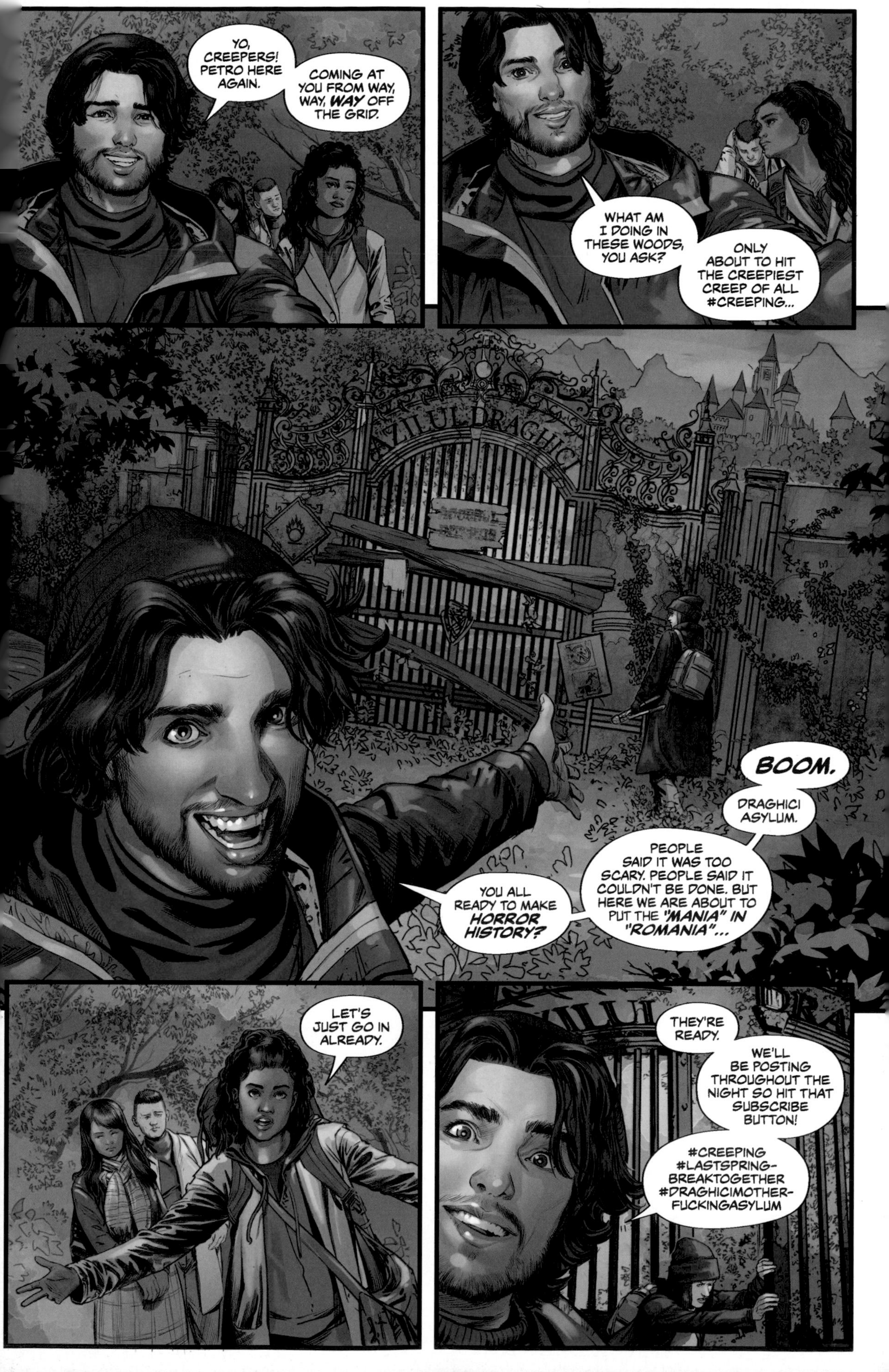
YO, CREEPERS! PETRO HERE AGAIN.
COMING AT YOU FROM WAY, WAY, WAY OFF THE GRID.
WHAT AM I DOING IN THESE WOODS, YOU ASK?
ONLY ABOUT TO HIT THE CREEPIEST CREEP OF ALL #CREEPING...
AZILUL DRAGHICI
BOOM.
DRAGHICI ASYLUM.
PEOPLE SAID IT WAS TOO SCARY. PEOPLE SAID IT COULDN'T BE DONE. BUT HERE WE ARE ABOUT TO PUT THE "MANIA" IN "ROMANIA"...
YOU ALL READY TO MAKE HORROR HISTORY?
LET'S JUST GO IN ALREADY.
THEY'RE READY.
WE'LL BE POSTING THROUGHOUT THE NIGHT SO HIT THAT SUBSCRIBE BUTTON!
#CREEPING #LASTSPRING-BREAKTOGETHER #DRAGHICIMOTHER-FUCKINGASYLUM

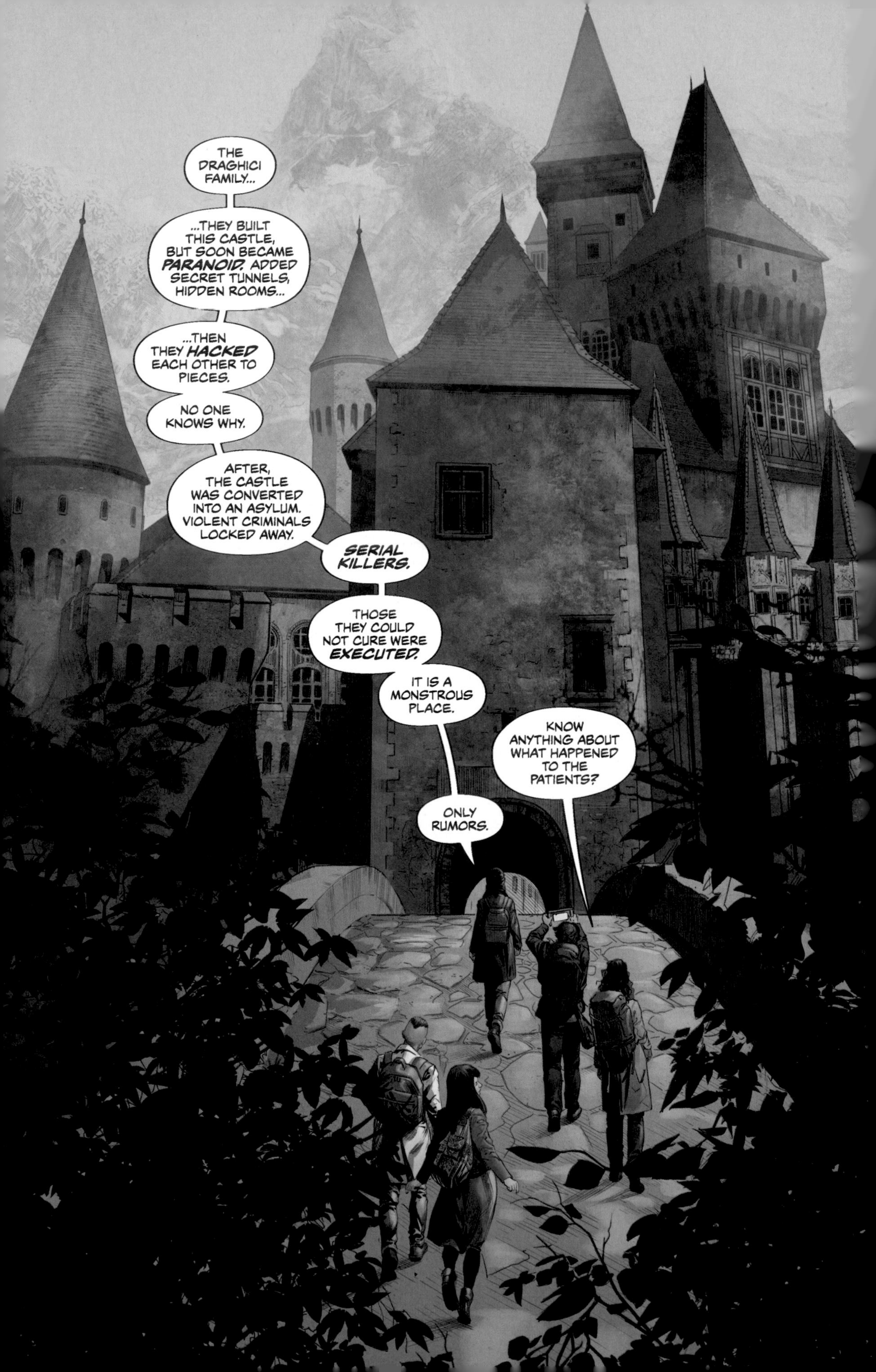
THE DRAGHICI FAMILY...
...THEY BUILT THIS CASTLE, BUT SOON BECAME **PARANOID.** ADDED SECRET TUNNELS, HIDDEN ROOMS...
...THEN THEY **HACKED** EACH OTHER TO PIECES.
NO ONE KNOWS WHY.
AFTER, THE CASTLE WAS CONVERTED INTO AN ASYLUM. VIOLENT CRIMINALS LOCKED AWAY.
SERIAL KILLERS.
THOSE THEY COULD NOT CURE WERE **EXECUTED.**
IT IS A MONSTROUS PLACE.
KNOW ANYTHING ABOUT WHAT HAPPENED TO THE PATIENTS?
ONLY RUMORS.

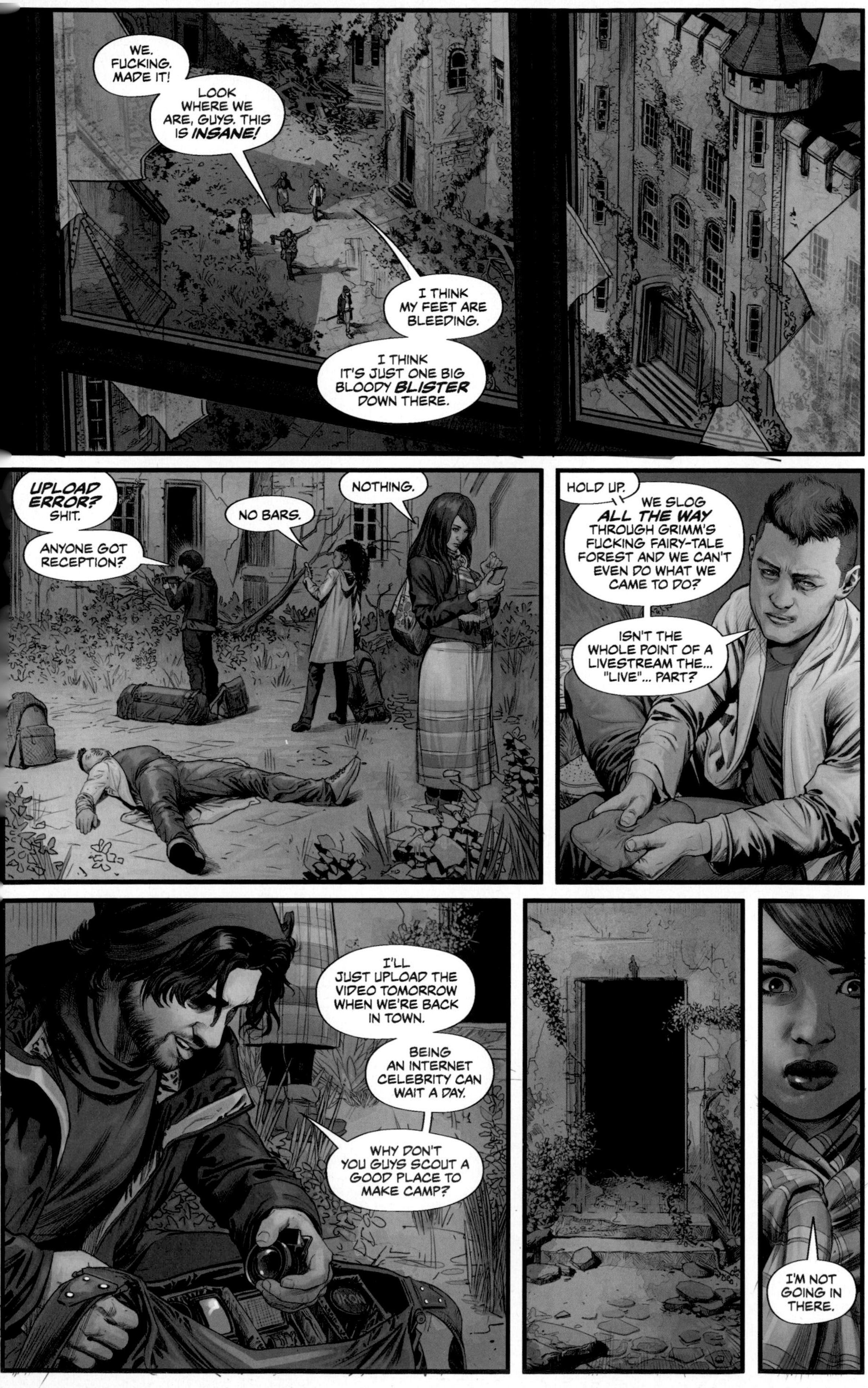
WE. FUCKING. MADE IT!
LOOK WHERE WE ARE, GUYS. THIS IS *INSANE!*
I THINK MY FEET ARE BLEEDING.
I THINK IT'S JUST ONE BIG BLOODY *BLISTER* DOWN THERE.
UPLOAD ERROR? SHIT.
ANYONE GOT RECEPTION?
NO BARS.
NOTHING.
HOLD UP.
WE SLOG *ALL THE WAY* THROUGH GRIMM'S FUCKING FAIRY-TALE FOREST AND WE CAN'T EVEN DO WHAT WE CAME TO DO?
ISN'T THE WHOLE POINT OF A LIVESTREAM THE... "LIVE"... PART?
I'LL JUST UPLOAD THE VIDEO TOMORROW WHEN WE'RE BACK IN TOWN.
BEING AN INTERNET CELEBRITY CAN WAIT A DAY.
WHY DON'T YOU GUYS SCOUT A GOOD PLACE TO MAKE CAMP?
I'M NOT GOING IN THERE.

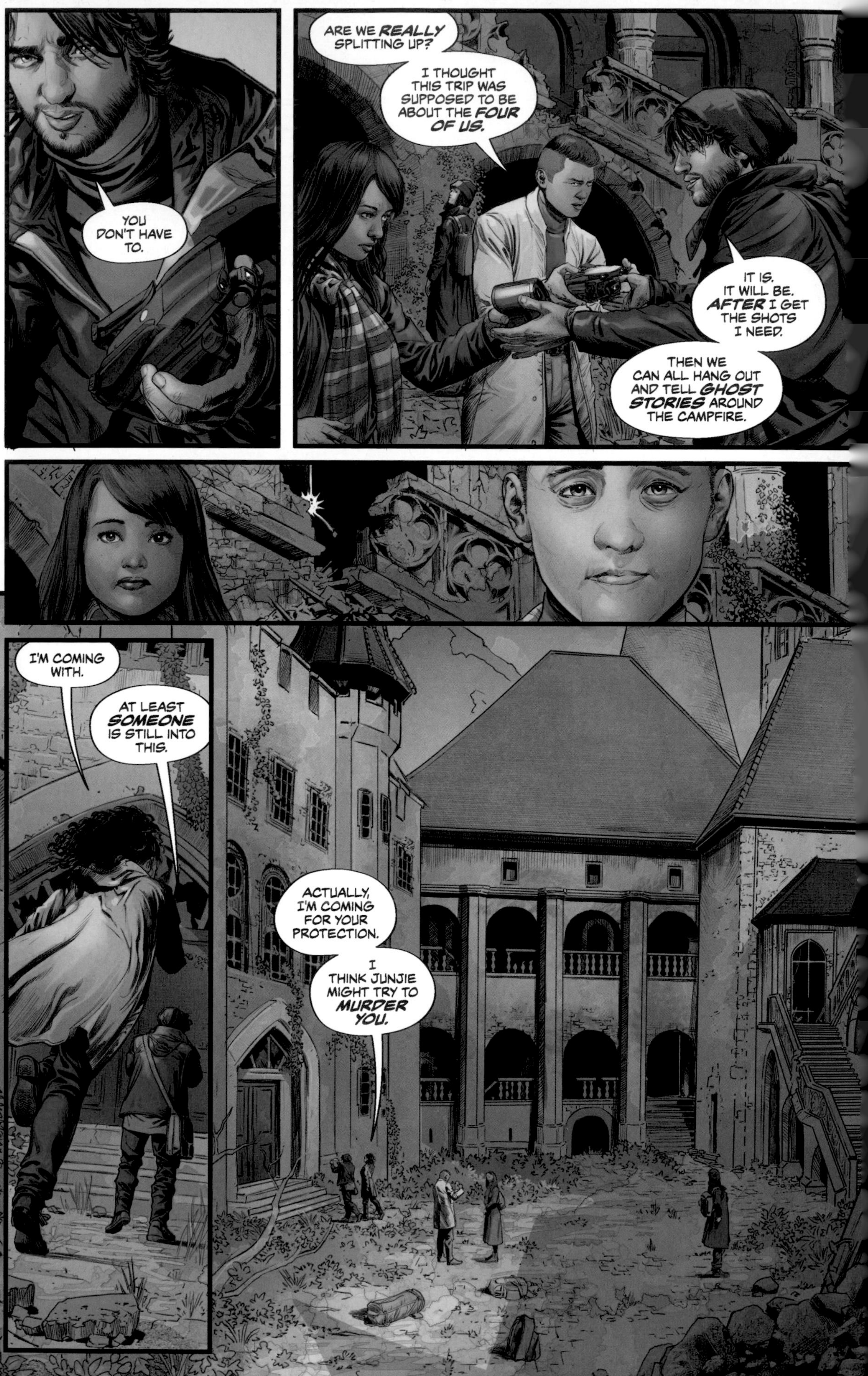
ARE WE REALLY SPLITTING UP?
I THOUGHT THIS TRIP WAS SUPPOSED TO BE ABOUT THE FOUR OF US.
YOU DON'T HAVE TO.
IT IS. IT WILL BE. AFTER I GET THE SHOTS I NEED.
THEN WE CAN ALL HANG OUT AND TELL GHOST STORIES AROUND THE CAMPFIRE.
I'M COMING WITH.
AT LEAST SOMEONE IS STILL INTO THIS.
ACTUALLY, I'M COMING FOR YOUR PROTECTION.
I THINK JUNJIE MIGHT TRY TO MURDER YOU.

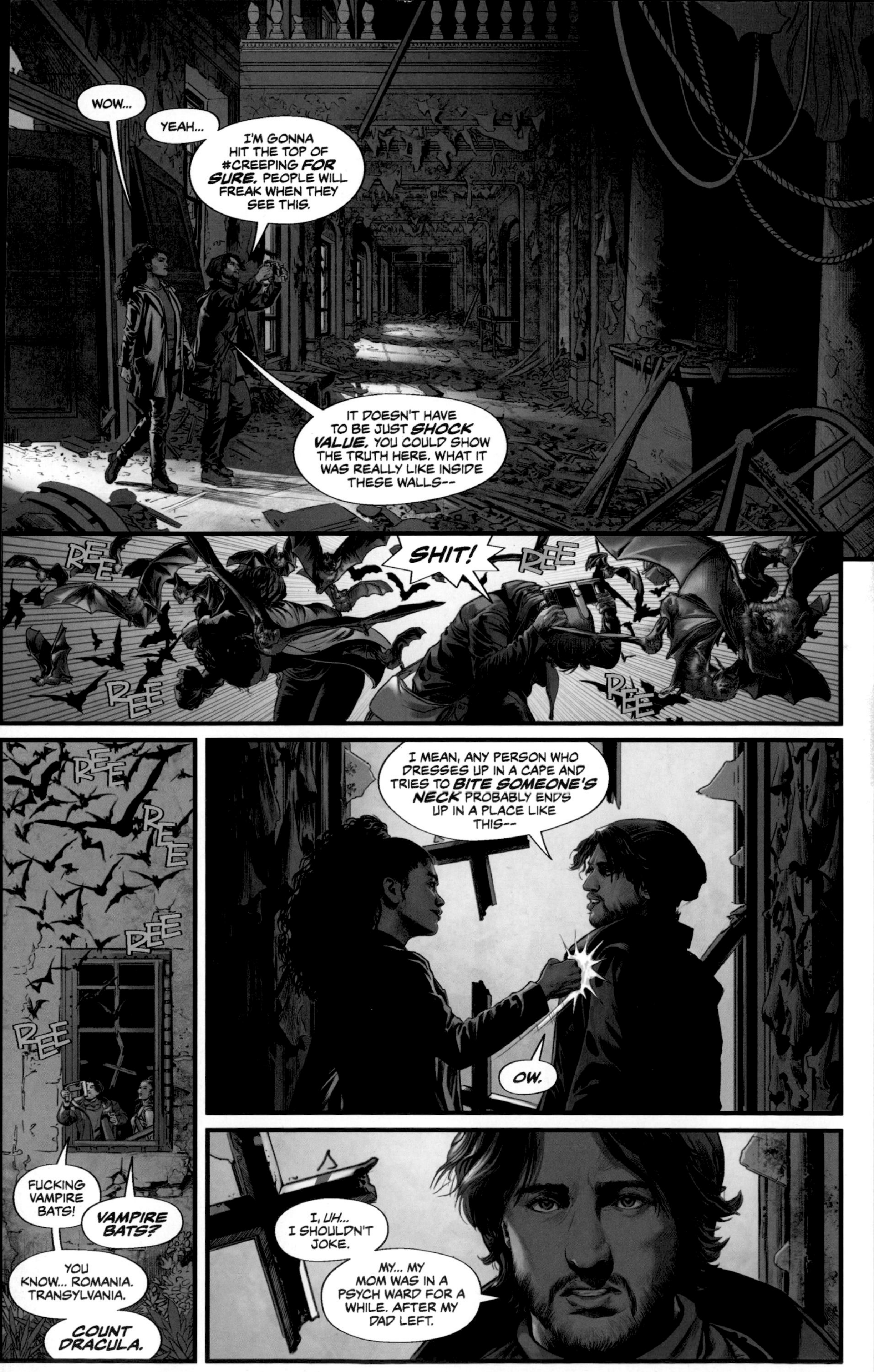
WOW...
YEAH...
I'M GONNA HIT THE TOP OF #CREEPING FOR SURE. PEOPLE WILL FREAK WHEN THEY SEE THIS.
IT DOESN'T HAVE TO BE JUST SHOCK VALUE. YOU COULD SHOW THE TRUTH HERE. WHAT IT WAS REALLY LIKE INSIDE THESE WALLS--
REE
SHIT!
REE
REE
REE
REE
REE
REE
REE
REE
FUCKING VAMPIRE BATS!
VAMPIRE BATS?
YOU KNOW... ROMANIA. TRANSYLVANIA.
COUNT DRACULA.
I MEAN, ANY PERSON WHO DRESSES UP IN A CAPE AND TRIES TO BITE SOMEONE'S NECK PROBABLY ENDS UP IN A PLACE LIKE THIS--
OW.
I, UH... I SHOULDN'T JOKE.
MY... MY MOM WAS IN A PSYCH WARD FOR A WHILE. AFTER MY DAD LEFT.

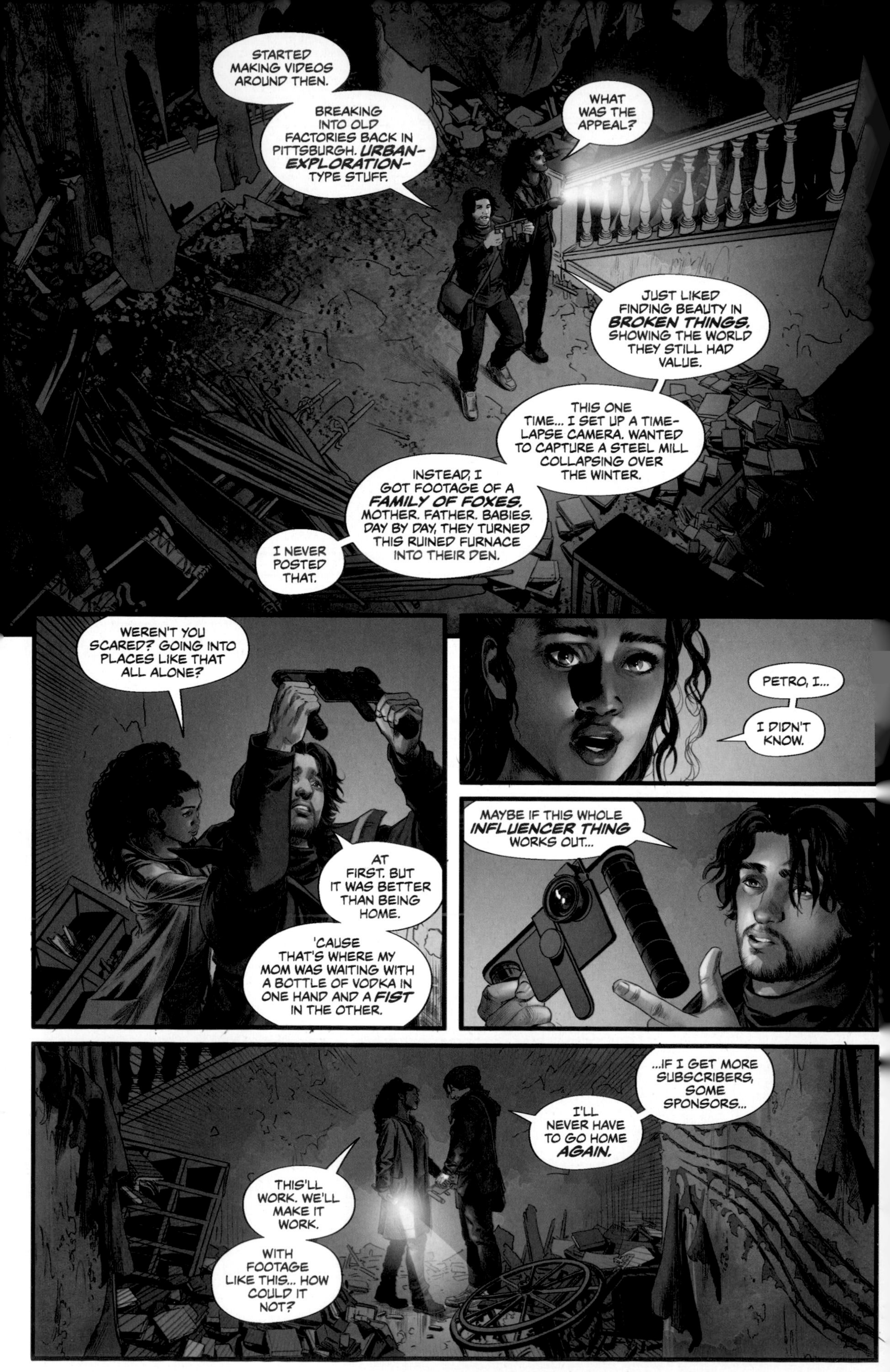
STARTED MAKING VIDEOS AROUND THEN.
BREAKING INTO OLD FACTORIES BACK IN PITTSBURGH. URBAN-EXPLORATION-TYPE STUFF.
WHAT WAS THE APPEAL?
JUST LIKED FINDING BEAUTY IN BROKEN THINGS. SHOWING THE WORLD THEY STILL HAD VALUE.
THIS ONE TIME... I SET UP A TIME-LAPSE CAMERA. WANTED TO CAPTURE A STEEL MILL COLLAPSING OVER THE WINTER.
INSTEAD, I GOT FOOTAGE OF A FAMILY OF FOXES. MOTHER. FATHER. BABIES. DAY BY DAY, THEY TURNED THIS RUINED FURNACE INTO THEIR DEN.
I NEVER POSTED THAT.
WEREN'T YOU SCARED? GOING INTO PLACES LIKE THAT ALL ALONE?
AT FIRST. BUT IT WAS BETTER THAN BEING HOME.
'CAUSE THAT'S WHERE MY MOM WAS WAITING WITH A BOTTLE OF VODKA IN ONE HAND AND A FIST IN THE OTHER.
PETRO, I...
I DIDN'T KNOW.
MAYBE IF THIS WHOLE INFLUENCER THING WORKS OUT...
...IF I GET MORE SUBSCRIBERS, SOME SPONSORS...
I'LL NEVER HAVE TO GO HOME AGAIN.
THIS'LL WORK. WE'LL MAKE IT WORK.
WITH FOOTAGE LIKE THIS... HOW COULD IT NOT?

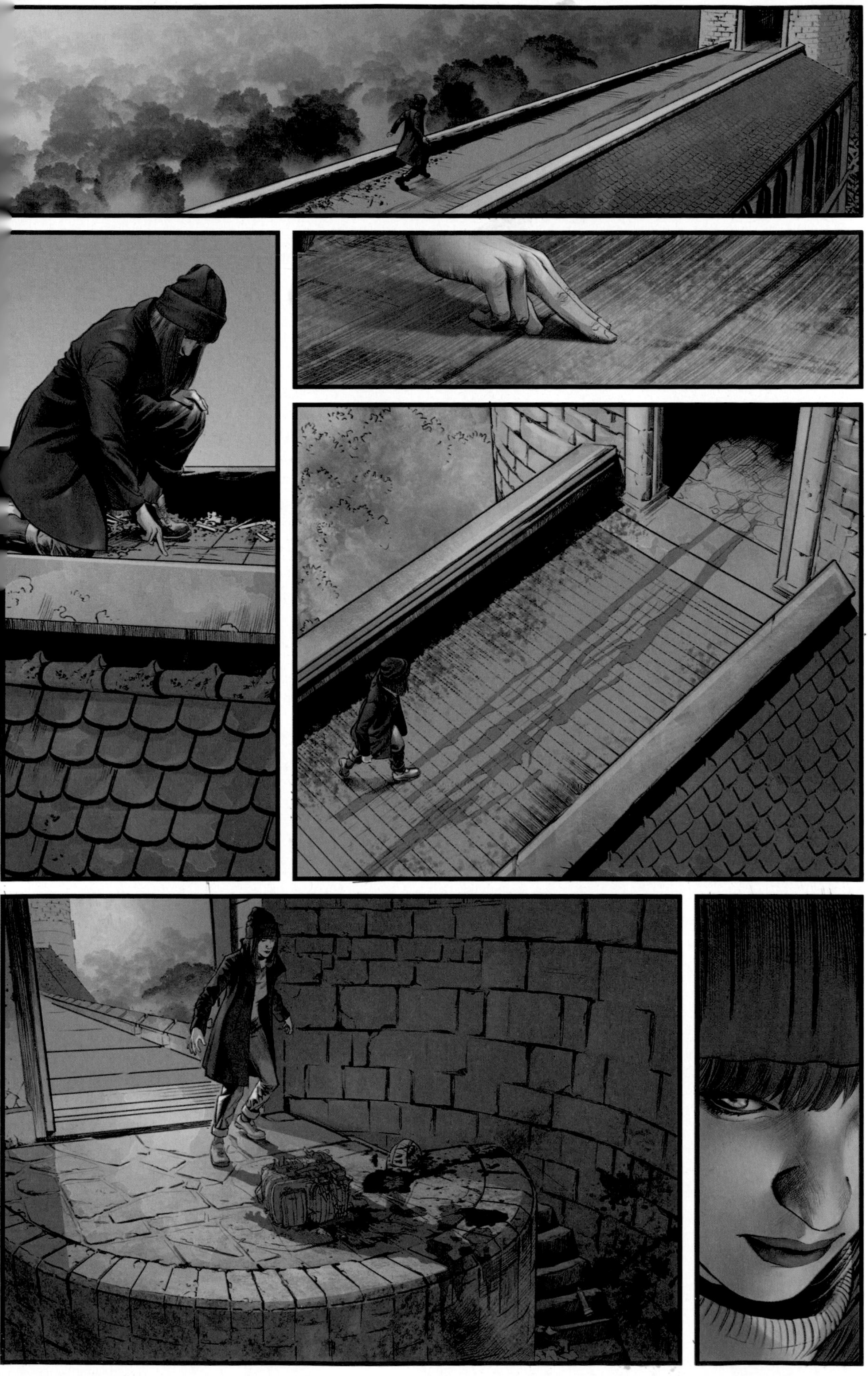

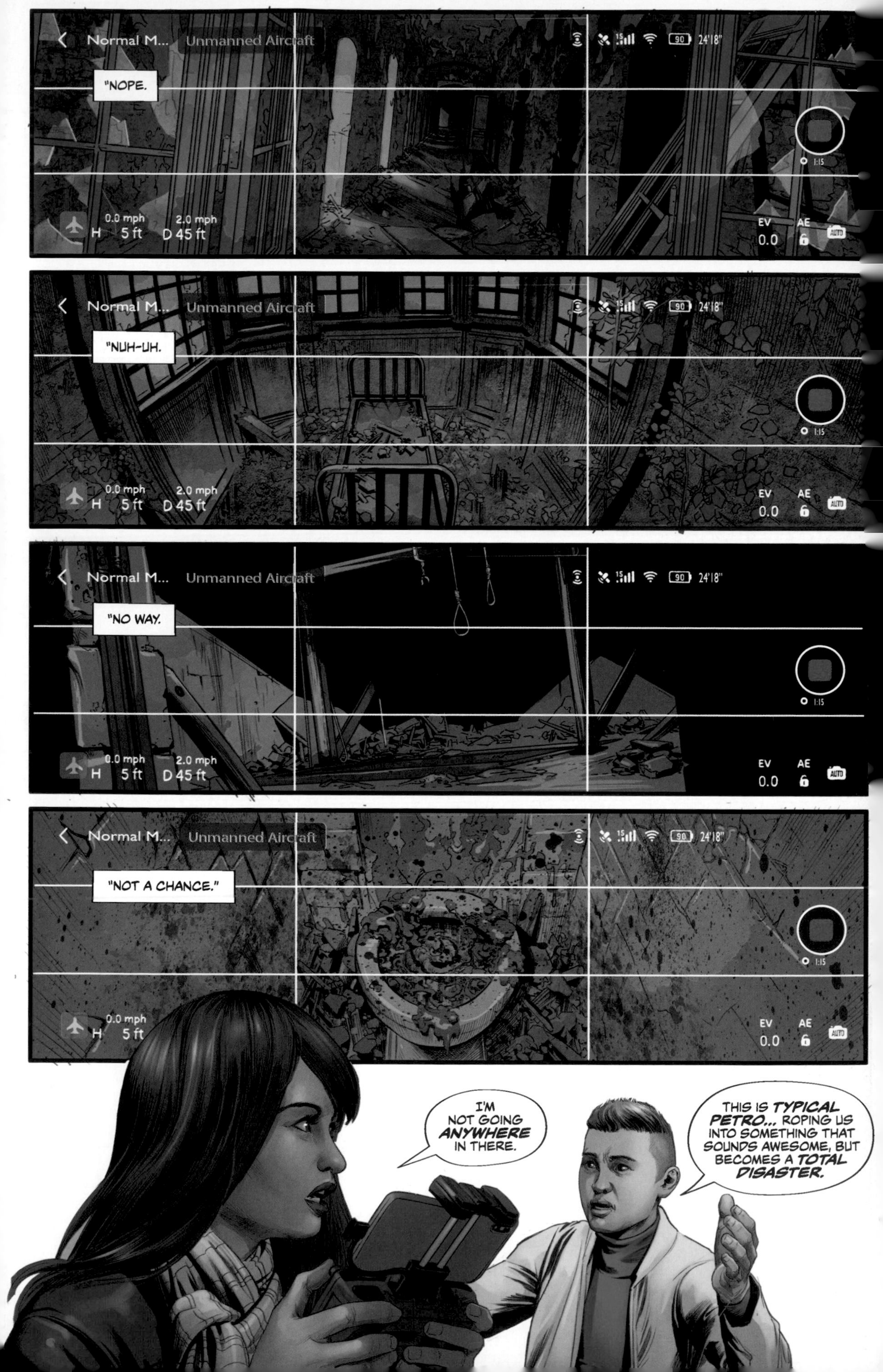

Normal M... Unmanned Aircraft
"NOPE.
0.0 mph 2.0 mph
H 5 ft D 45 ft
EV AE
0.0
"NUH-UH.
"NO WAY.
"NOT A CHANCE."
I'M NOT GOING ANYWHERE IN THERE.
THIS IS TYPICAL PETRO... ROPING US INTO SOMETHING THAT SOUNDS AWESOME, BUT BECOMES A TOTAL DISASTER.

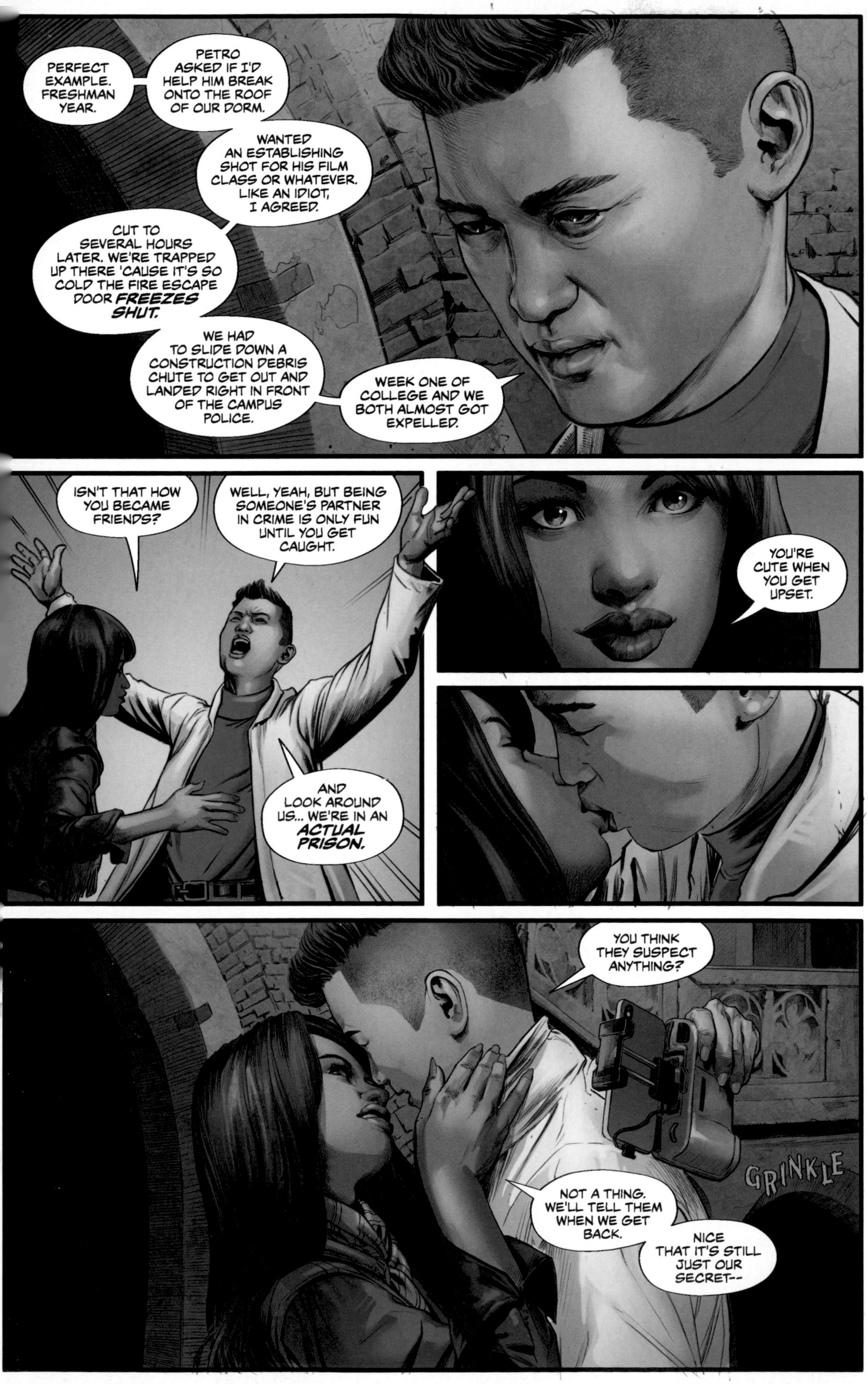
PERFECT EXAMPLE. FRESHMAN YEAR.
PETRO ASKED IF I'D HELP HIM BREAK ONTO THE ROOF OF OUR DORM.
WANTED AN ESTABLISHING SHOT FOR HIS FILM CLASS OR WHATEVER. LIKE AN IDIOT, I AGREED.
CUT TO SEVERAL HOURS LATER. WE'RE TRAPPED UP THERE 'CAUSE IT'S SO COLD THE FIRE ESCAPE DOOR FREEZES SHUT.
WE HAD TO SLIDE DOWN A CONSTRUCTION DEBRIS CHUTE TO GET OUT AND LANDED RIGHT IN FRONT OF THE CAMPUS POLICE.
WEEK ONE OF COLLEGE AND WE BOTH ALMOST GOT EXPELLED.
ISN'T THAT HOW YOU BECAME FRIENDS?
WELL, YEAH, BUT BEING SOMEONE'S PARTNER IN CRIME IS ONLY FUN UNTIL YOU GET CAUGHT.
AND LOOK AROUND US... WE'RE IN AN ACTUAL PRISON.
YOU'RE CUTE WHEN YOU GET UPSET.
YOU THINK THEY SUSPECT ANYTHING?
GRINKLE
NOT A THING. WE'LL TELL THEM WHEN WE GET BACK.
NICE THAT IT'S STILL JUST OUR SECRET--

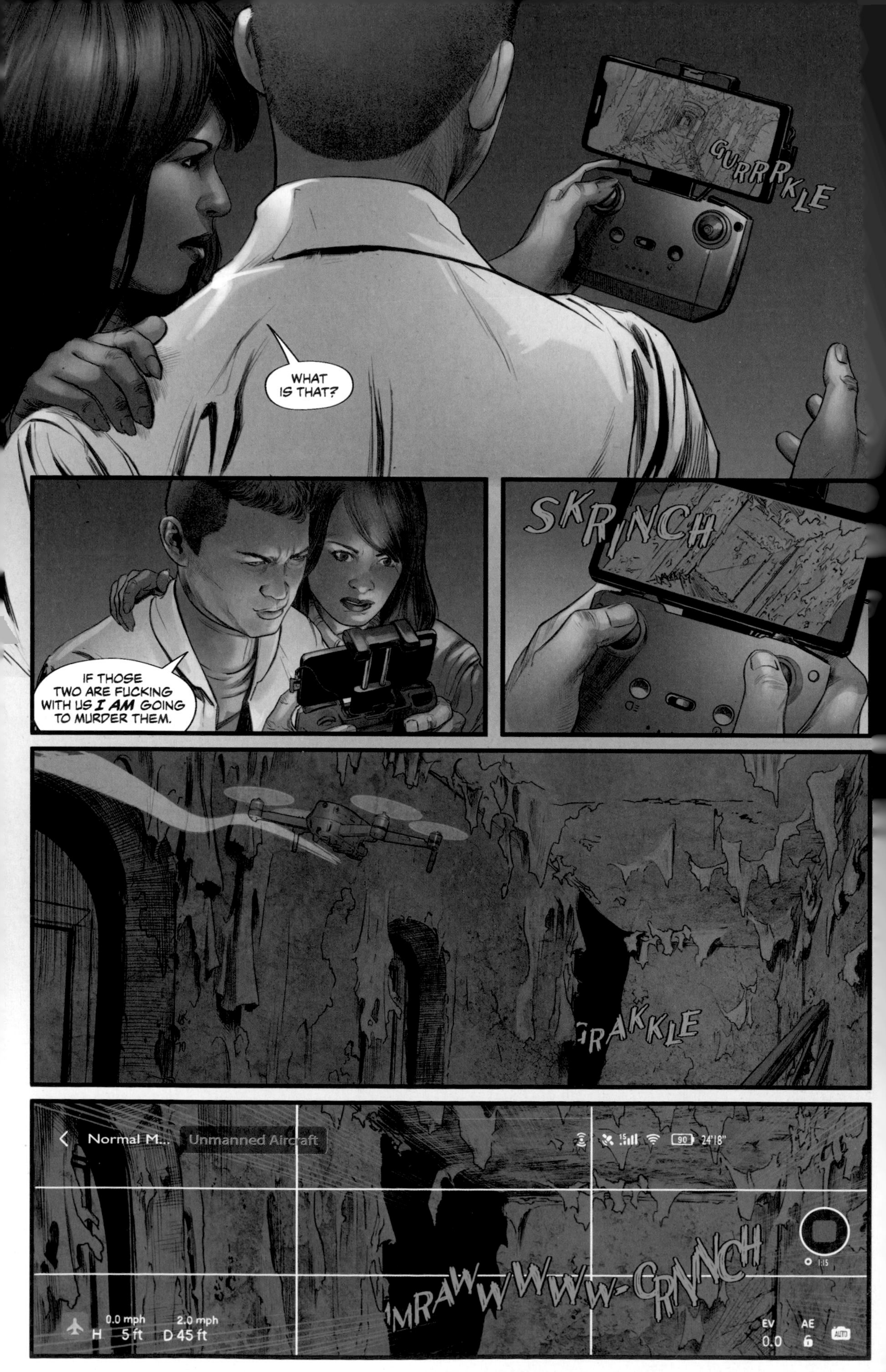
GURRRKLE
WHAT IS THAT?
IF THOSE TWO ARE FUCKING WITH US **I AM** GOING TO MURDER THEM.
SKRINCH
GRAKKLE
Normal M...
Unmanned Aircraft
24'18"
0.0 mph
2.0 mph
H 5 ft
D 45 ft
MRAWWWWW-CRNNCH
EV
0.0
AE

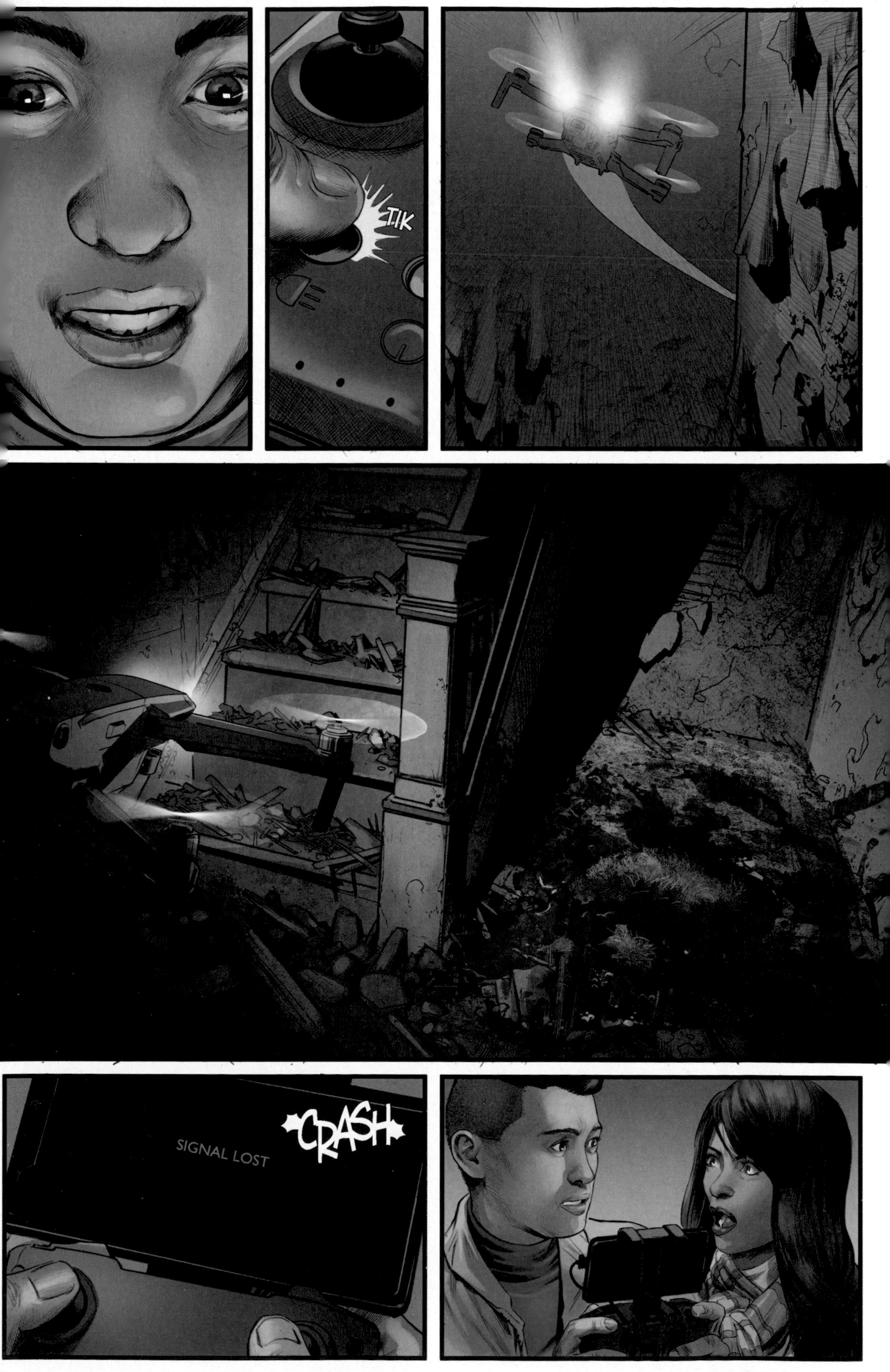
TIK
SIGNAL LOST
CRASH

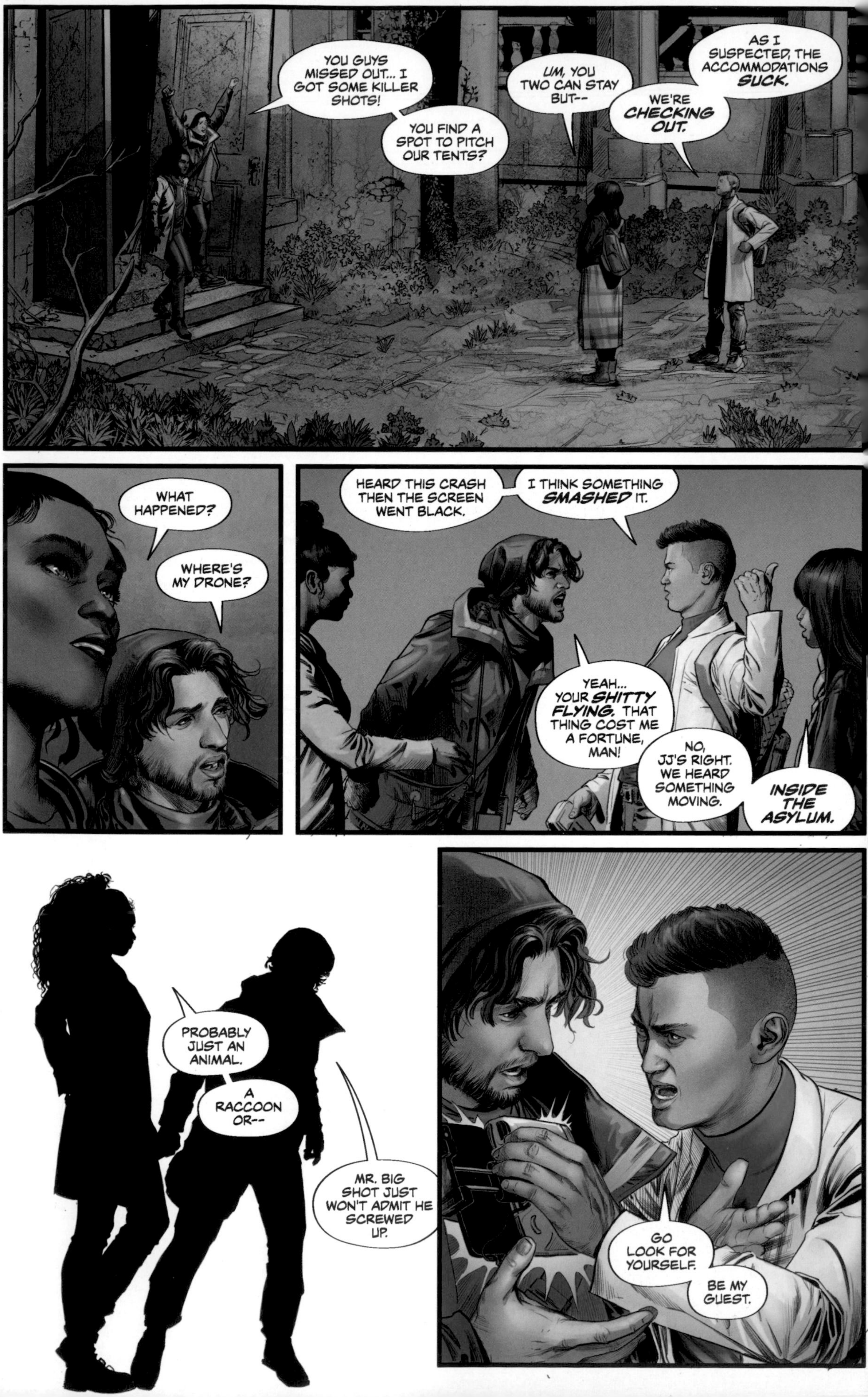
YOU GUYS MISSED OUT... I GOT SOME KILLER SHOTS!
YOU FIND A SPOT TO PITCH OUR TENTS?
UM, YOU TWO CAN STAY BUT--
AS I SUSPECTED, THE ACCOMMODATIONS SUCK.
WE'RE CHECKING OUT.
WHAT HAPPENED?
WHERE'S MY DRONE?
HEARD THIS CRASH THEN THE SCREEN WENT BLACK.
I THINK SOMETHING SMASHED IT.
YEAH... YOUR SHITTY FLYING. THAT THING COST ME A FORTUNE, MAN!
NO, JJ'S RIGHT. WE HEARD SOMETHING MOVING.
INSIDE THE ASYLUM.
PROBABLY JUST AN ANIMAL.
A RACCOON OR--
MR. BIG SHOT JUST WON'T ADMIT HE SCREWED UP.
GO LOOK FOR YOURSELF.
BE MY GUEST.

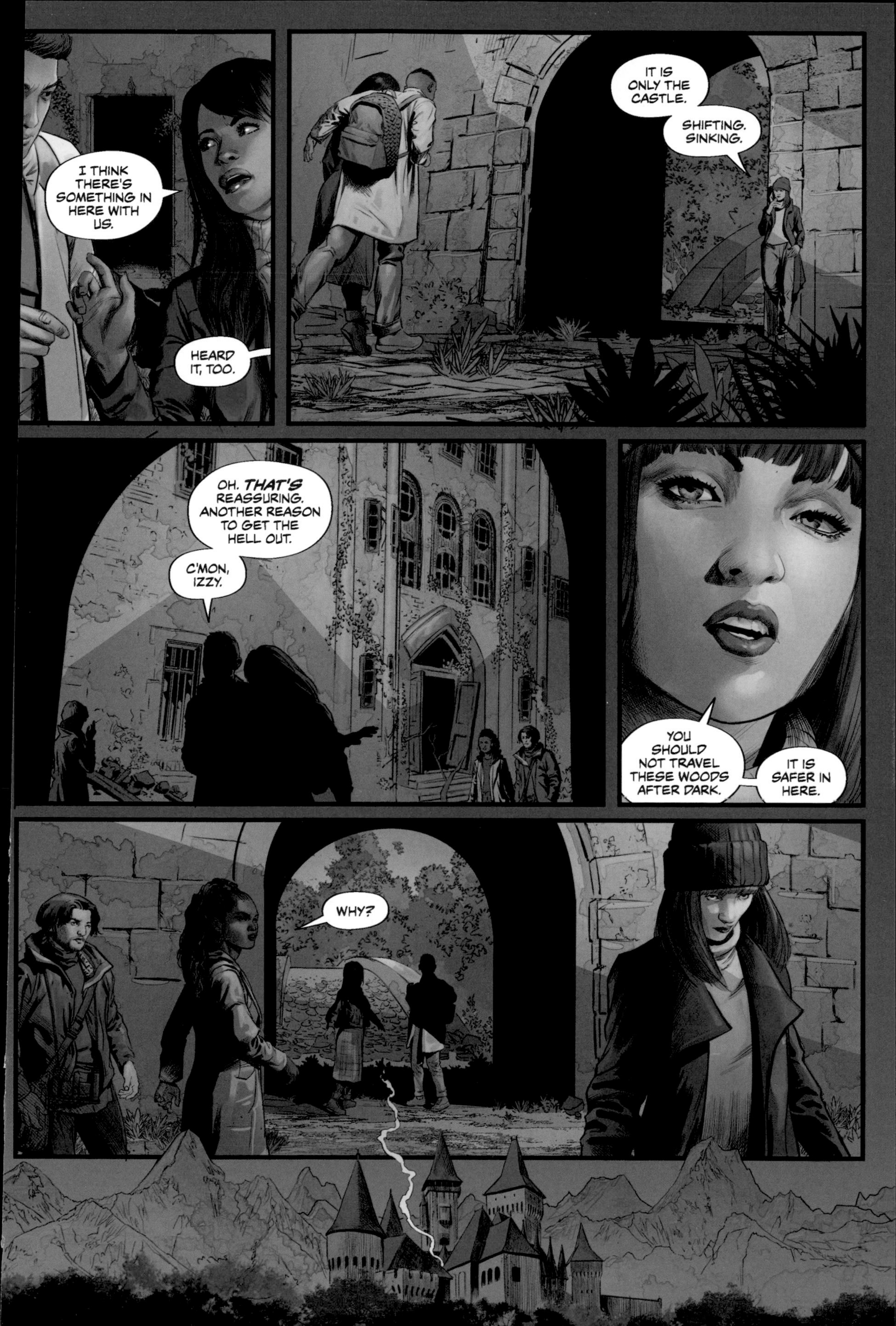
I THINK THERE'S SOMETHING IN HERE WITH US.
HEARD IT, TOO.
IT IS ONLY THE CASTLE.
SHIFTING. SINKING.
OH. *THAT'S* REASSURING. ANOTHER REASON TO GET THE HELL OUT.
C'MON, IZZY.
YOU SHOULD NOT TRAVEL THESE WOODS AFTER DARK.
IT IS SAFER IN HERE.
WHY?

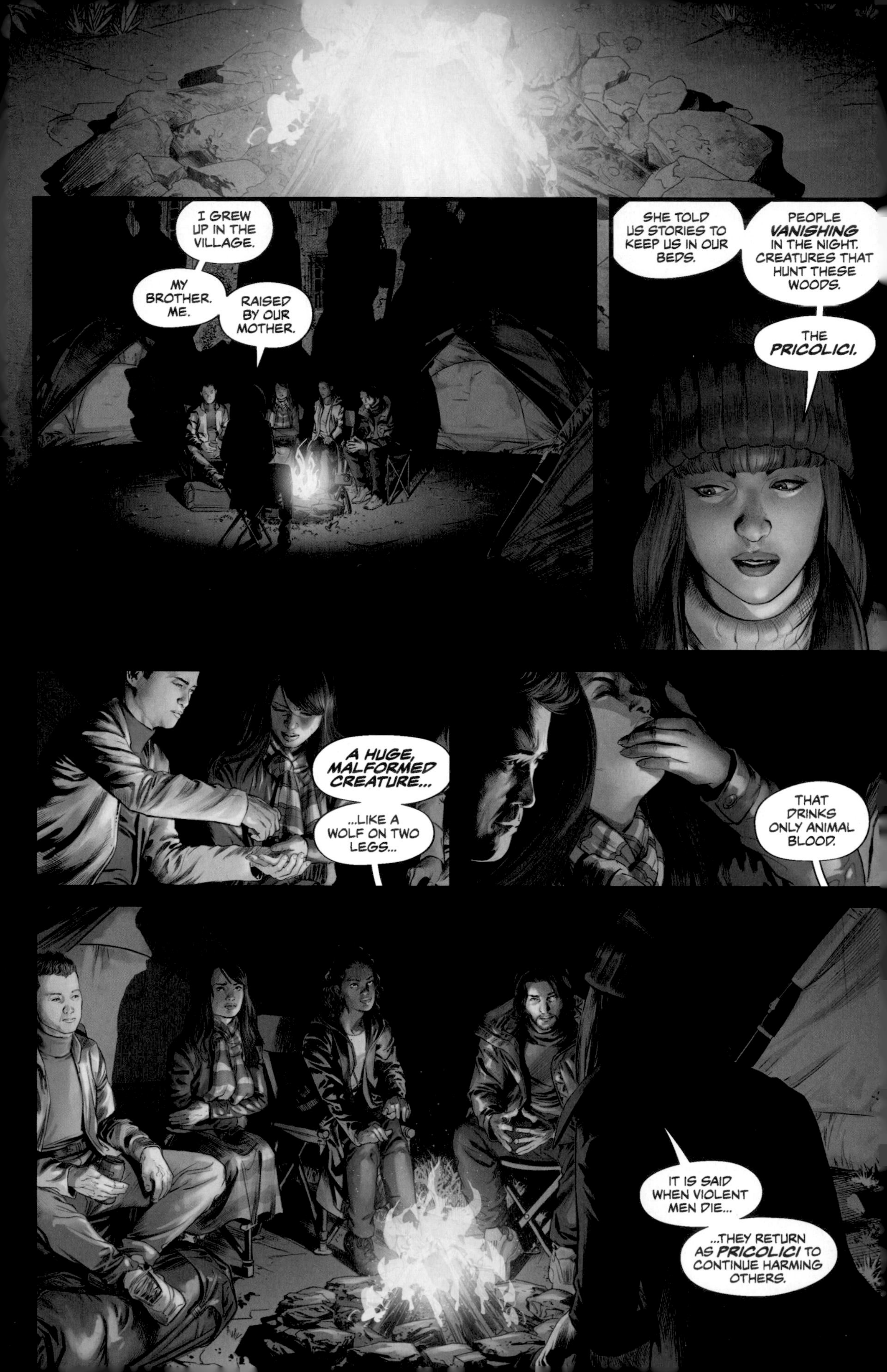
I GREW UP IN THE VILLAGE.
MY BROTHER. ME.
RAISED BY OUR MOTHER.
SHE TOLD US STORIES TO KEEP US IN OUR BEDS.
PEOPLE VANISHING IN THE NIGHT. CREATURES THAT HUNT THESE WOODS.
THE PRICOLICI.
A HUGE, MALFORMED CREATURE...
...LIKE A WOLF ON TWO LEGS...
THAT DRINKS ONLY ANIMAL BLOOD.
IT IS SAID WHEN VIOLENT MEN DIE...
...THEY RETURN AS PRICOLICI TO CONTINUE HARMING OTHERS.

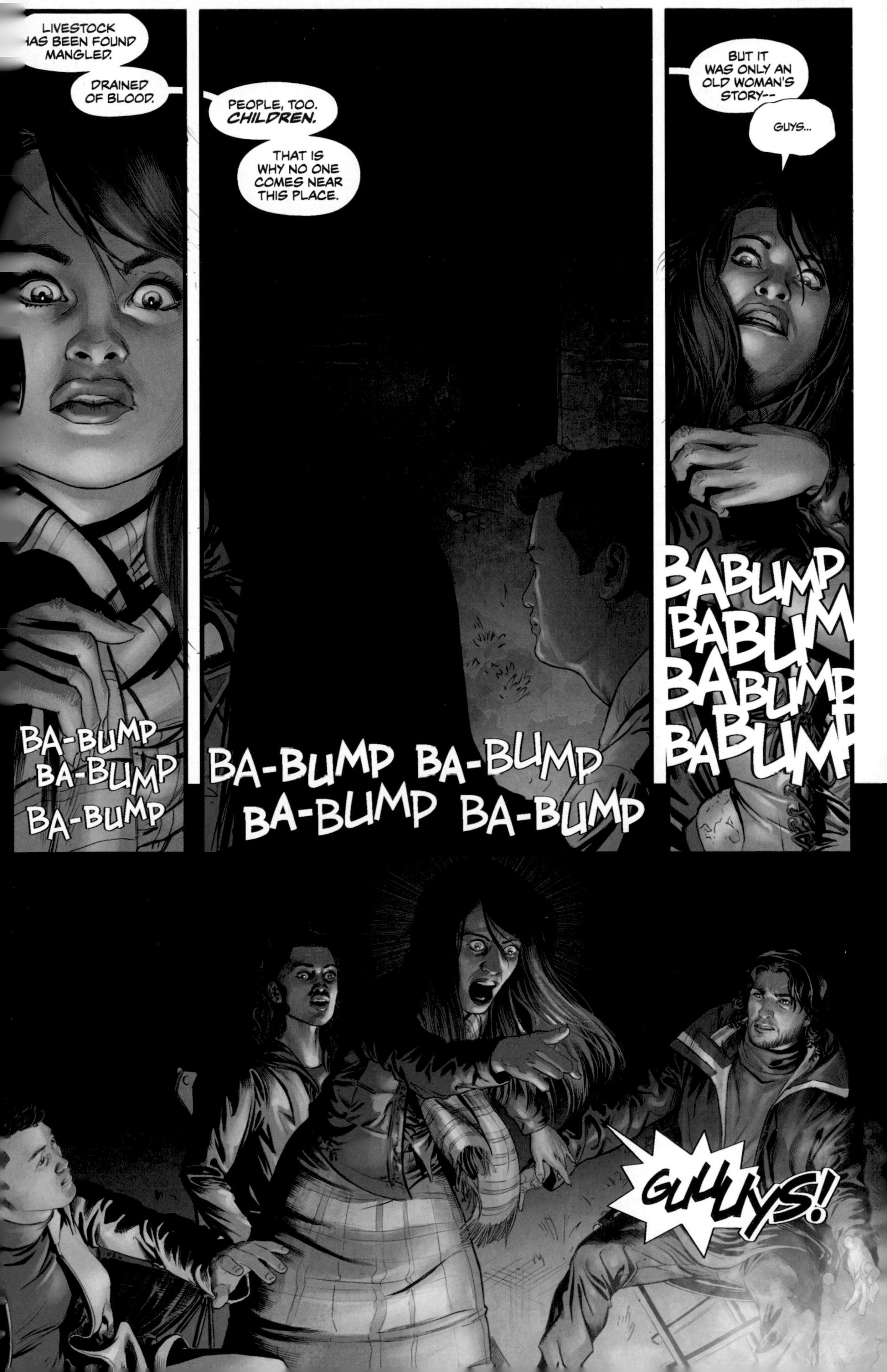

LIVESTOCK HAS BEEN FOUND MANGLED.
DRAINED OF BLOOD.
BA-BUMP BA-BUMP BA-BUMP
PEOPLE, TOO. CHILDREN.
THAT IS WHY NO ONE COMES NEAR THIS PLACE.
BA-BUMP BA-BUMP BA-BUMP BA-BUMP
BUT IT WAS ONLY AN OLD WOMAN'S STORY--
GUYS...
BABUMP BABUM BABUMP BABUMP
GUUUYS!

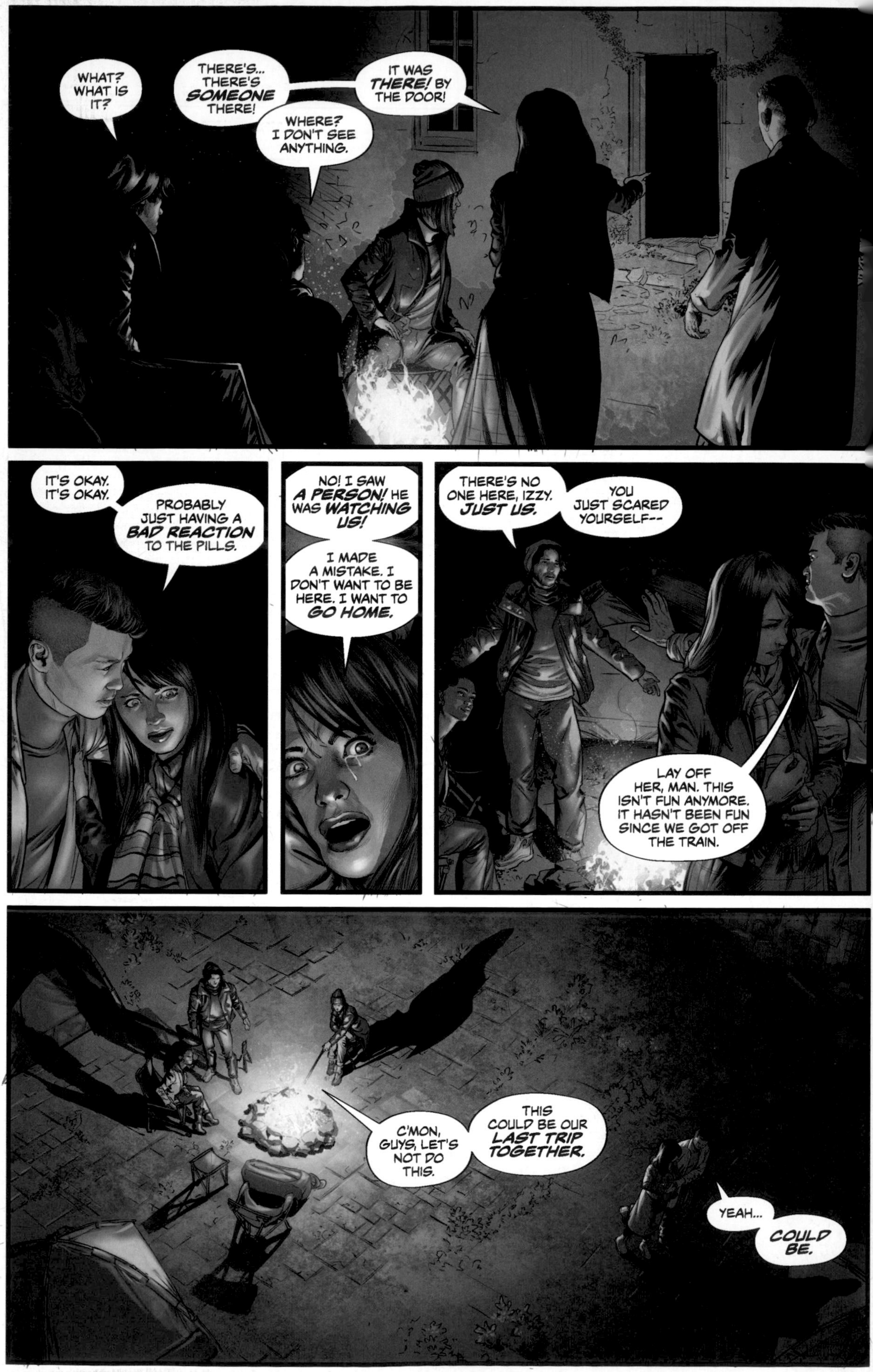
WHAT? WHAT IS IT?
THERE'S... THERE'S SOMEONE THERE!
IT WAS THERE! BY THE DOOR!
WHERE? I DON'T SEE ANYTHING.
IT'S OKAY. IT'S OKAY.
PROBABLY JUST HAVING A BAD REACTION TO THE PILLS.
NO! I SAW A PERSON! HE WAS WATCHING US!
I MADE A MISTAKE. I DON'T WANT TO BE HERE. I WANT TO GO HOME.
THERE'S NO ONE HERE, IZZY. JUST US.
YOU JUST SCARED YOURSELF--
LAY OFF HER, MAN. THIS ISN'T FUN ANYMORE. IT HASN'T BEEN FUN SINCE WE GOT OFF THE TRAIN.
C'MON, GUYS, LET'S NOT DO THIS.
THIS COULD BE OUR LAST TRIP TOGETHER.
YEAH... COULD BE.

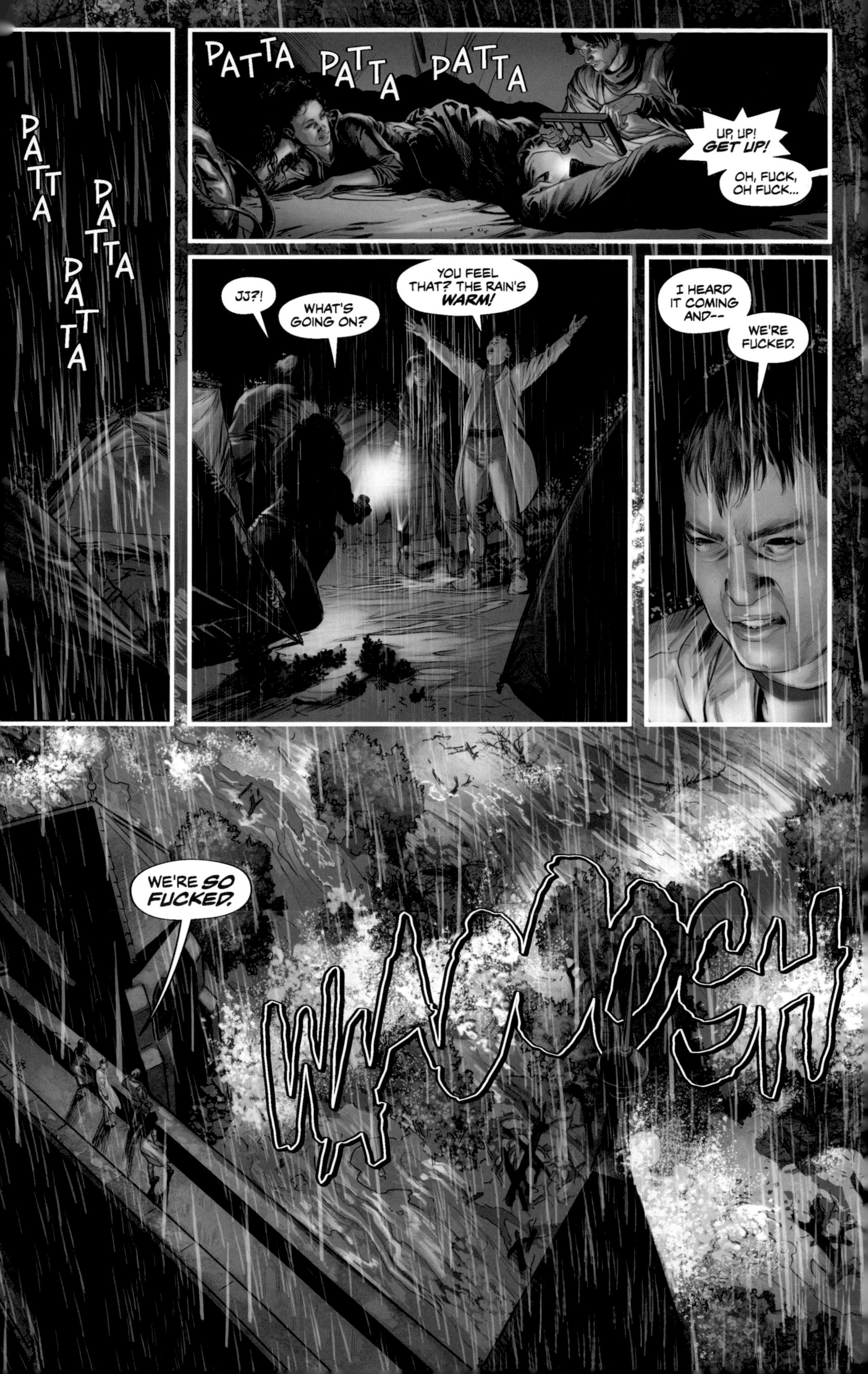
PATTA PATTA PATTA
PATTA PATTA PATTA
UP, UP! GET UP!
OH, FUCK, OH FUCK...
JJ?!
WHAT'S GOING ON?
YOU FEEL THAT? THE RAIN'S WARM!
I HEARD IT COMING AND--
WE'RE FUCKED.
WE'RE SO FUCKED.
WHOOSH

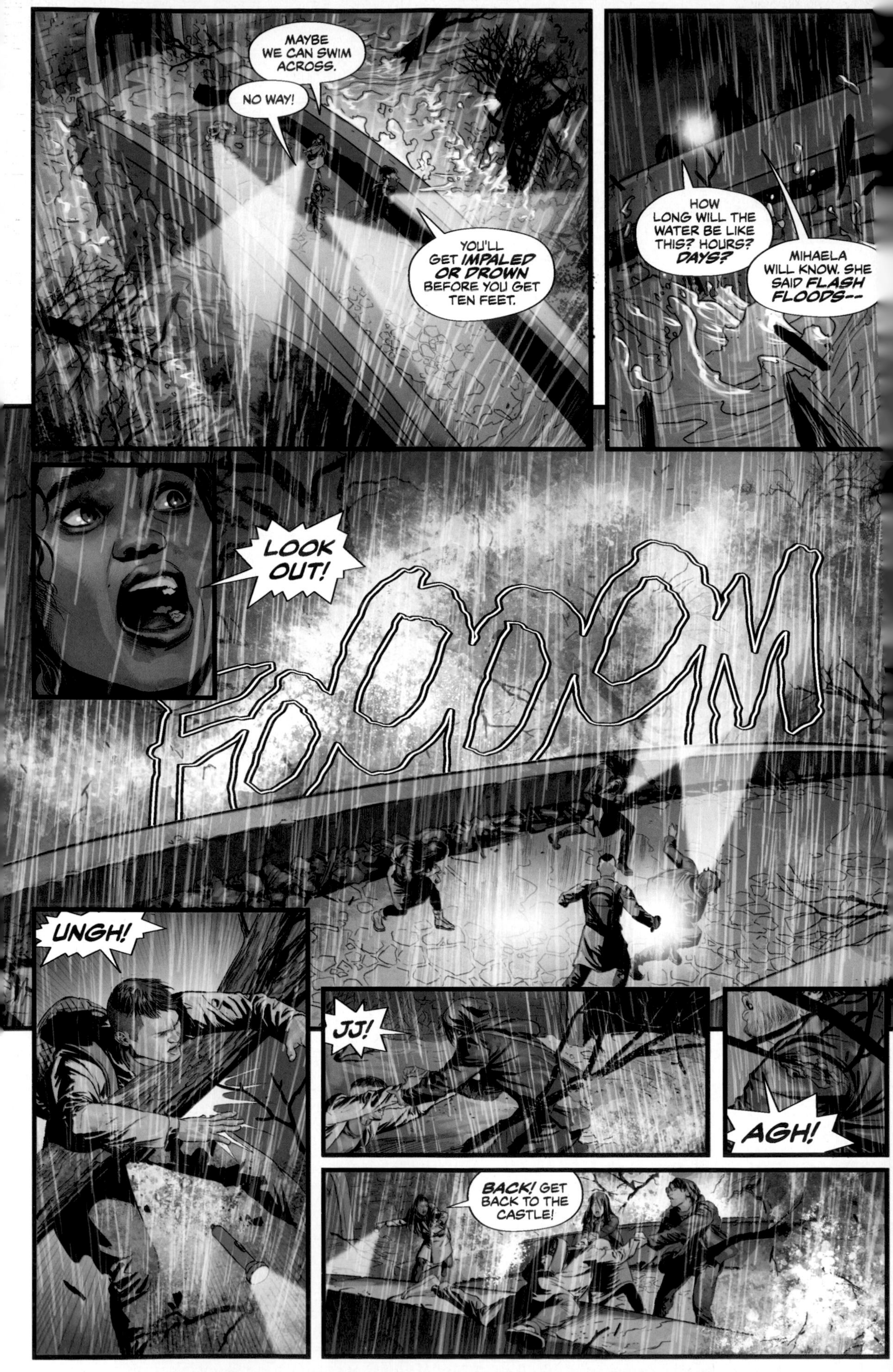
MAYBE WE CAN SWIM ACROSS.
NO WAY!
YOU'LL GET IMPALED OR DROWN BEFORE YOU GET TEN FEET.
HOW LONG WILL THE WATER BE LIKE THIS? HOURS? DAYS?
MIHAELA WILL KNOW. SHE SAID FLASH FLOODS--
LOOK OUT!
FOOOOM
UNGH!
JJ!
AGH!
BACK! GET BACK TO THE CASTLE!

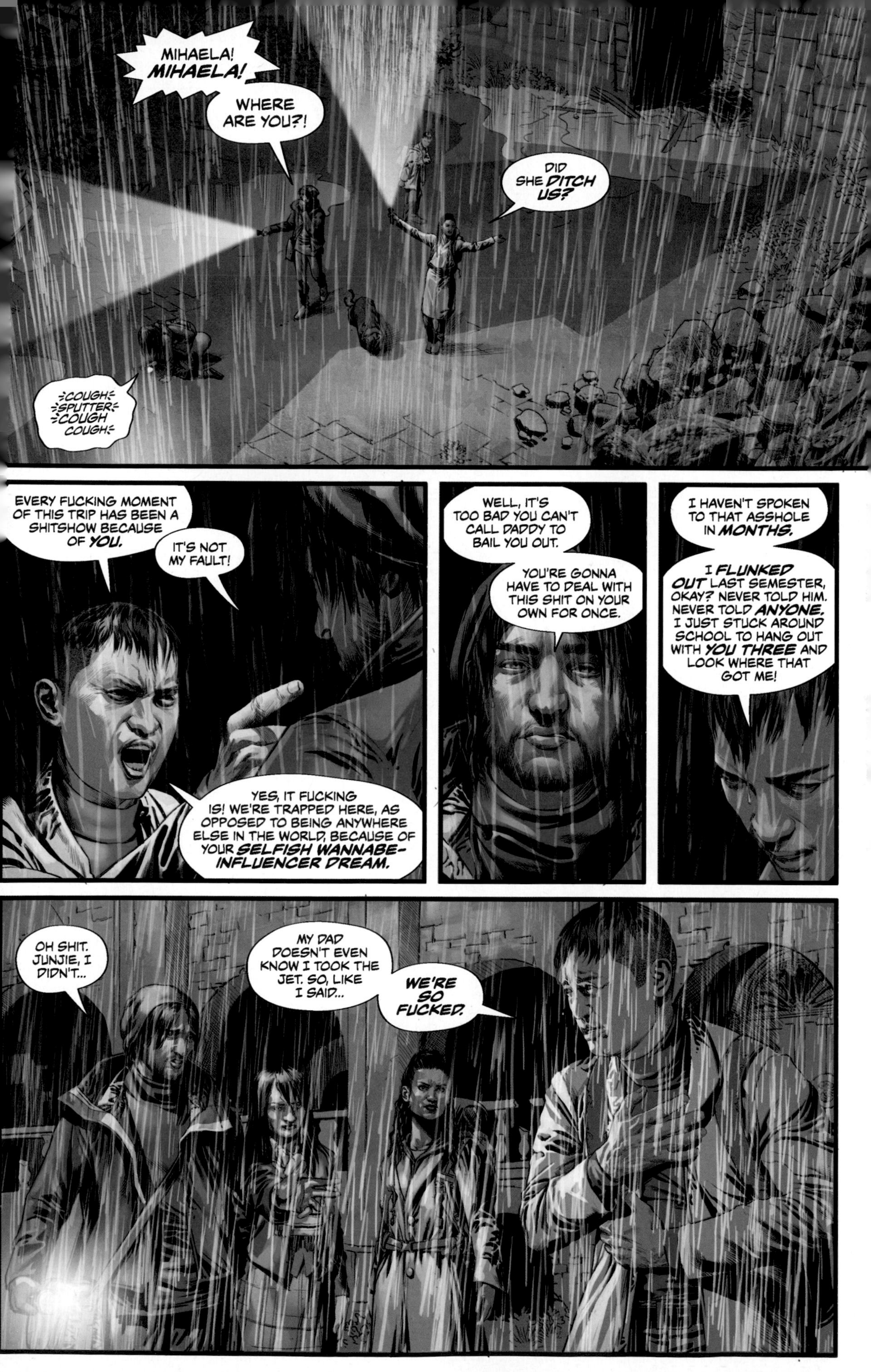
MIHAELA! MIHAELA!
WHERE ARE YOU?!
DID SHE DITCH US?
COUGH SPUTTER COUGH COUGH
EVERY FUCKING MOMENT OF THIS TRIP HAS BEEN A SHITSHOW BECAUSE OF YOU.
IT'S NOT MY FAULT!
YES, IT FUCKING IS! WE'RE TRAPPED HERE, AS OPPOSED TO BEING ANYWHERE ELSE IN THE WORLD, BECAUSE OF YOUR SELFISH WANNABE-INFLUENCER DREAM.
WELL, IT'S TOO BAD YOU CAN'T CALL DADDY TO BAIL YOU OUT.
YOU'RE GONNA HAVE TO DEAL WITH THIS SHIT ON YOUR OWN FOR ONCE.
I HAVEN'T SPOKEN TO THAT ASSHOLE IN MONTHS.
I FLUNKED OUT LAST SEMESTER, OKAY? NEVER TOLD HIM. NEVER TOLD ANYONE. I JUST STUCK AROUND SCHOOL TO HANG OUT WITH YOU THREE AND LOOK WHERE THAT GOT ME!
OH SHIT. JUNJIE, I DIDN'T...
MY DAD DOESN'T EVEN KNOW I TOOK THE JET. SO, LIKE I SAID...
WE'RE SO FUCKED.

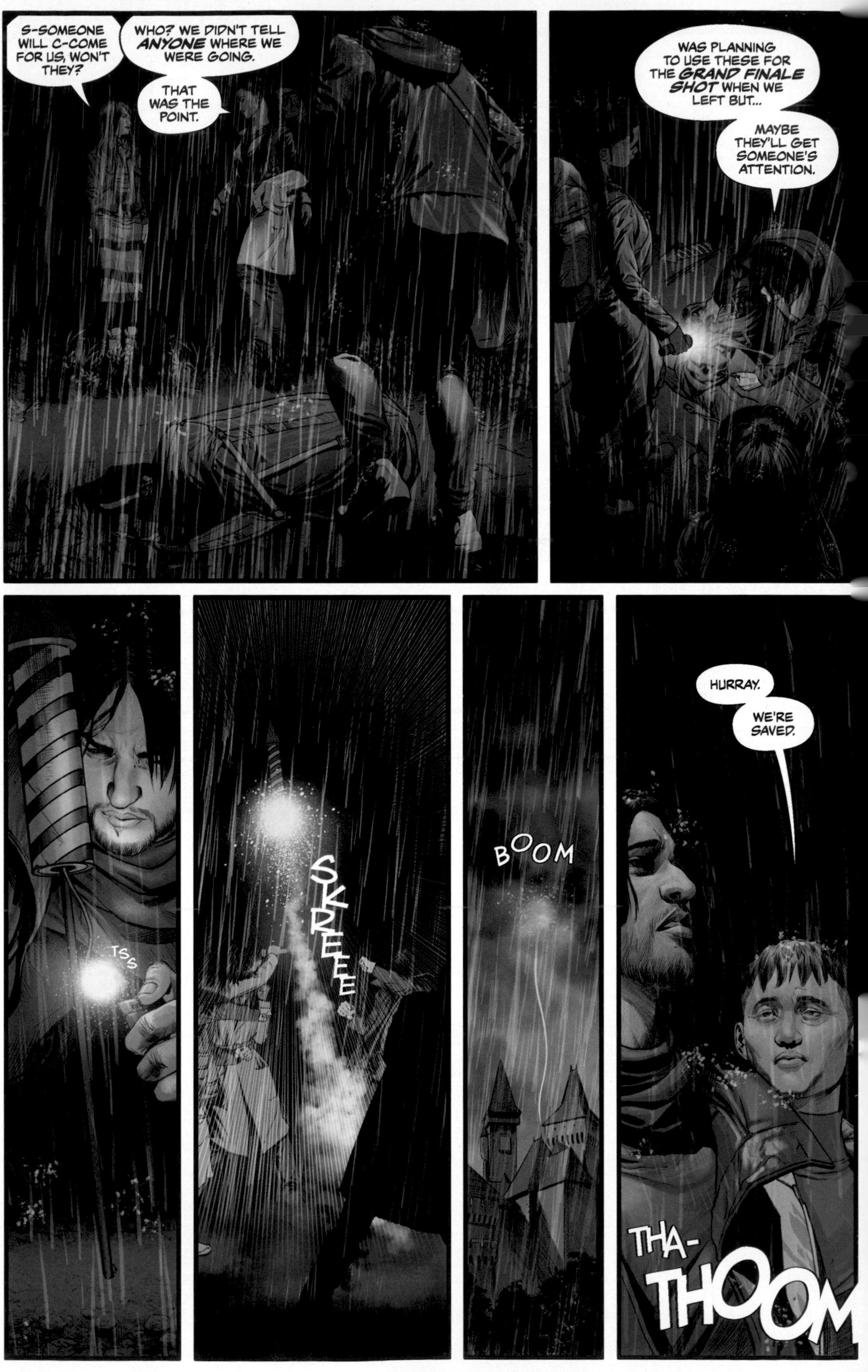
S-SOMEONE WILL C-COME FOR US, WON'T THEY?
WHO? WE DIDN'T TELL ANYONE WHERE WE WERE GOING.
THAT WAS THE POINT.
WAS PLANNING TO USE THESE FOR THE GRAND FINALE SHOT WHEN WE LEFT BUT...
MAYBE THEY'LL GET SOMEONE'S ATTENTION.
TSS
SKREEE
BOOM
HURRAY.
WE'RE SAVED.
THA-THOOM

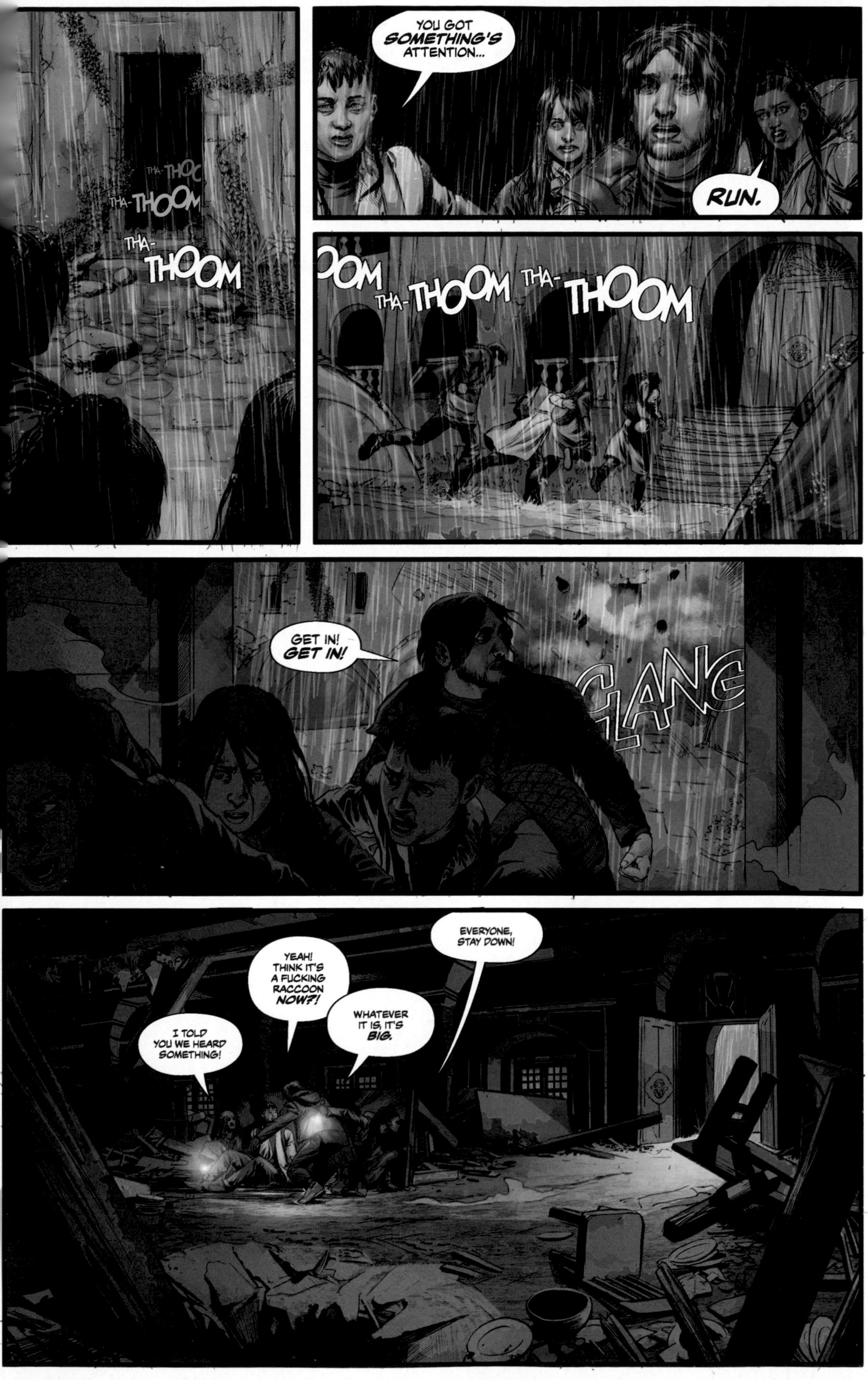
THA-THOO
THA-THOOM
THA-THOOM
YOU GOT SOMETHING'S ATTENTION...
RUN.
OOM
THA-THOOM
THA-THOOM
GET IN! GET IN!
CLANG
EVERYONE, STAY DOWN!
YEAH! THINK IT'S A FUCKING RACCOON NOW?!
WHATEVER IT IS, IT'S BIG.
I TOLD YOU WE HEARD SOMETHING!

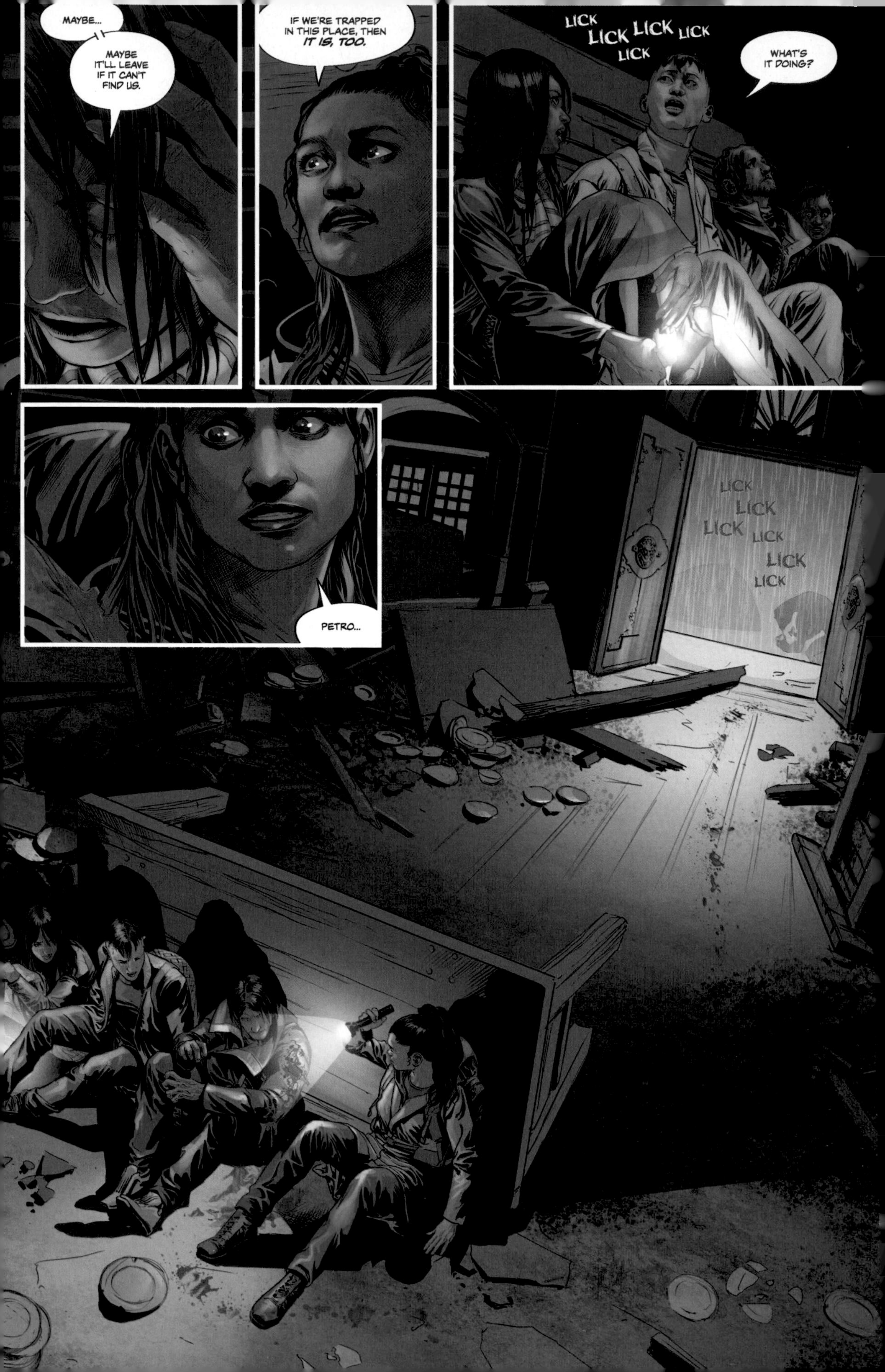
MAYBE...
MAYBE IT'LL LEAVE IF IT CAN'T FIND US.
IF WE'RE TRAPPED IN THIS PLACE, THEN *IT IS, TOO.*
LICK LICK LICK LICK LICK
WHAT'S IT DOING?
PETRO...
LICK LICK LICK LICK LICK LICK

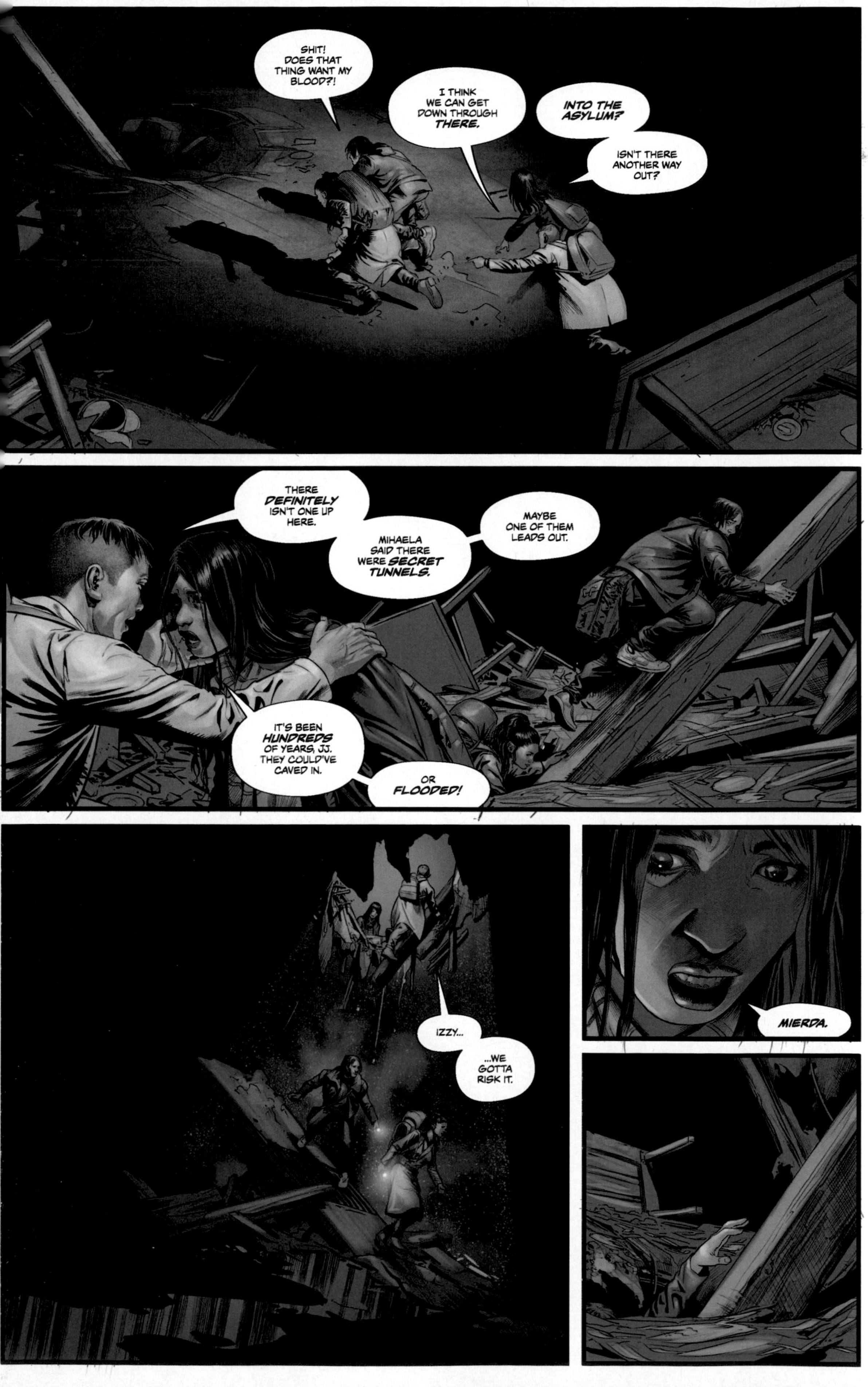
SHIT! DOES THAT THING WANT MY BLOOD?!
I THINK WE CAN GET DOWN THROUGH THERE.
INTO THE ASYLUM?
ISN'T THERE ANOTHER WAY OUT?
THERE DEFINITELY ISN'T ONE UP HERE.
MIHAELA SAID THERE WERE SECRET TUNNELS.
MAYBE ONE OF THEM LEADS OUT.
IT'S BEEN HUNDREDS OF YEARS, JJ. THEY COULD'VE CAVED IN.
OR FLOODED!
IZZY...
...WE GOTTA RISK IT.
MIERDA.

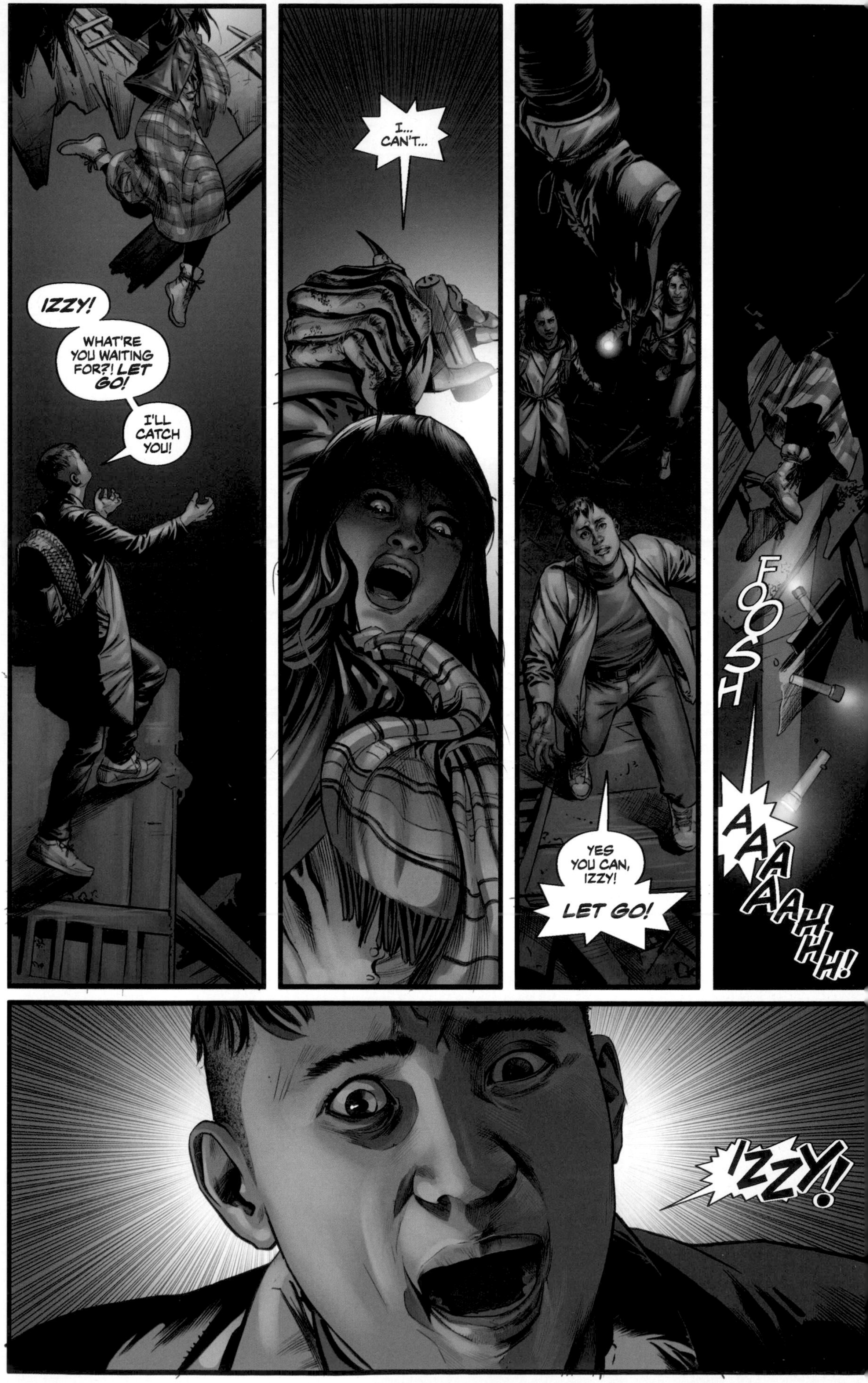
IZZY!
WHAT'RE YOU WAITING FOR?! LET GO!
I'LL CATCH YOU!
I... CAN'T...
YES YOU CAN, IZZY!
LET GO!
FOOSH
AAAAAHHHH!
IZZY!

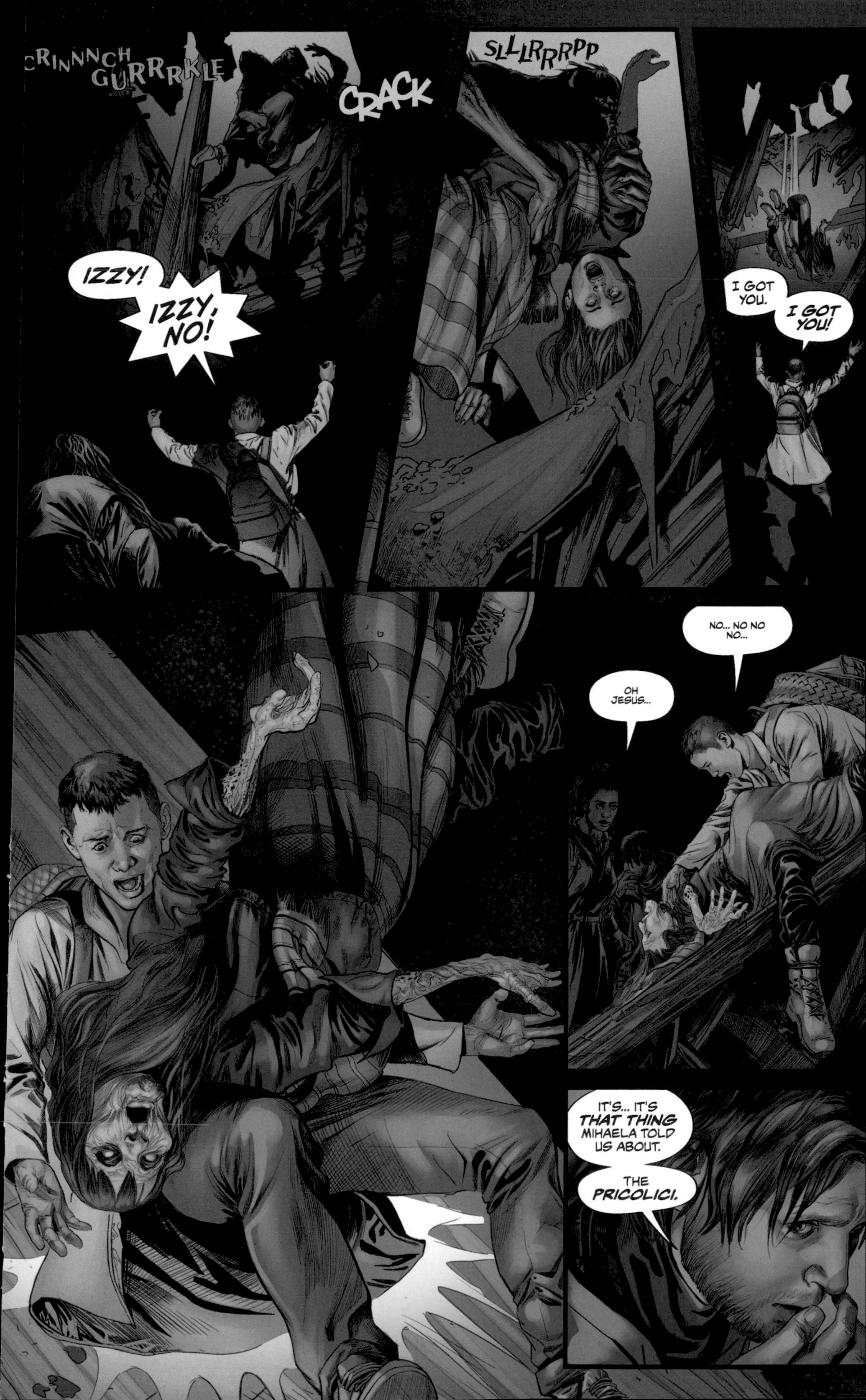
CRINNNCH
GURRRKLE
CRACK
IZZY!
IZZY, NO!
SLLLRRRPP
I GOT YOU.
I GOT YOU!
OH JESUS...
NO... NO NO NO...
IT'S... IT'S THAT THING MIHAELA TOLD US ABOUT.
THE PRICOLICI.

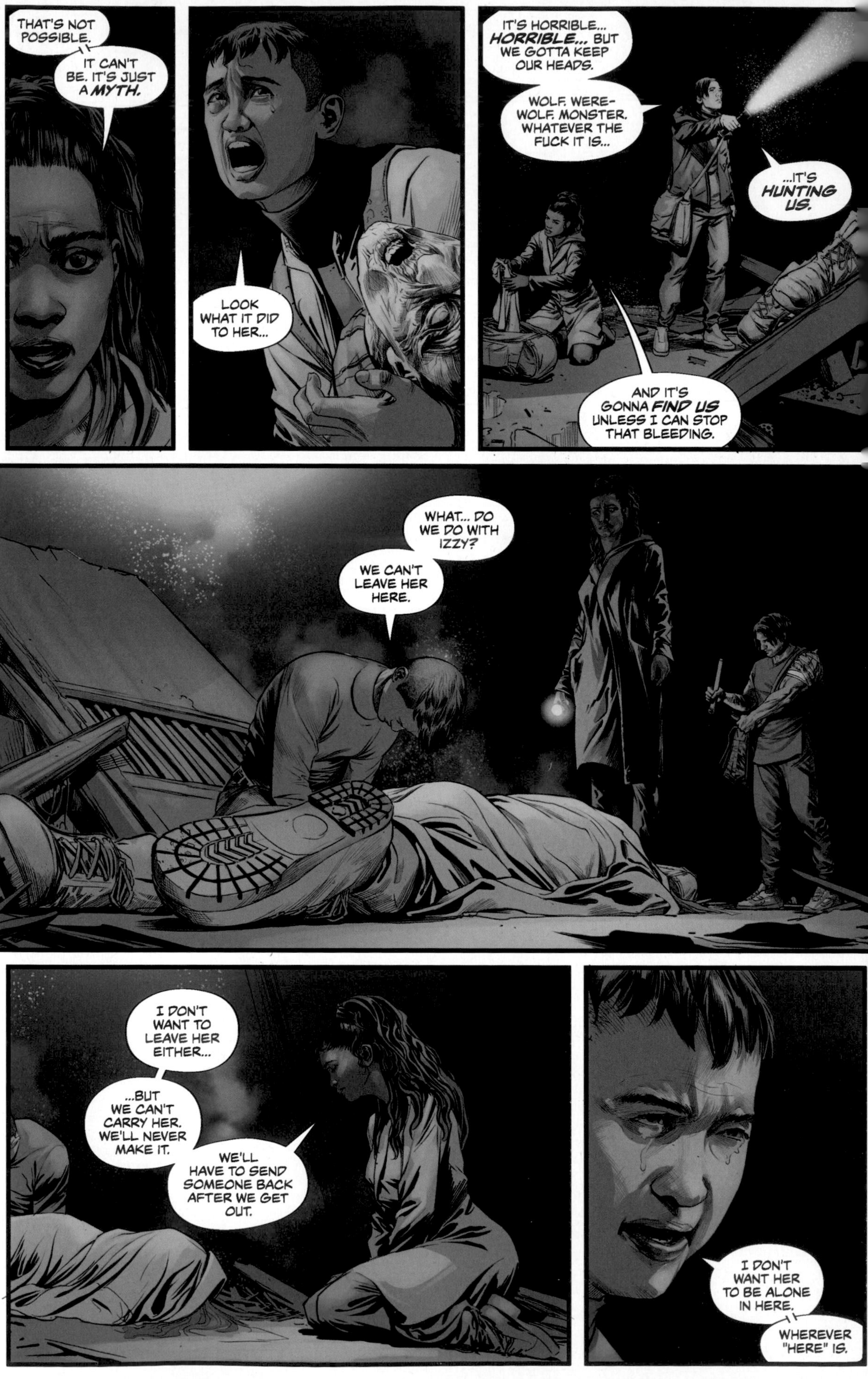
THAT'S NOT POSSIBLE.
IT CAN'T BE. IT'S JUST A MYTH.
LOOK WHAT IT DID TO HER...
IT'S HORRIBLE... HORRIBLE... BUT WE GOTTA KEEP OUR HEADS.
WOLF. WERE-WOLF. MONSTER. WHATEVER THE FUCK IT IS...
...IT'S HUNTING US.
AND IT'S GONNA FIND US UNLESS I CAN STOP THAT BLEEDING.
WHAT... DO WE DO WITH IZZY?
WE CAN'T LEAVE HER HERE.
I DON'T WANT TO LEAVE HER EITHER...
...BUT WE CAN'T CARRY HER. WE'LL NEVER MAKE IT.
WE'LL HAVE TO SEND SOMEONE BACK AFTER WE GET OUT.
I DON'T WANT HER TO BE ALONE IN HERE.
WHEREVER "HERE" IS.

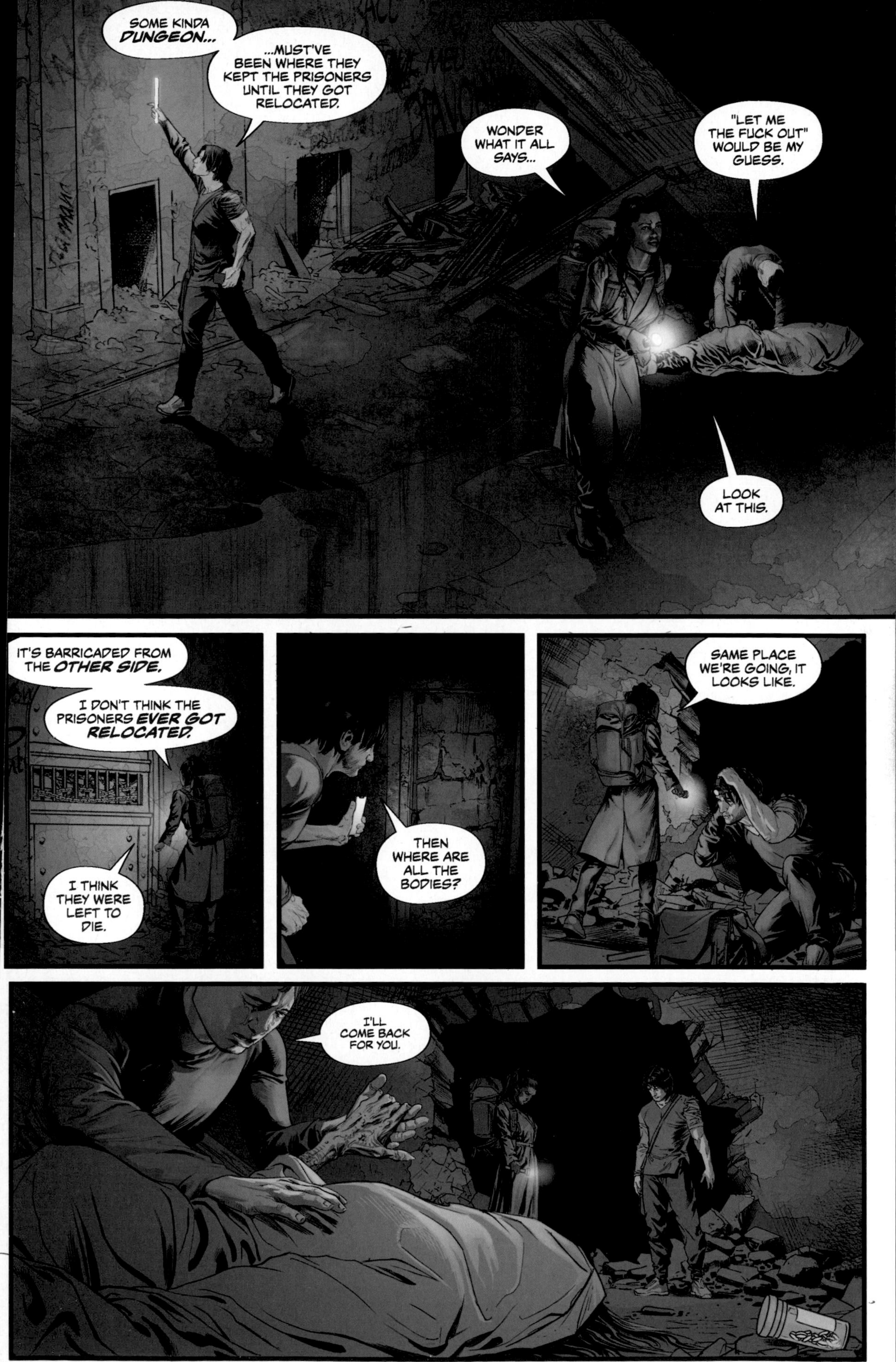
SOME KINDA DUNGEON...
...MUST'VE BEEN WHERE THEY KEPT THE PRISONERS UNTIL THEY GOT RELOCATED.
WONDER WHAT IT ALL SAYS...
"LET ME THE FUCK OUT" WOULD BE MY GUESS.
LOOK AT THIS.
IT'S BARRICADED FROM THE OTHER SIDE.
I DON'T THINK THE PRISONERS EVER GOT RELOCATED.
I THINK THEY WERE LEFT TO DIE.
THEN WHERE ARE ALL THE BODIES?
SAME PLACE WE'RE GOING, IT LOOKS LIKE.
I'LL COME BACK FOR YOU.

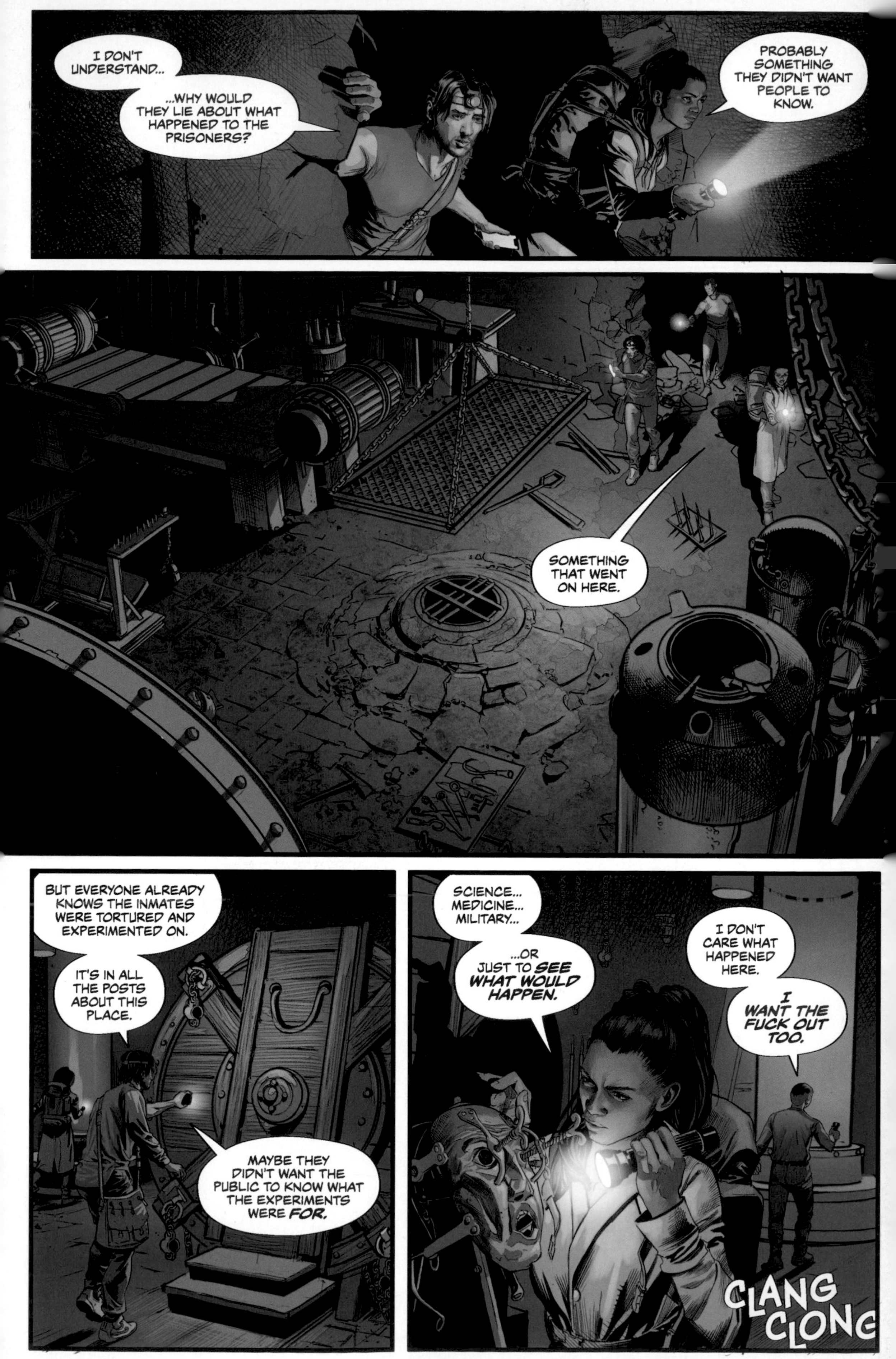
I DON'T UNDERSTAND...
...WHY WOULD THEY LIE ABOUT WHAT HAPPENED TO THE PRISONERS?
PROBABLY SOMETHING THEY DIDN'T WANT PEOPLE TO KNOW.
SOMETHING THAT WENT ON HERE.
BUT EVERYONE ALREADY KNOWS THE INMATES WERE TORTURED AND EXPERIMENTED ON.
IT'S IN ALL THE POSTS ABOUT THIS PLACE.
MAYBE THEY DIDN'T WANT THE PUBLIC TO KNOW WHAT THE EXPERIMENTS WERE FOR.
SCIENCE... MEDICINE... MILITARY...
...OR JUST TO SEE WHAT WOULD HAPPEN.
I DON'T CARE WHAT HAPPENED HERE.
I WANT THE FUCK OUT TOO.
CLANG CLONG

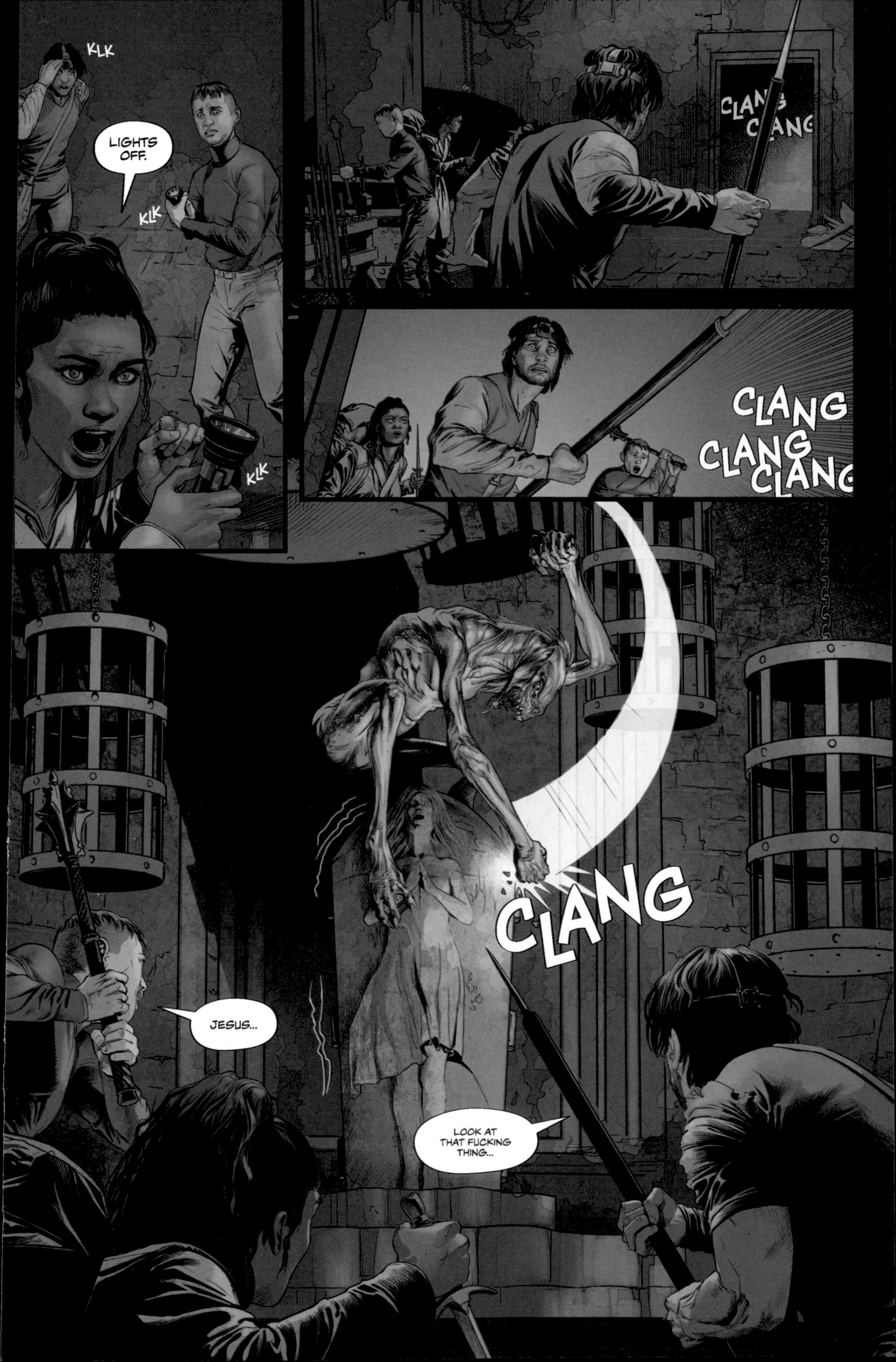
KLK
LIGHTS OFF.
KLK
KLK
CLANG CLANG
CLANG
CLANG
CLANG
CLANG
JESUS...
LOOK AT THAT FUCKING THING...

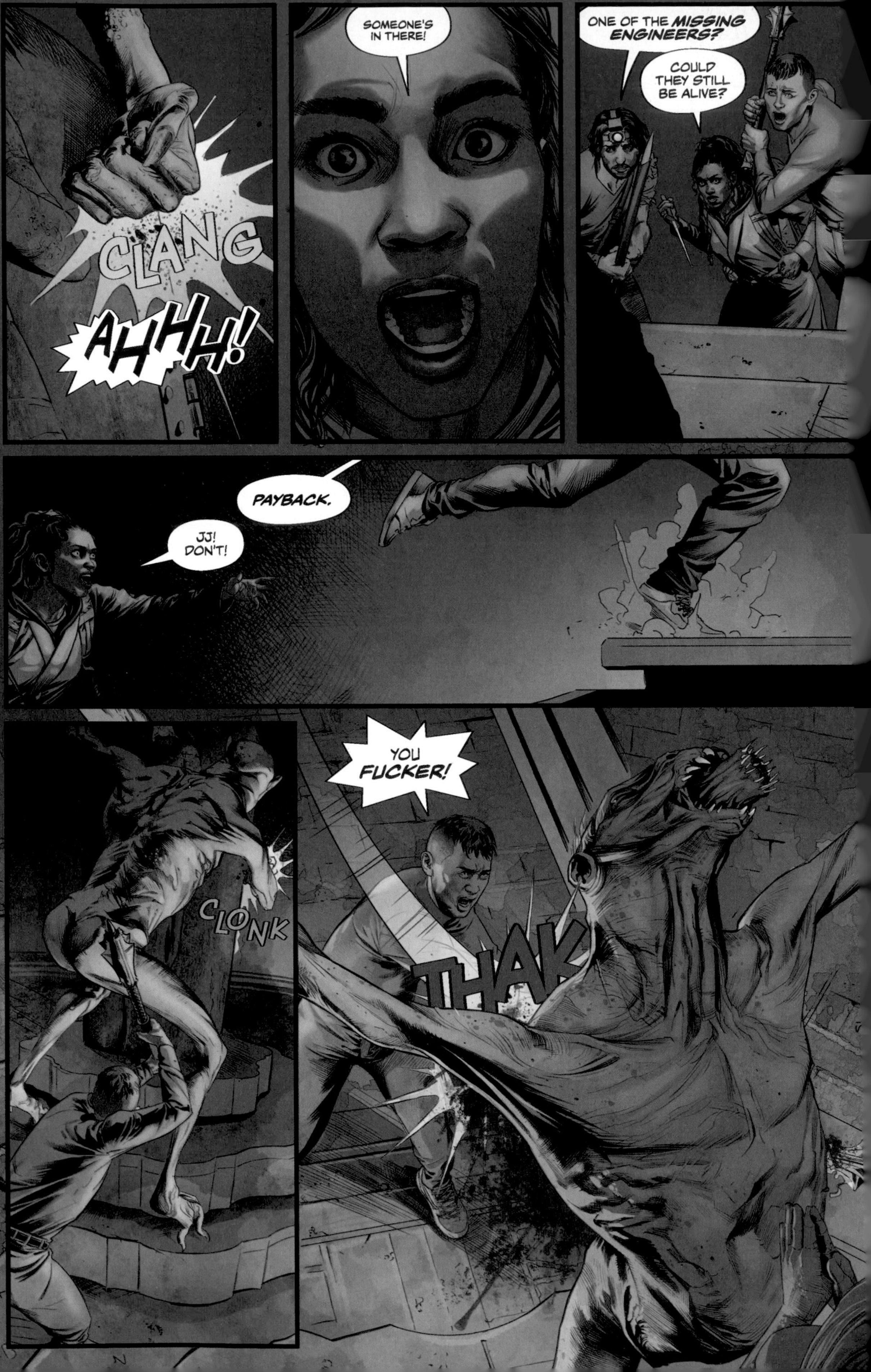
CLANG
AHHHH!
SOMEONE'S IN THERE!
ONE OF THE MISSING ENGINEERS?
COULD THEY STILL BE ALIVE?
PAYBACK.
JJ! DON'T!
CLONK
YOU FUCKER!
THAK

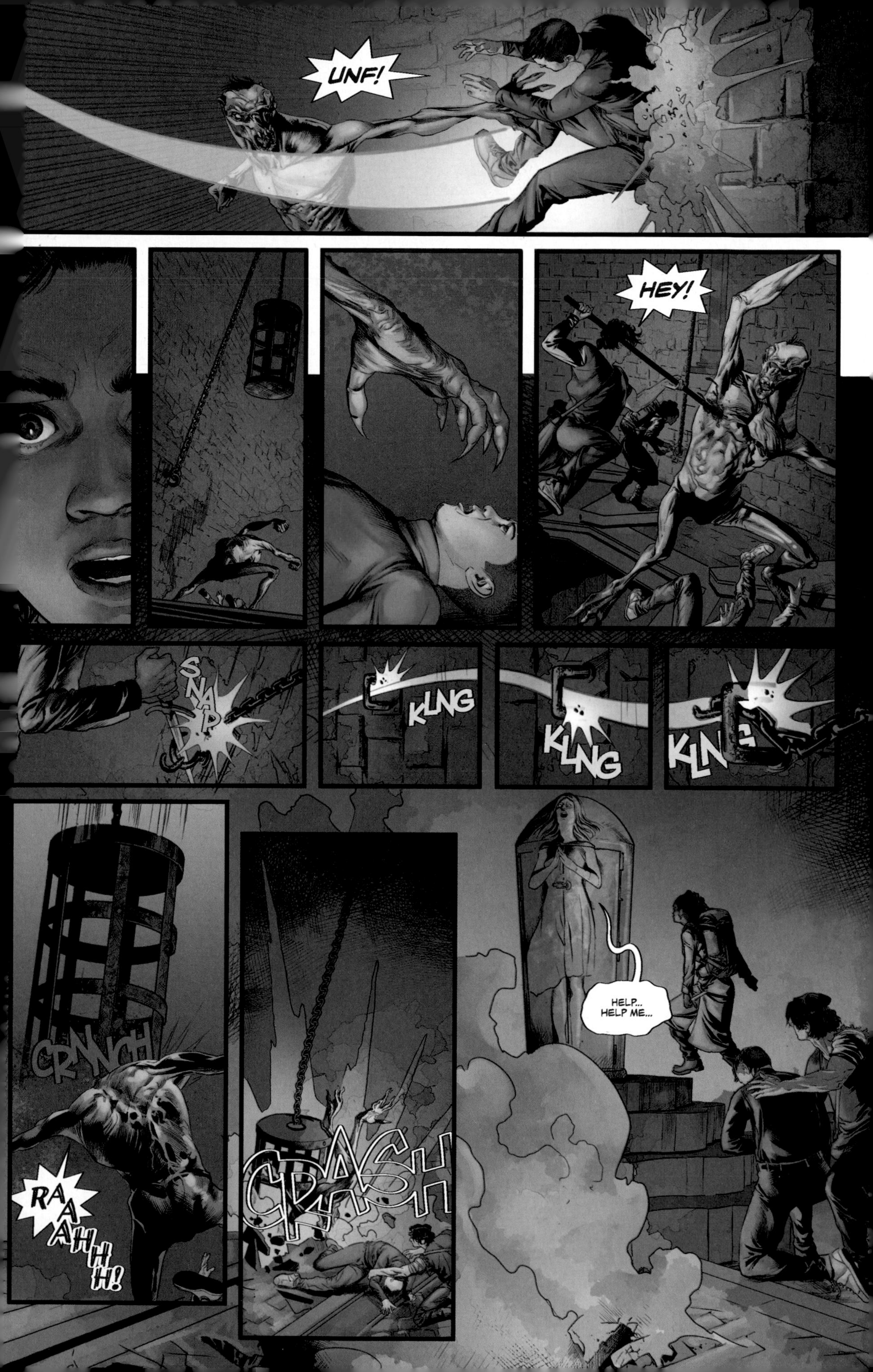
UNF!
HEY!
SNAP
KLNG
KLNG
KLNG
CRNNCH
RAAAHHHH!
CRASH
HELP... HELP ME...

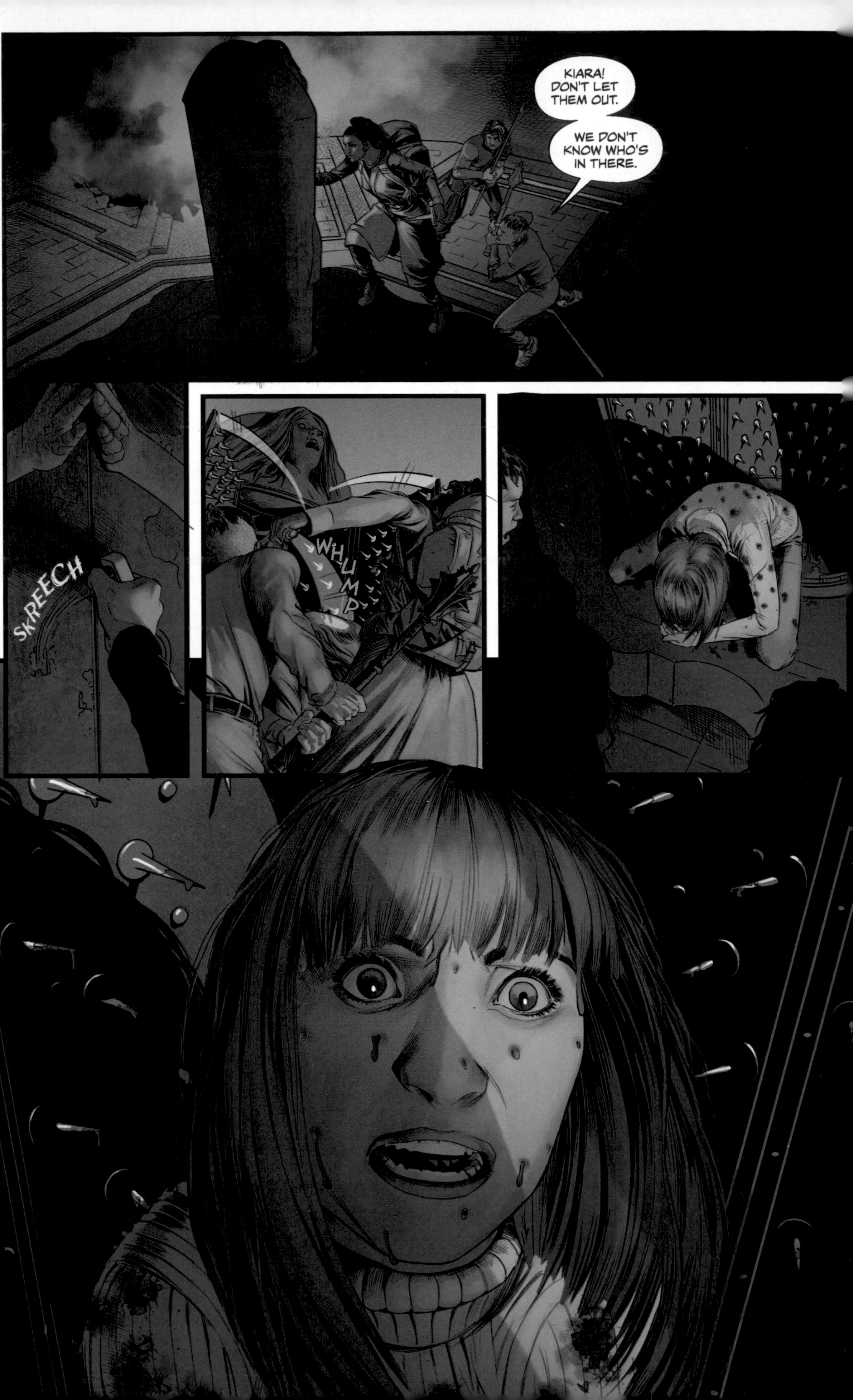
KIARA! DON'T LET THEM OUT.
WE DON'T KNOW WHO'S IN THERE.
SKREECH
WHUMP

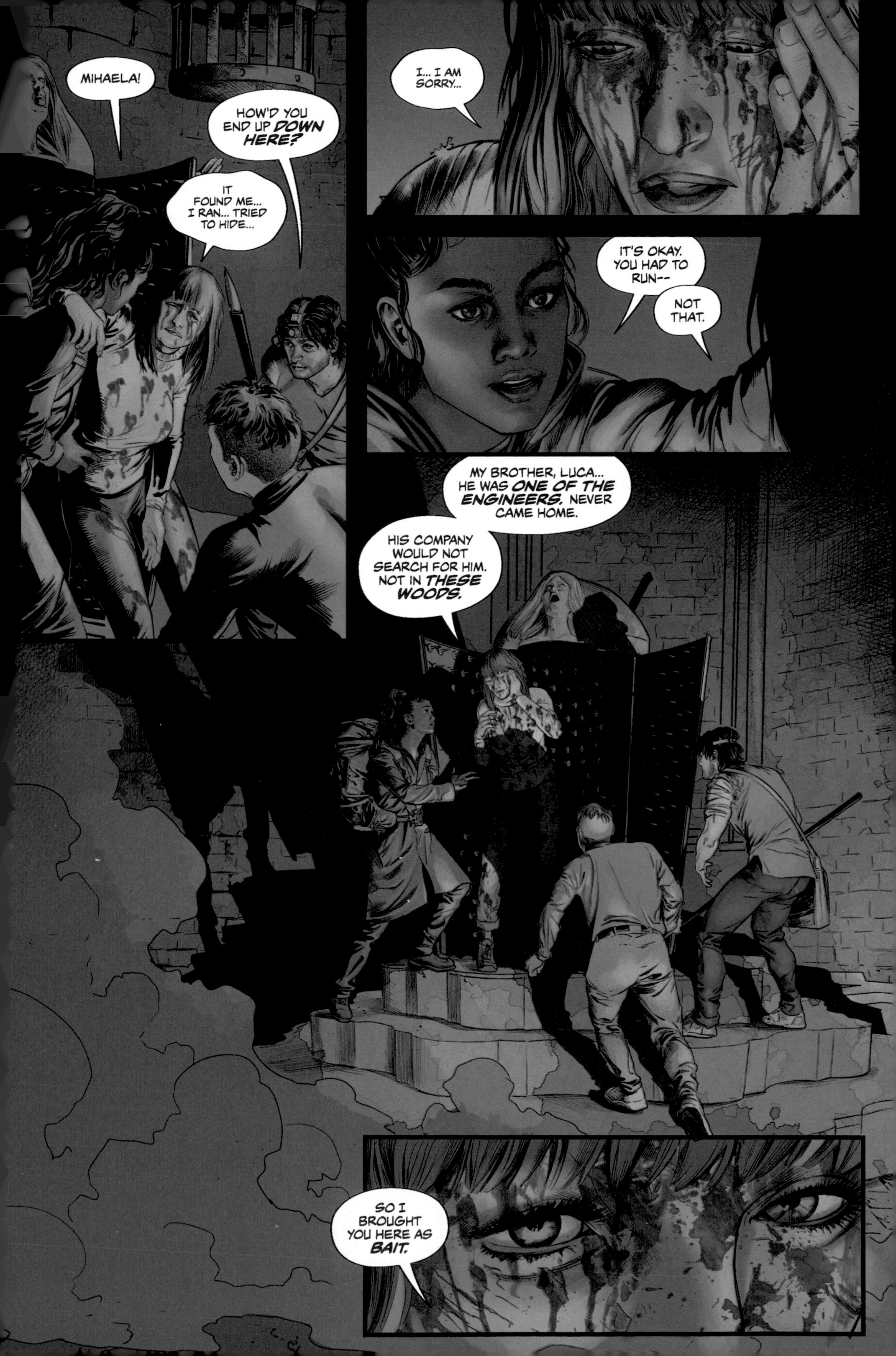
MIHAELA!
HOW'D YOU END UP DOWN HERE?
IT FOUND ME... I RAN... TRIED TO HIDE...
I... I AM SORRY...
IT'S OKAY. YOU HAD TO RUN--
NOT THAT.
MY BROTHER, LUCA... HE WAS ONE OF THE ENGINEERS. NEVER CAME HOME.
HIS COMPANY WOULD NOT SEARCH FOR HIM. NOT IN THESE WOODS.
SO I BROUGHT YOU HERE AS BAIT.

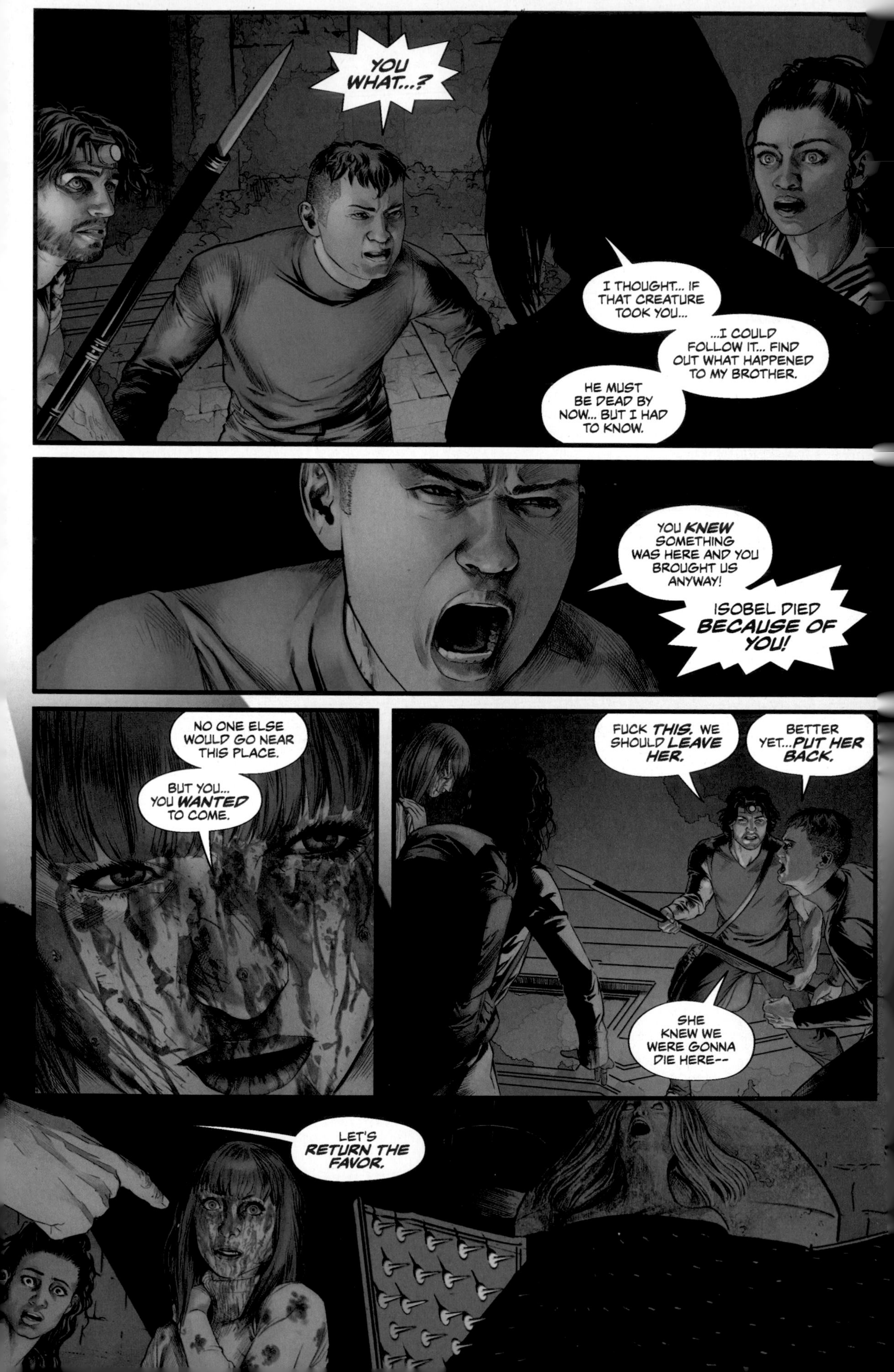
YOU WHAT...?
I THOUGHT... IF THAT CREATURE TOOK YOU...
...I COULD FOLLOW IT... FIND OUT WHAT HAPPENED TO MY BROTHER.
HE MUST BE DEAD BY NOW... BUT I HAD TO KNOW.
YOU KNEW SOMETHING WAS HERE AND YOU BROUGHT US ANYWAY!
ISOBEL DIED BECAUSE OF YOU!
NO ONE ELSE WOULD GO NEAR THIS PLACE.
BUT YOU... YOU WANTED TO COME.
FUCK THIS. WE SHOULD LEAVE HER.
BETTER YET...PUT HER BACK.
SHE KNEW WE WERE GONNA DIE HERE--
LET'S RETURN THE FAVOR.

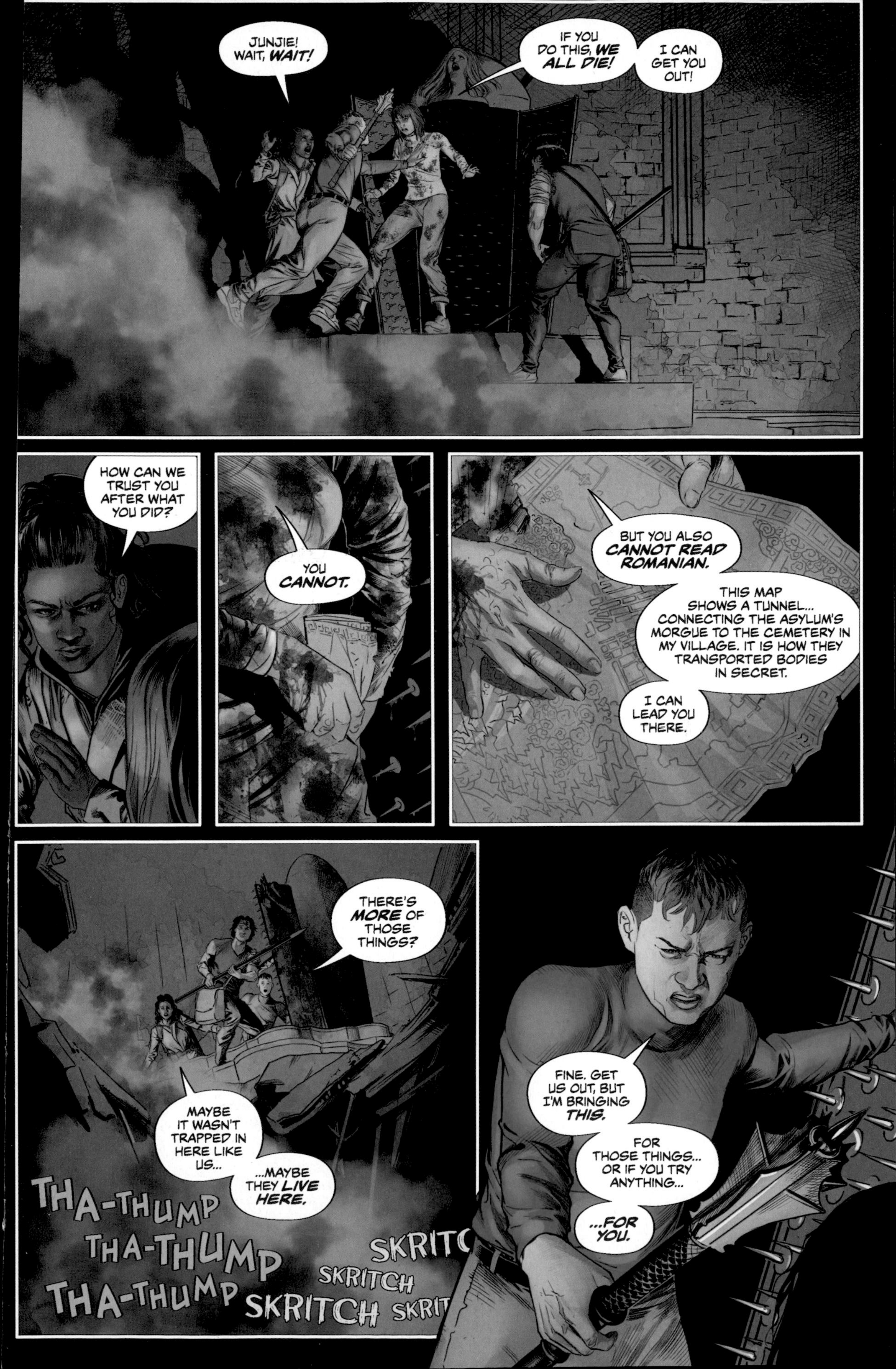
JUNJIE! WAIT, WAIT!
IF YOU DO THIS, WE ALL DIE!
I CAN GET YOU OUT!
HOW CAN WE TRUST YOU AFTER WHAT YOU DID?
YOU CANNOT.
BUT YOU ALSO CANNOT READ ROMANIAN.
THIS MAP SHOWS A TUNNEL... CONNECTING THE ASYLUM'S MORGUE TO THE CEMETERY IN MY VILLAGE. IT IS HOW THEY TRANSPORTED BODIES IN SECRET.
I CAN LEAD YOU THERE.
THERE'S MORE OF THOSE THINGS?
MAYBE IT WASN'T TRAPPED IN HERE LIKE US...
...MAYBE THEY LIVE HERE.
THA-THUMP
THA-THUMP
THA-THUMP
SKRITC
SKRITCH
SKRITCH
SKRIT
FINE. GET US OUT, BUT I'M BRINGING THIS.
FOR THOSE THINGS... OR IF YOU TRY ANYTHING...
...FOR YOU.

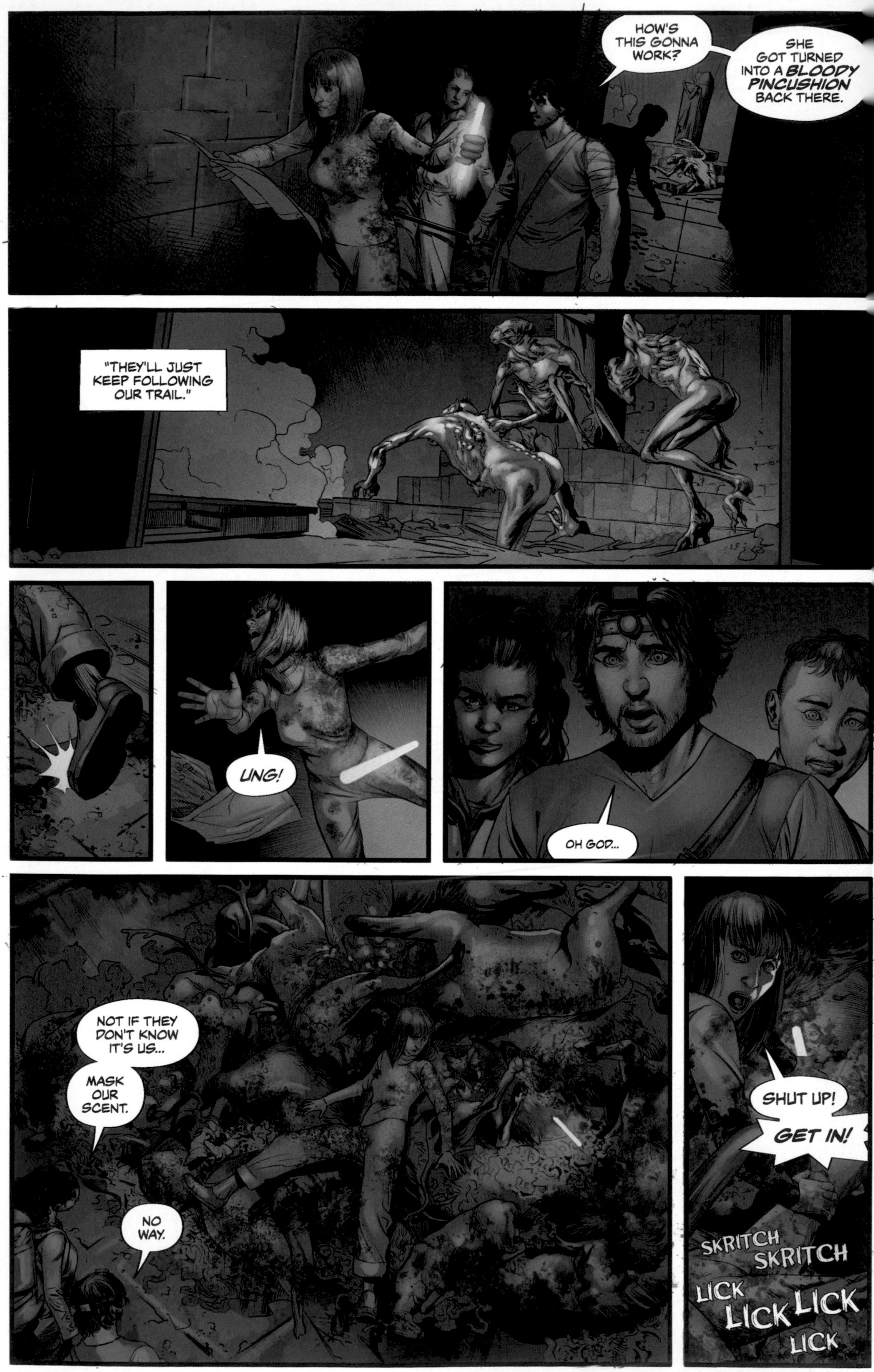
HOW'S THIS GONNA WORK?
SHE GOT TURNED INTO A BLOODY PINCUSHION BACK THERE.
"THEY'LL JUST KEEP FOLLOWING OUR TRAIL."
UNG!
OH GOD...
NOT IF THEY DON'T KNOW IT'S US...
MASK OUR SCENT.
NO WAY.
SHUT UP!
GET IN!
SKRITCH SKRITCH
LICK LICK LICK LICK

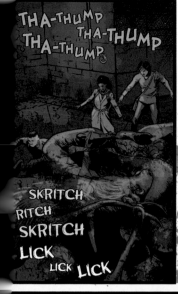

THA-THUMP THA-THUMP
THA-THUMP

SKRITCH
RITCH
SKRITCH
LICK
LICK LICK

LICK LICK LICK

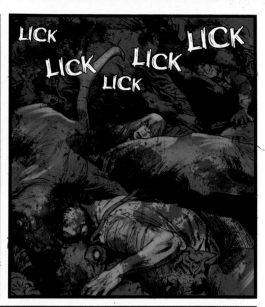

LICK
LICK LICK
LICK
LICK

MRRAWWW

ROOOAWWW

MAW W—

CRACK

FWOOSH

SKRITCH
RITCH
SKRITCH

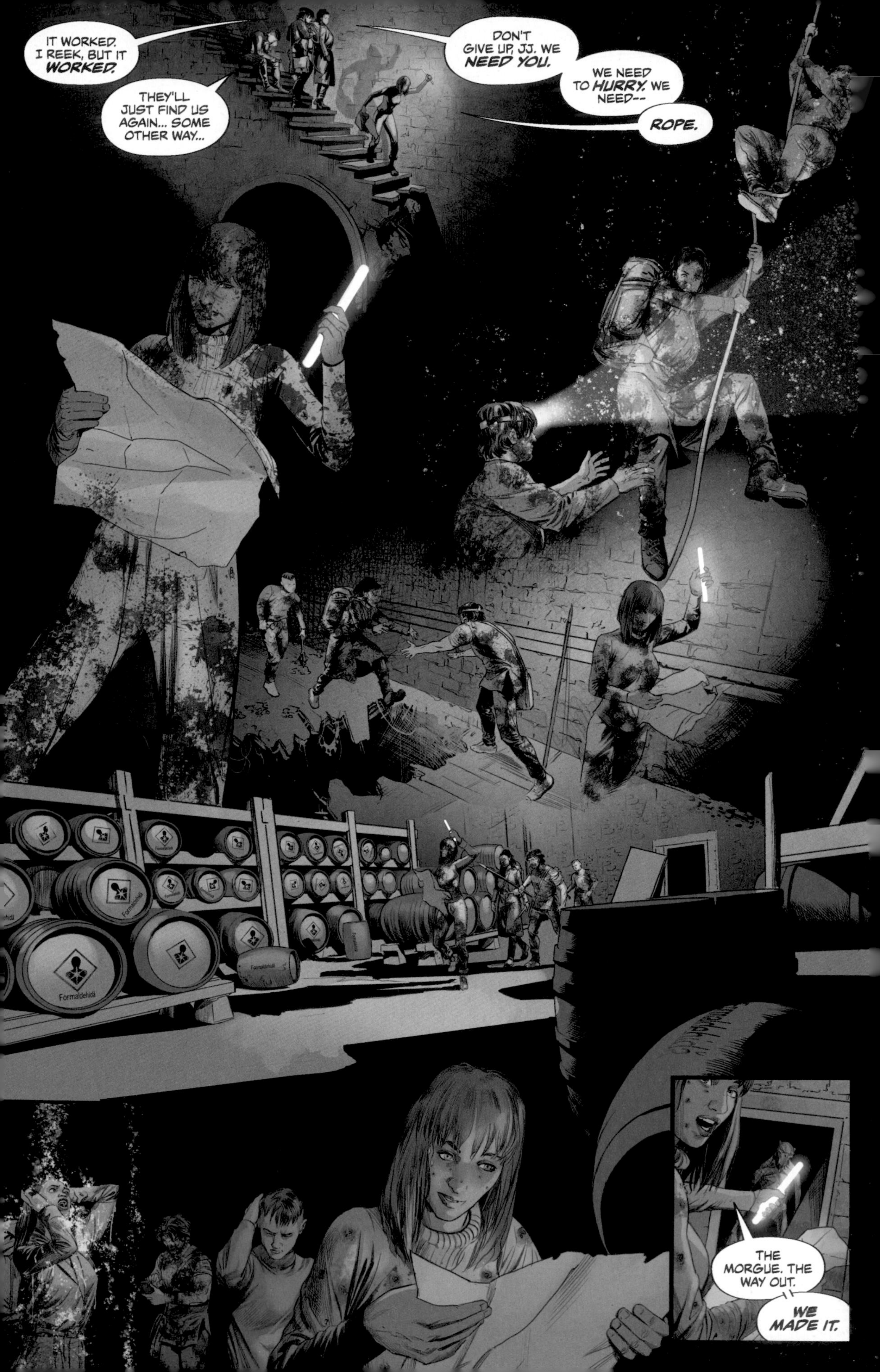
IT WORKED. I REEK, BUT IT WORKED.
THEY'LL JUST FIND US AGAIN... SOME OTHER WAY...
DON'T GIVE UP, JJ. WE NEED YOU.
WE NEED TO HURRY. WE NEED--
ROPE.
Formaldehidă
THE MORGUE. THE WAY OUT.
WE MADE IT.

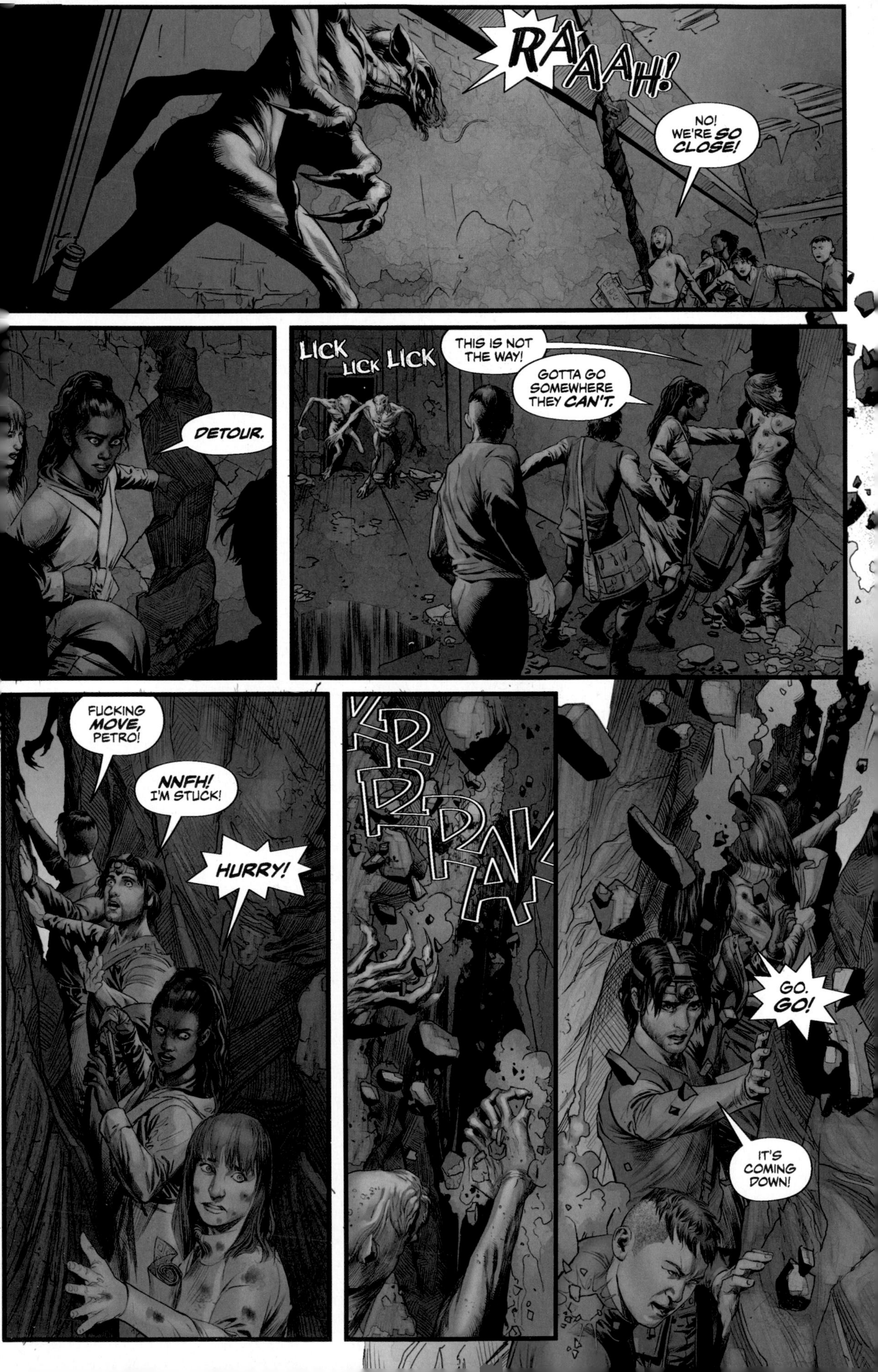
RAAAH!
NO! WE'RE SO CLOSE!
DETOUR.
LICK LICK LICK
THIS IS NOT THE WAY!
GOTTA GO SOMEWHERE THEY CAN'T.
FUCKING MOVE, PETRO!
NNFH! I'M STUCK!
HURRY!
GO. GO!
IT'S COMING DOWN!

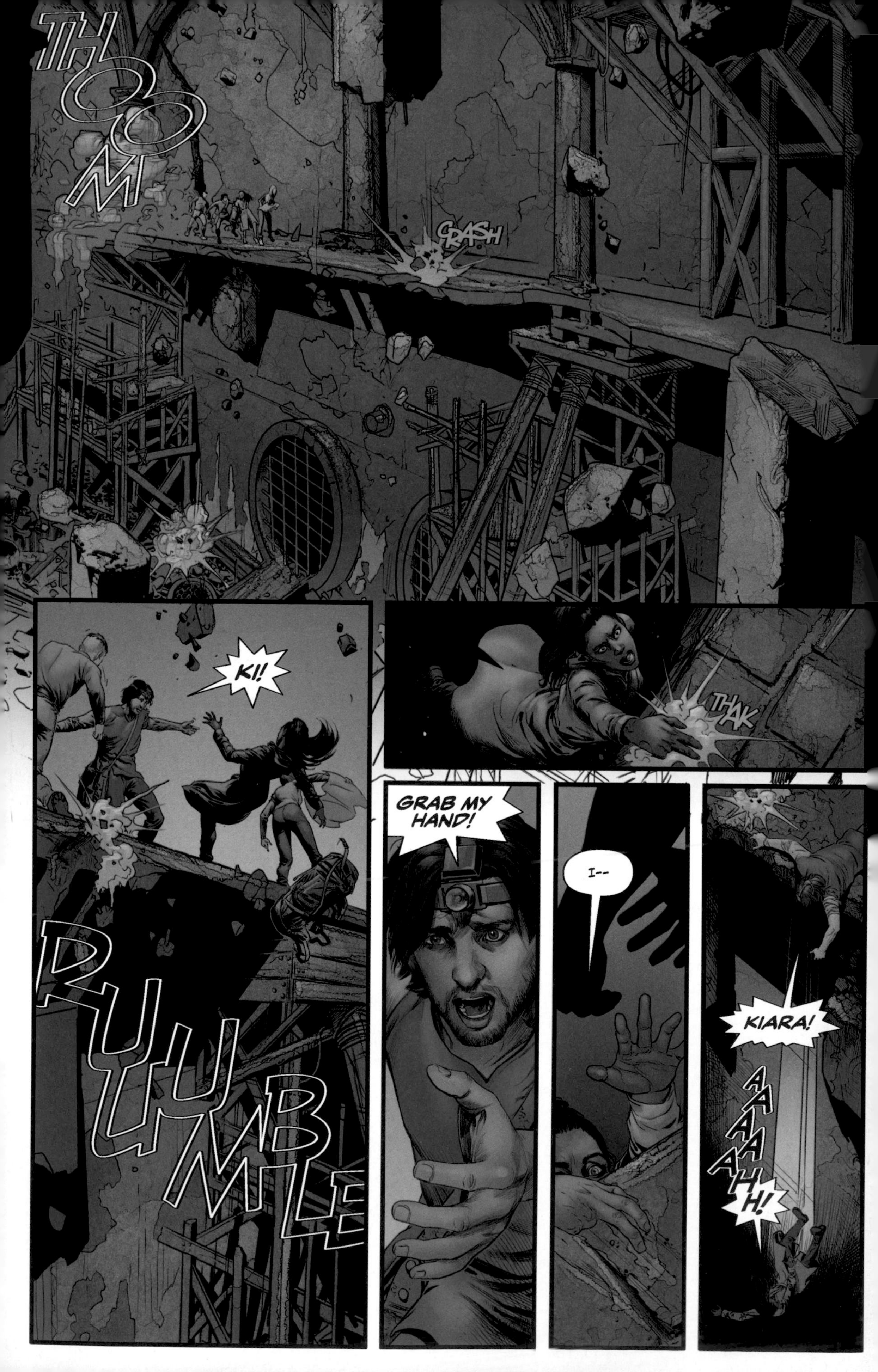
THOOOM
CRASH
KI!
RUUUMBLE
THAK
GRAB MY HAND!
I--
KIARA!
AAAAAHH!

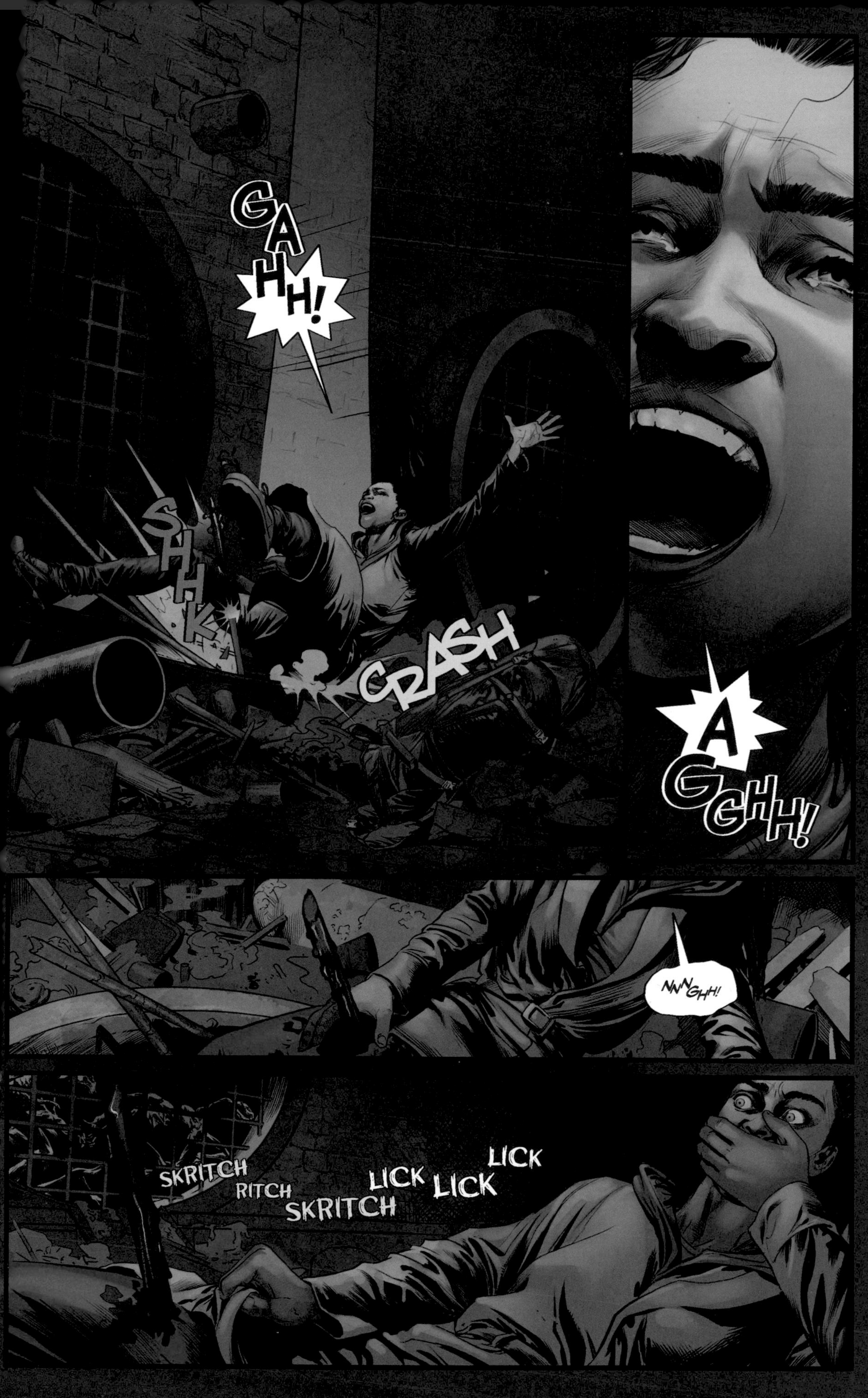
GAHH!
SHHK
CRASH
AGGHH!
NNNGHH!
SKRITCH
RITCH
SKRITCH
LICK
LICK
LICK

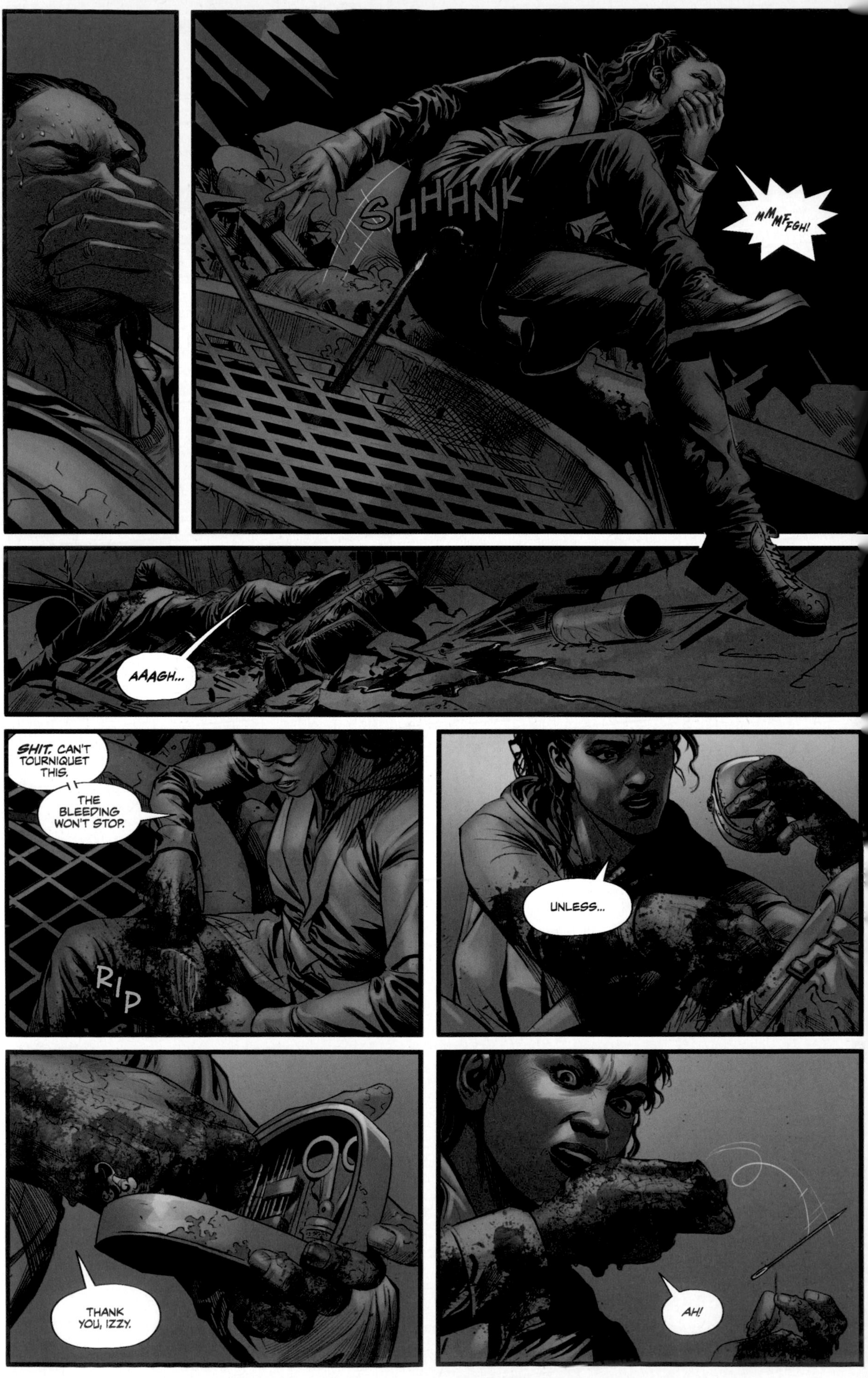
SHHHNK
MMMFFGH!
AAAGH...
SHIT. CAN'T TOURNIQUET THIS.
THE BLEEDING WON'T STOP.
RIP
UNLESS...
THANK YOU, IZZY.
AH!

THA-THUMP
THA-THUMP
THA-THUMP

C'MON...

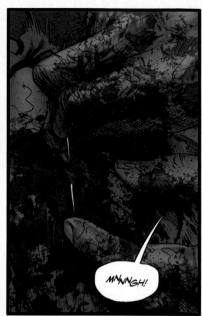

MNNNGH!

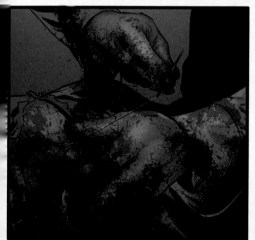

NNN...

SKRITCH
RITCH SKRITCH

HAVE TO DO FOR NOW...

LICK
LICK LICK

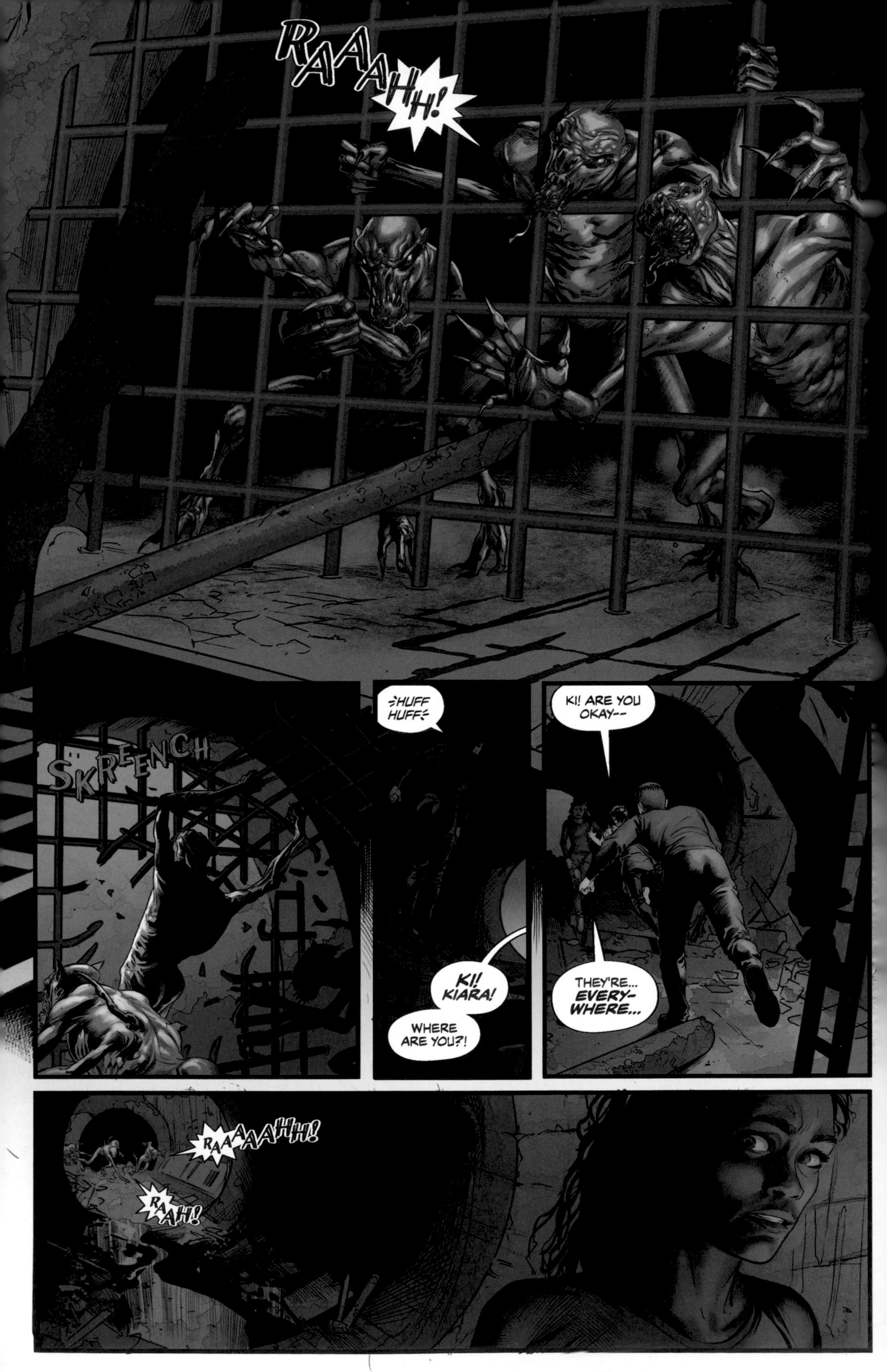
RAAAHHH!
SKREENCH
HUFF HUFF
KI! KIARA!
WHERE ARE YOU?!
KI! ARE YOU OKAY--
THEY'RE... EVERY-WHERE...
RAAAAAHHH!
RAAH!

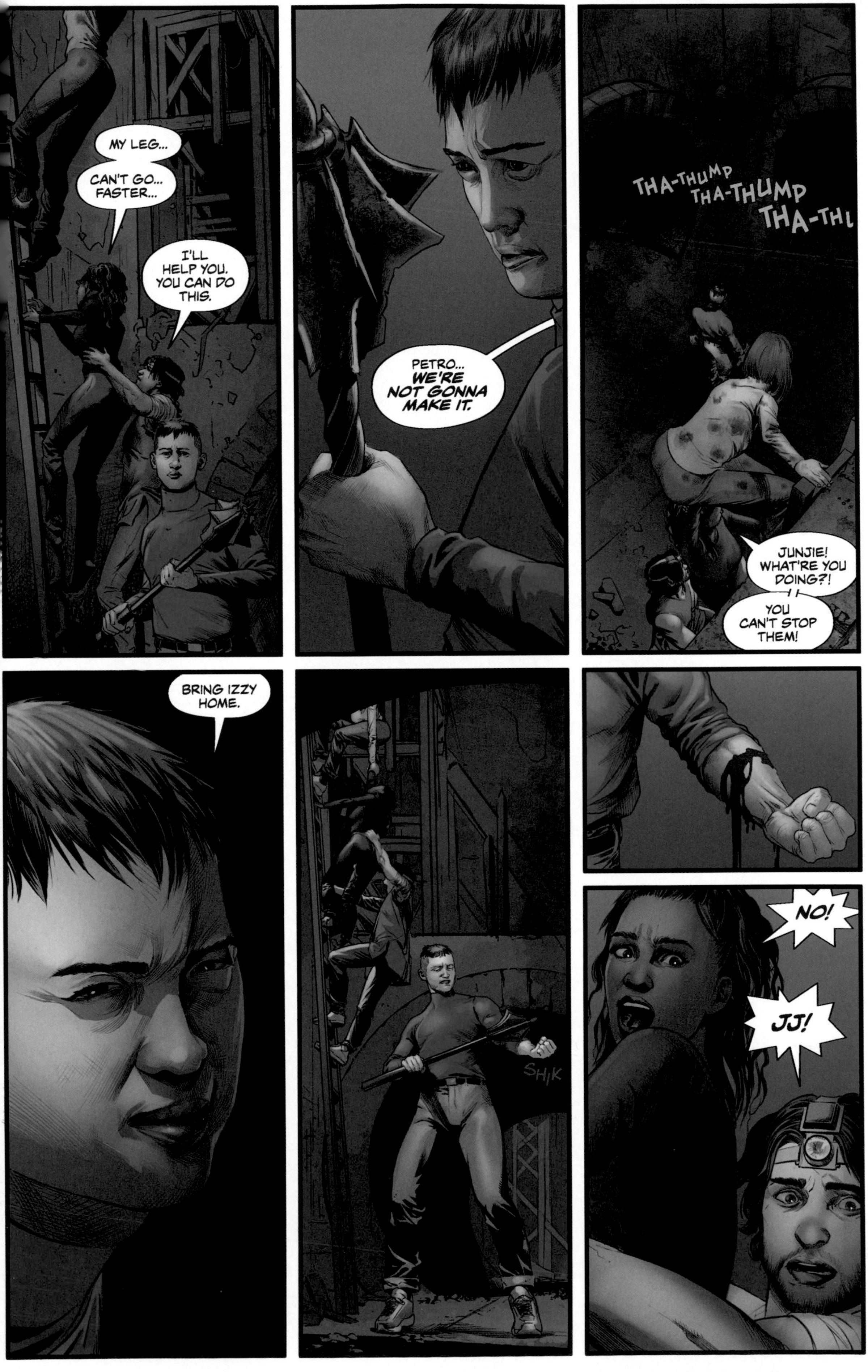

MY LEG...
CAN'T GO... FASTER...
I'LL HELP YOU. YOU CAN DO THIS.
PETRO... WE'RE NOT GONNA MAKE IT.
THA-THUMP THA-THUMP THA-THU
JUNJIE! WHAT'RE YOU DOING?!
YOU CAN'T STOP THEM!
BRING IZZY HOME.
SHIK
NO!
JJ!

CLANG

JUNJIE! DON'T DO THIS.

PLEASE DON'T DO THIS!

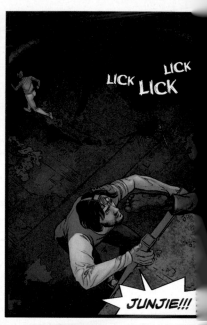

LICK LICK LICK

JUNJIE!!!

LICK LICK LICK

LICK LICK LICK LICK

NO...

HUNGRY?

TOO BAD.

DINNER'S FUCKING CANCELED!

THAK

CRNCH

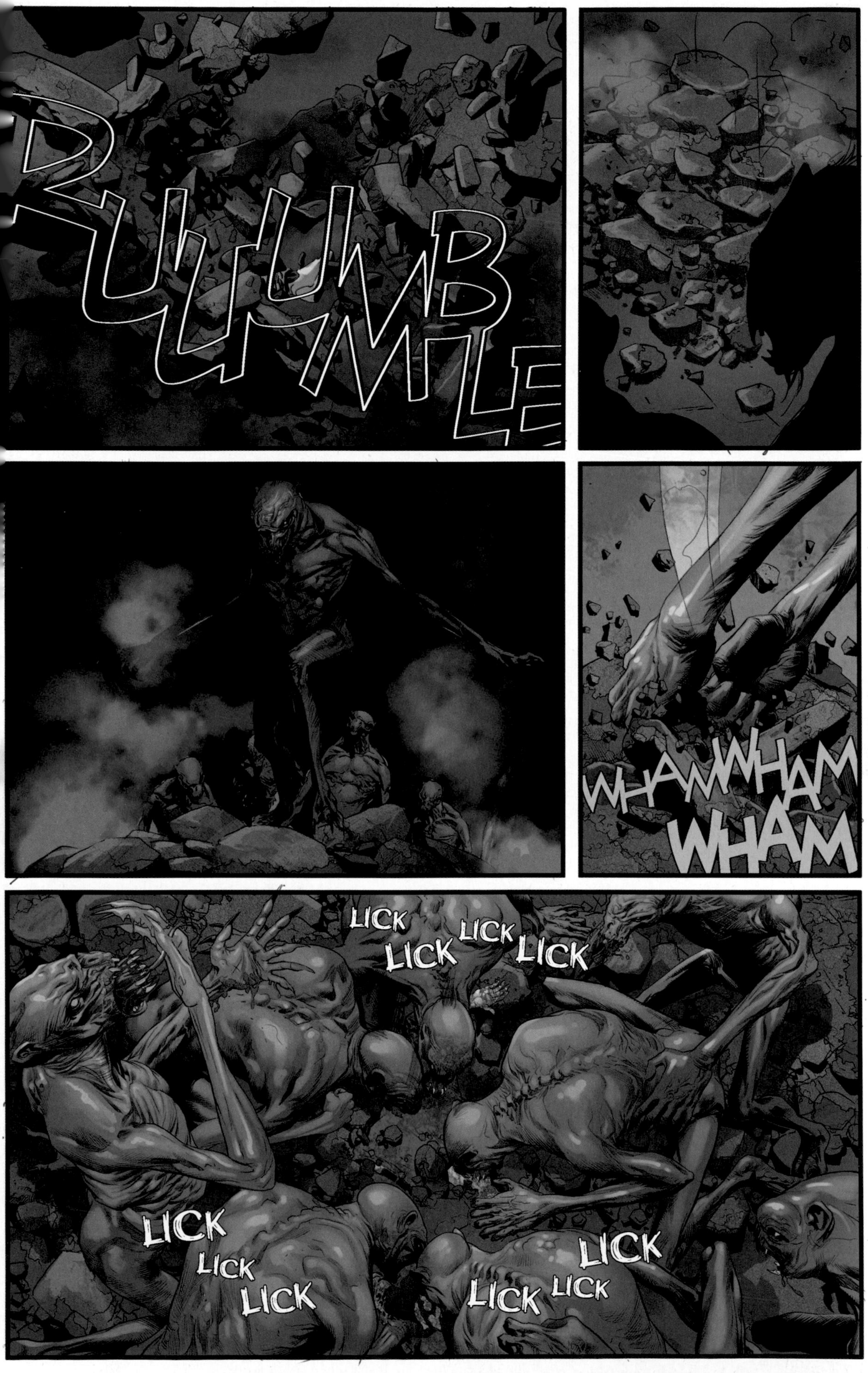
RUUUMBLE
RUMMLE
WHAM WHAM
WHAM
LICK
LICK
LICK
LICK
LICK
LICK
LICK
LICK
LICK
LICK

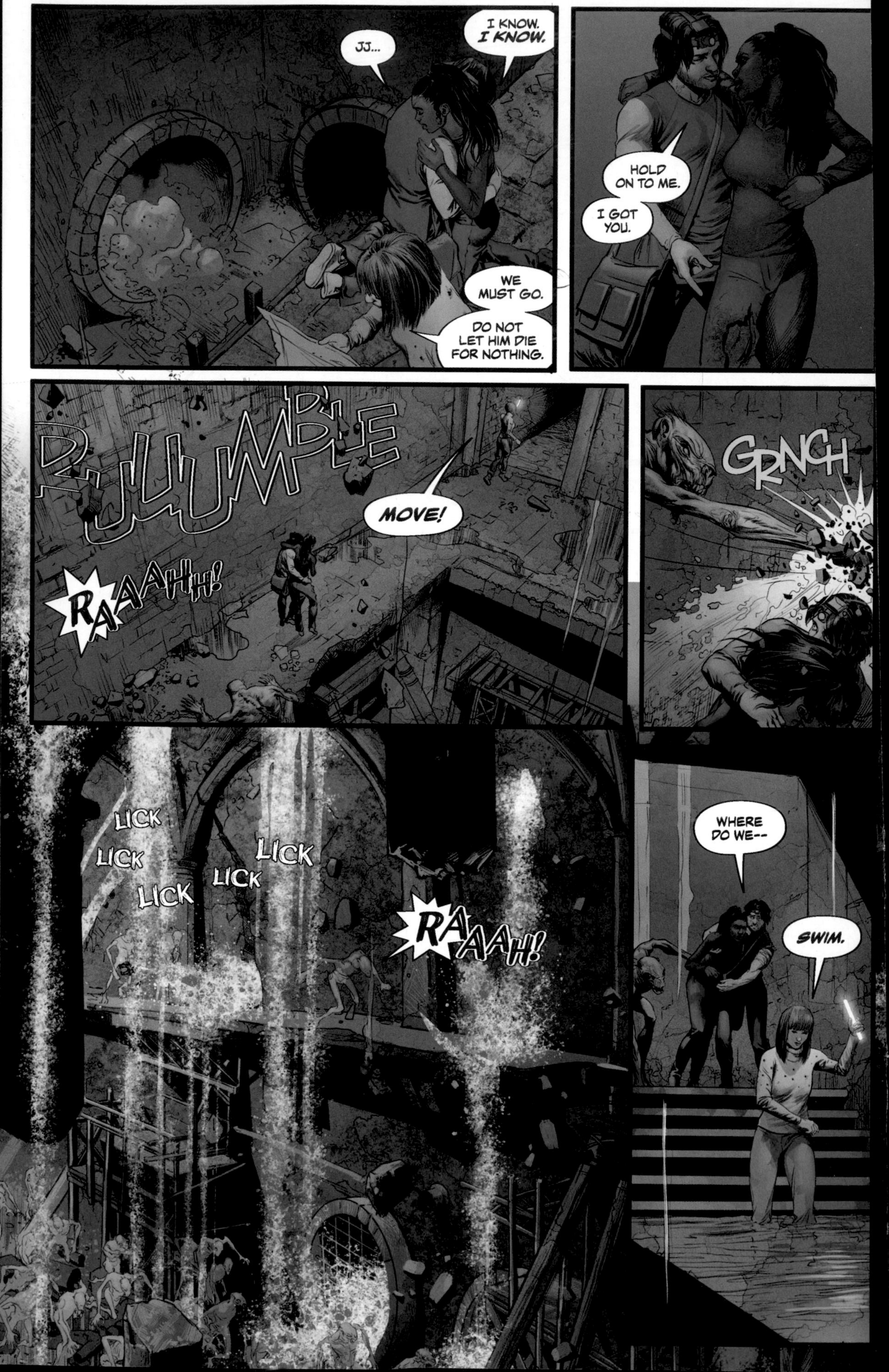
JJ...
I KNOW. I KNOW.
HOLD ON TO ME.
I GOT YOU.
WE MUST GO.
DO NOT LET HIM DIE FOR NOTHING.
RUUUMBLE
MOVE!
RAAAHHH!
GRNCH
LICK
LICK
LICK
LICK
LICK
RAAAH!
WHERE DO WE--
SWIM.

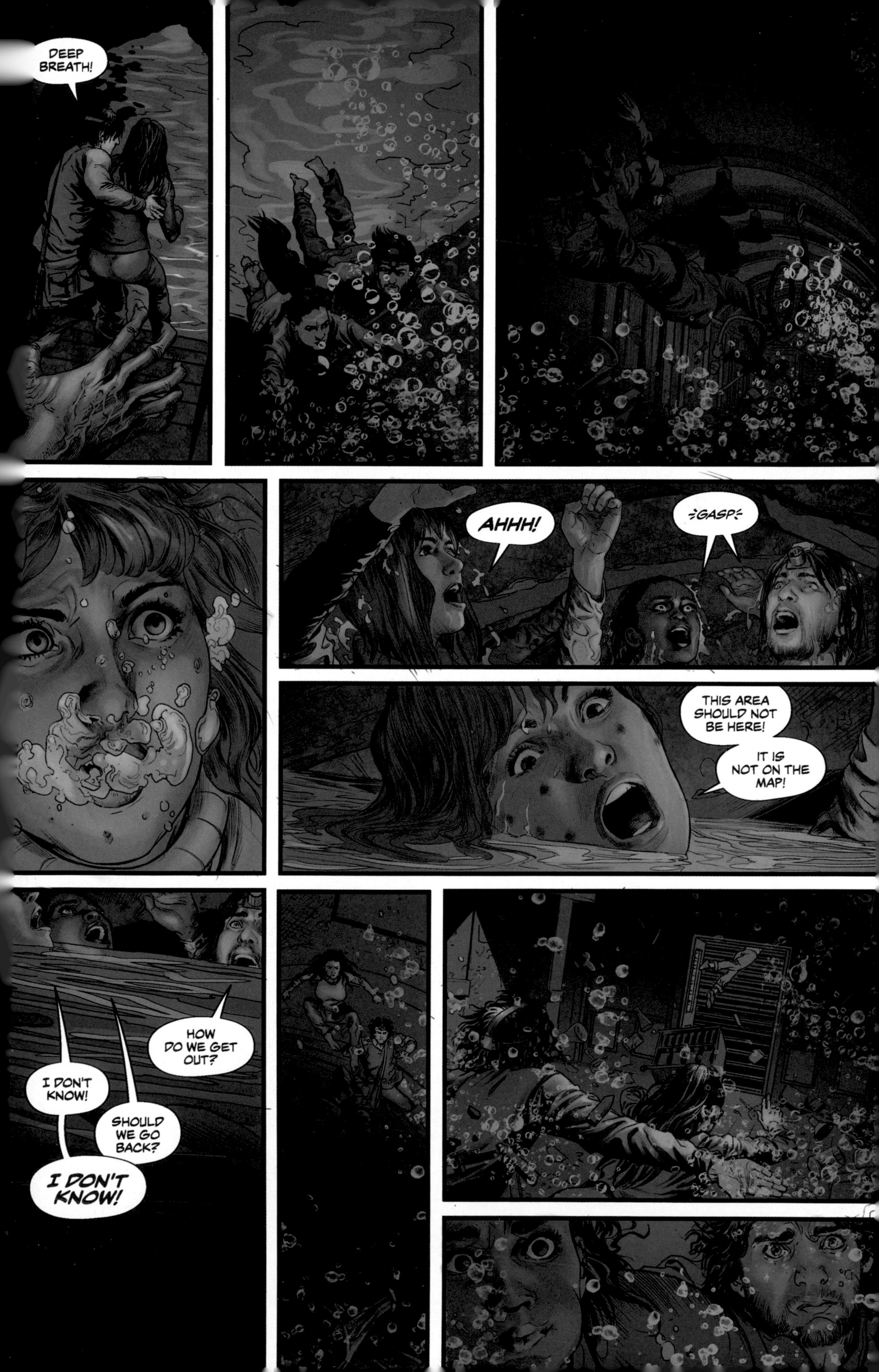
DEEP BREATH!
AHHH!
GASP
THIS AREA SHOULD NOT BE HERE!
IT IS NOT ON THE MAP!
HOW DO WE GET OUT?
I DON'T KNOW!
SHOULD WE GO BACK?
I DON'T KNOW!

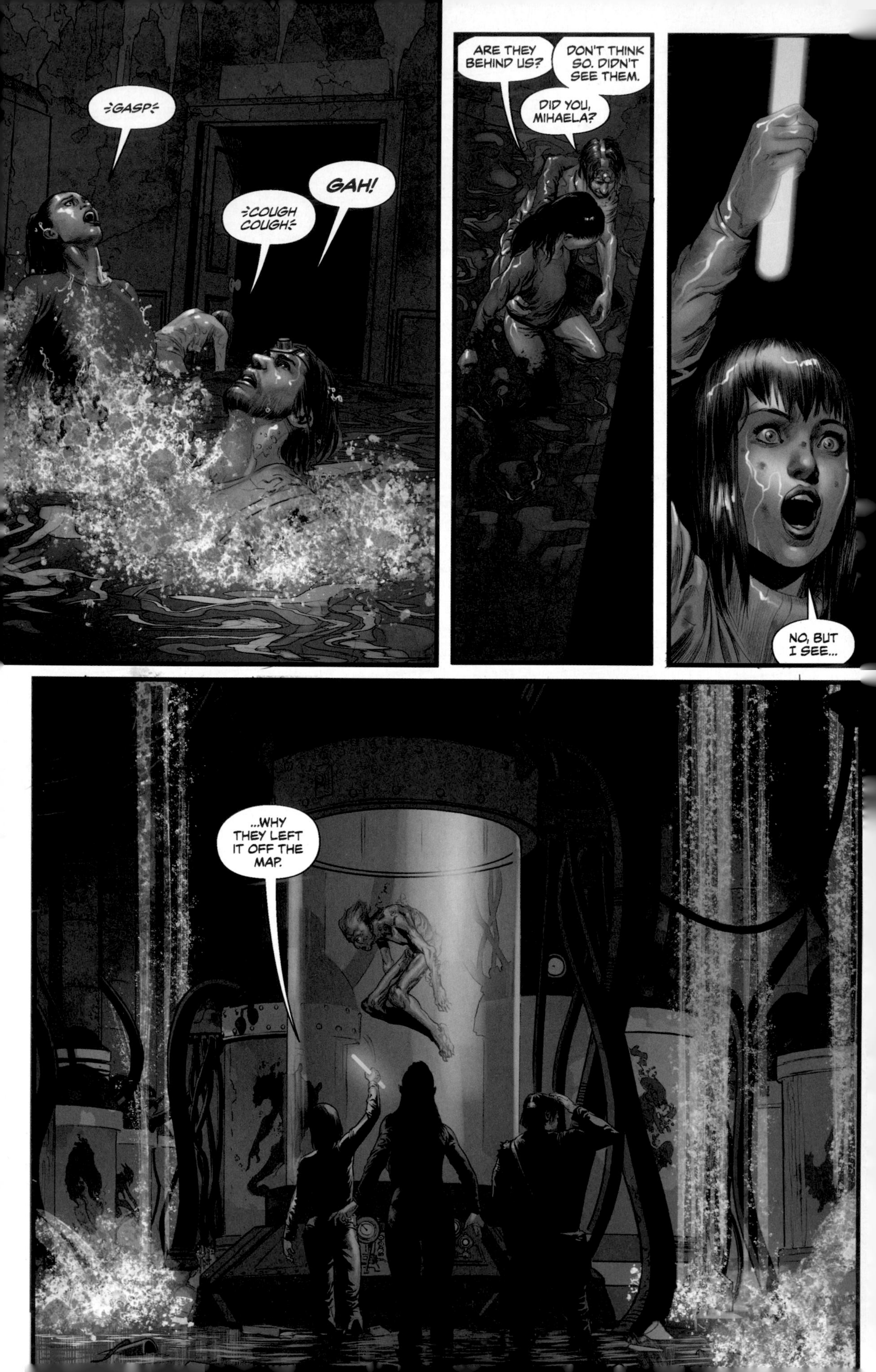

GASP
COUGH COUGH
GAH!
ARE THEY BEHIND US?
DON'T THINK SO. DIDN'T SEE THEM.
DID YOU, MIHAELA?
NO, BUT I SEE...
...WHY THEY LEFT IT OFF THE MAP.

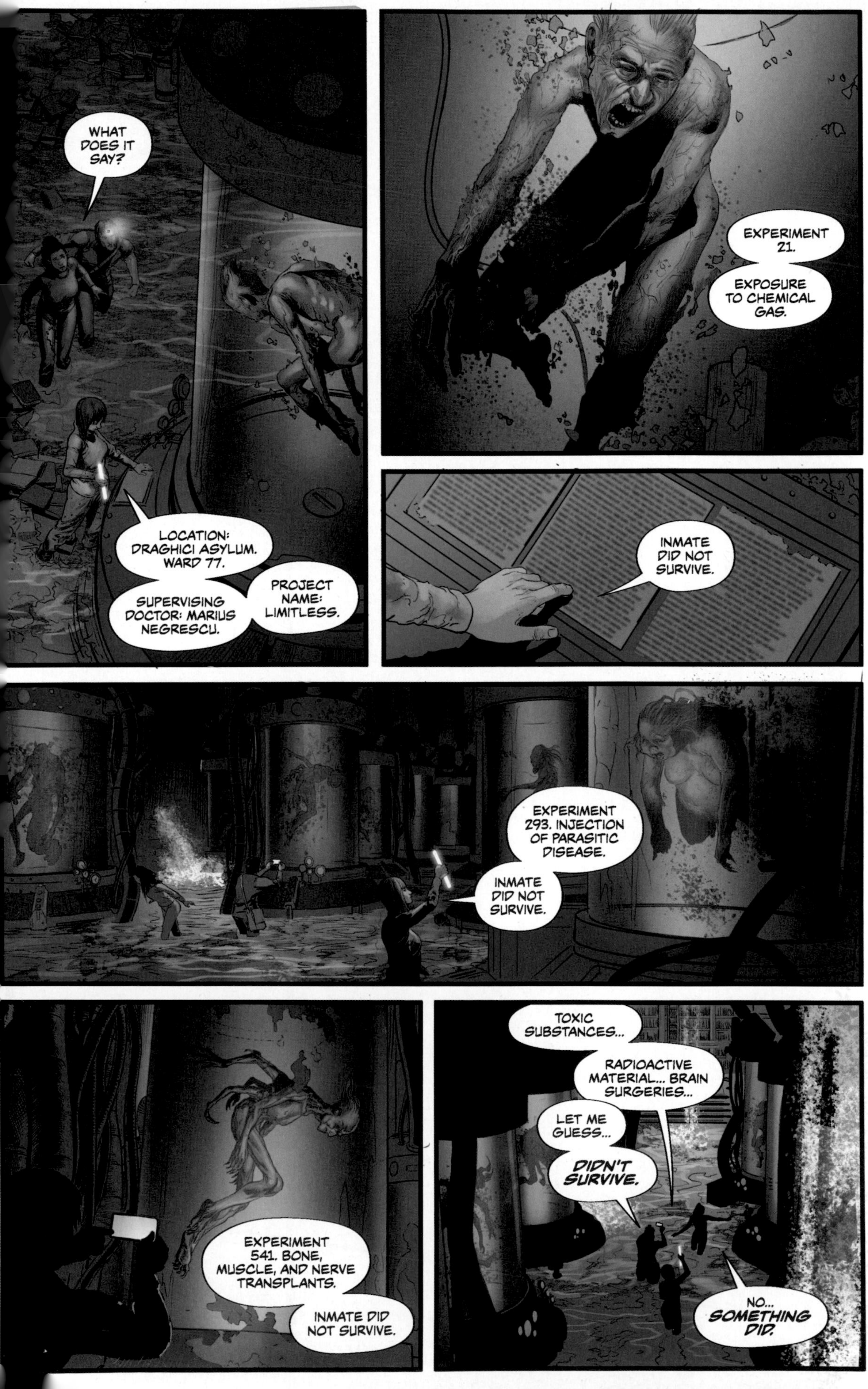
WHAT DOES IT SAY?
LOCATION: DRAGHICI ASYLUM. WARD 77.
SUPERVISING DOCTOR: MARIUS NEGRESCU.
PROJECT NAME: LIMITLESS.
EXPERIMENT 21.
EXPOSURE TO CHEMICAL GAS.
INMATE DID NOT SURVIVE.
EXPERIMENT 293. INJECTION OF PARASITIC DISEASE.
INMATE DID NOT SURVIVE.
EXPERIMENT 541. BONE, MUSCLE, AND NERVE TRANSPLANTS.
INMATE DID NOT SURVIVE.
TOXIC SUBSTANCES...
RADIOACTIVE MATERIAL... BRAIN SURGERIES...
LET ME GUESS...
DIDN'T SURVIVE.
NO... SOMETHING DID.

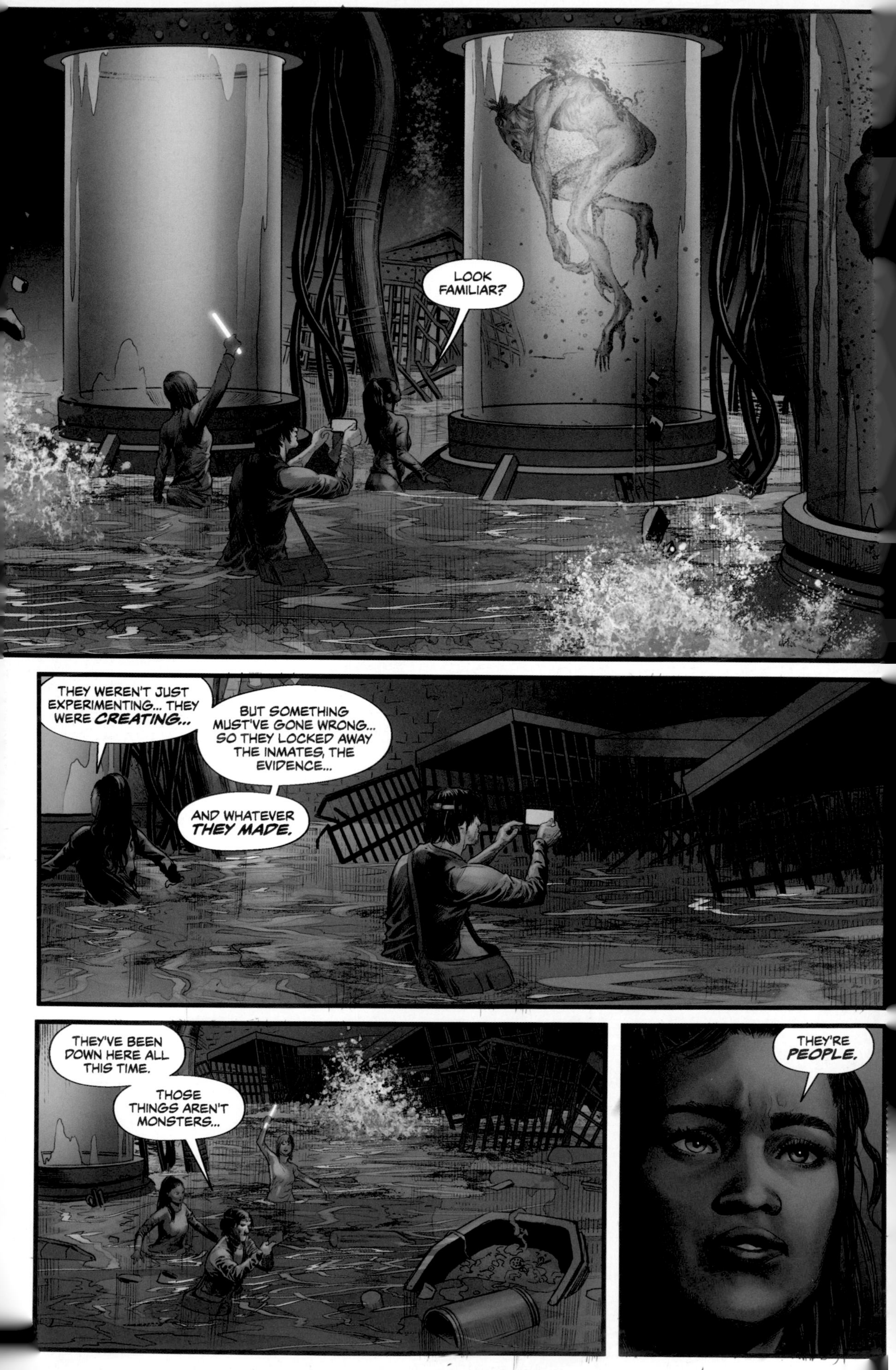
LOOK FAMILIAR?
THEY WEREN'T JUST EXPERIMENTING... THEY WERE CREATING...
BUT SOMETHING MUST'VE GONE WRONG... SO THEY LOCKED AWAY THE INMATES, THE EVIDENCE...
AND WHATEVER THEY MADE.
THEY'VE BEEN DOWN HERE ALL THIS TIME.
THOSE THINGS AREN'T MONSTERS...
THEY'RE PEOPLE.

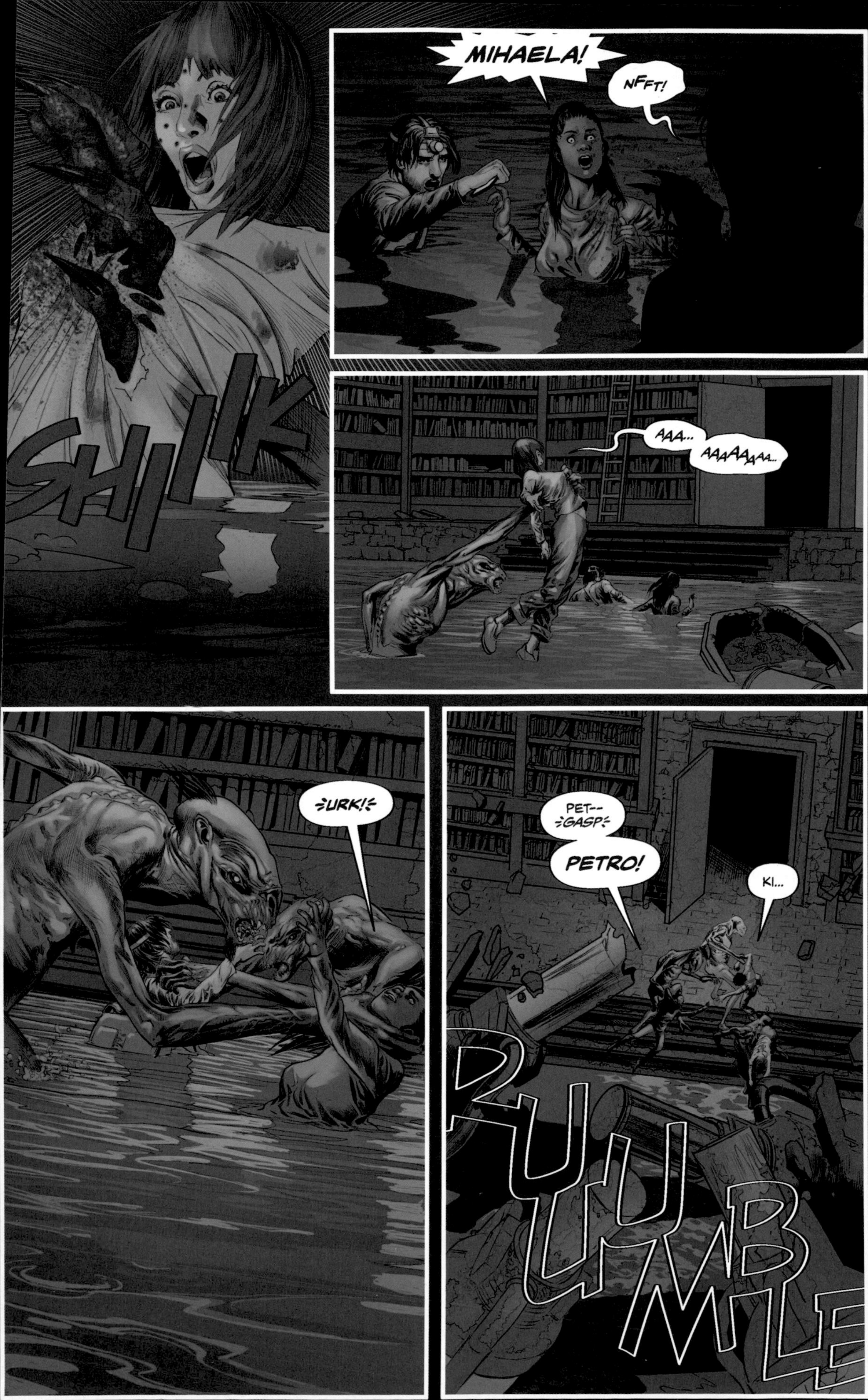
SHIIIK
MIHAELA!
NFFT!
AAA...
AAAAAAAA...
URK!
PET--
GASP
PETRO!
KI...
RUUUMBLE

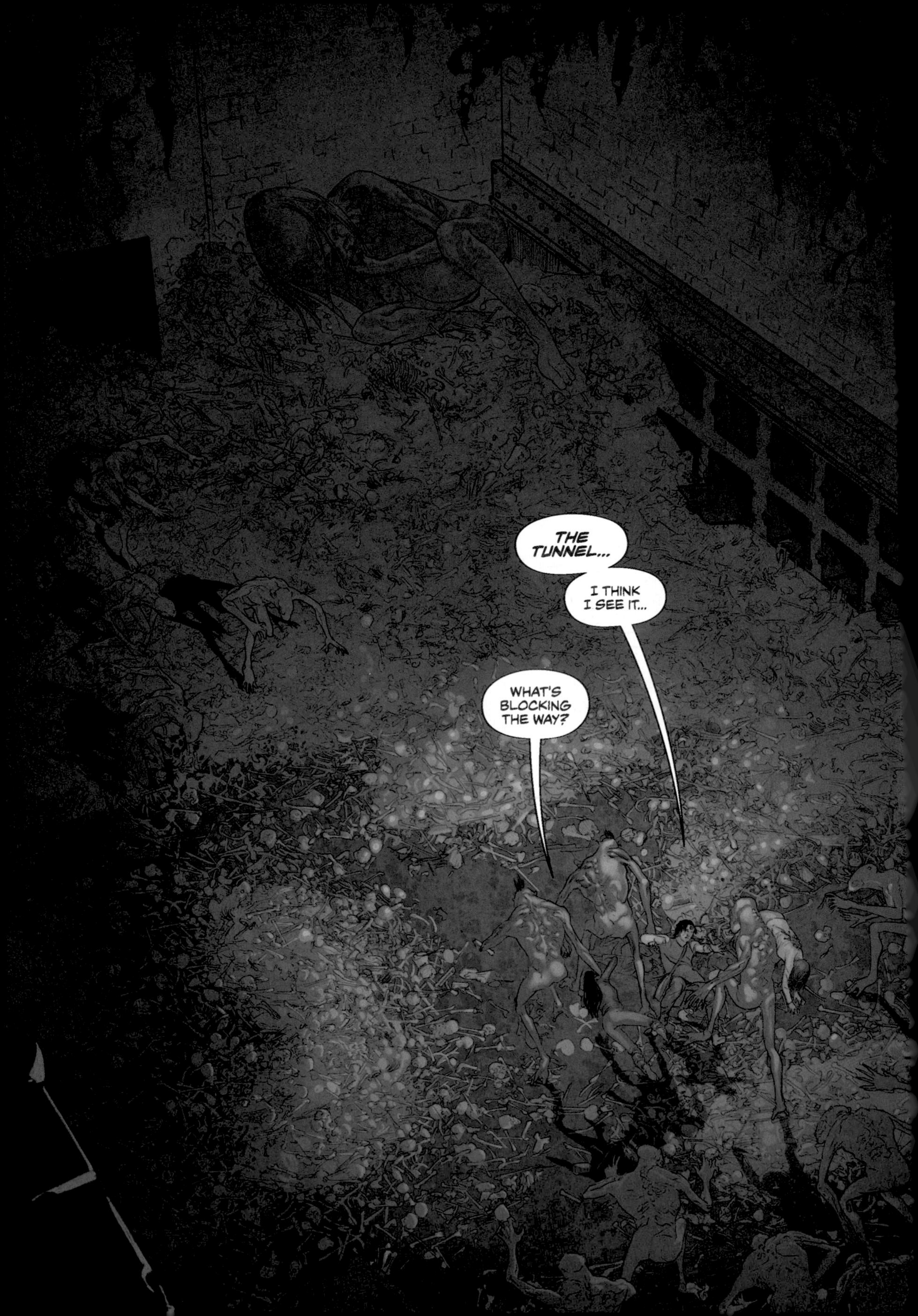
THE TUNNEL...
I THINK I SEE IT...
WHAT'S BLOCKING THE WAY?

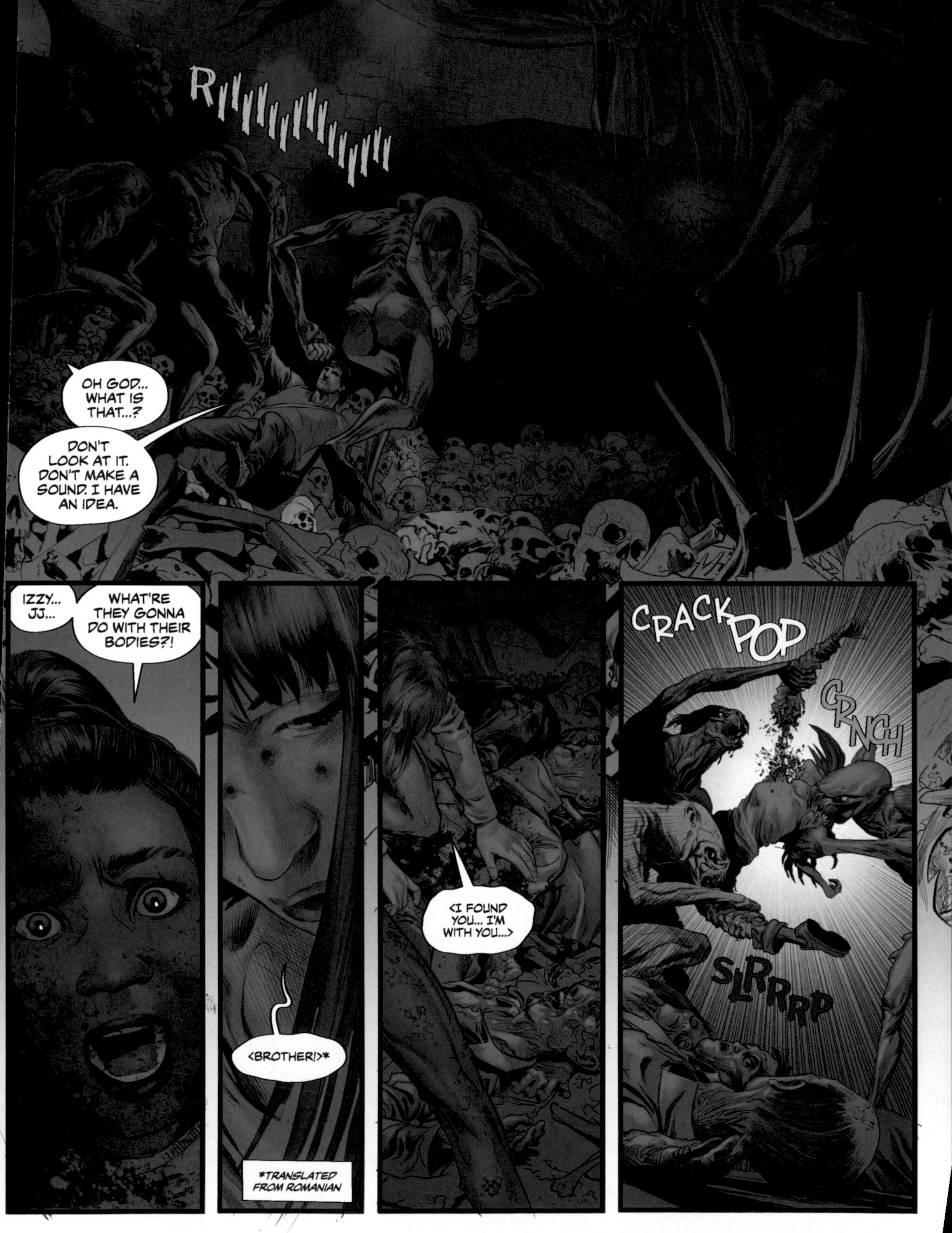
RIIIIIIIIIIIIIIII
OH GOD... WHAT IS THAT...?
DON'T LOOK AT IT. DON'T MAKE A SOUND. I HAVE AN IDEA.
IZZY... JJ...
WHAT'RE THEY GONNA DO WITH THEIR BODIES?!
<BROTHER!>*
*TRANSLATED FROM ROMANIAN
<I FOUND YOU... I'M WITH YOU...>
CRACK
POP
CRNCH
SLRRRP

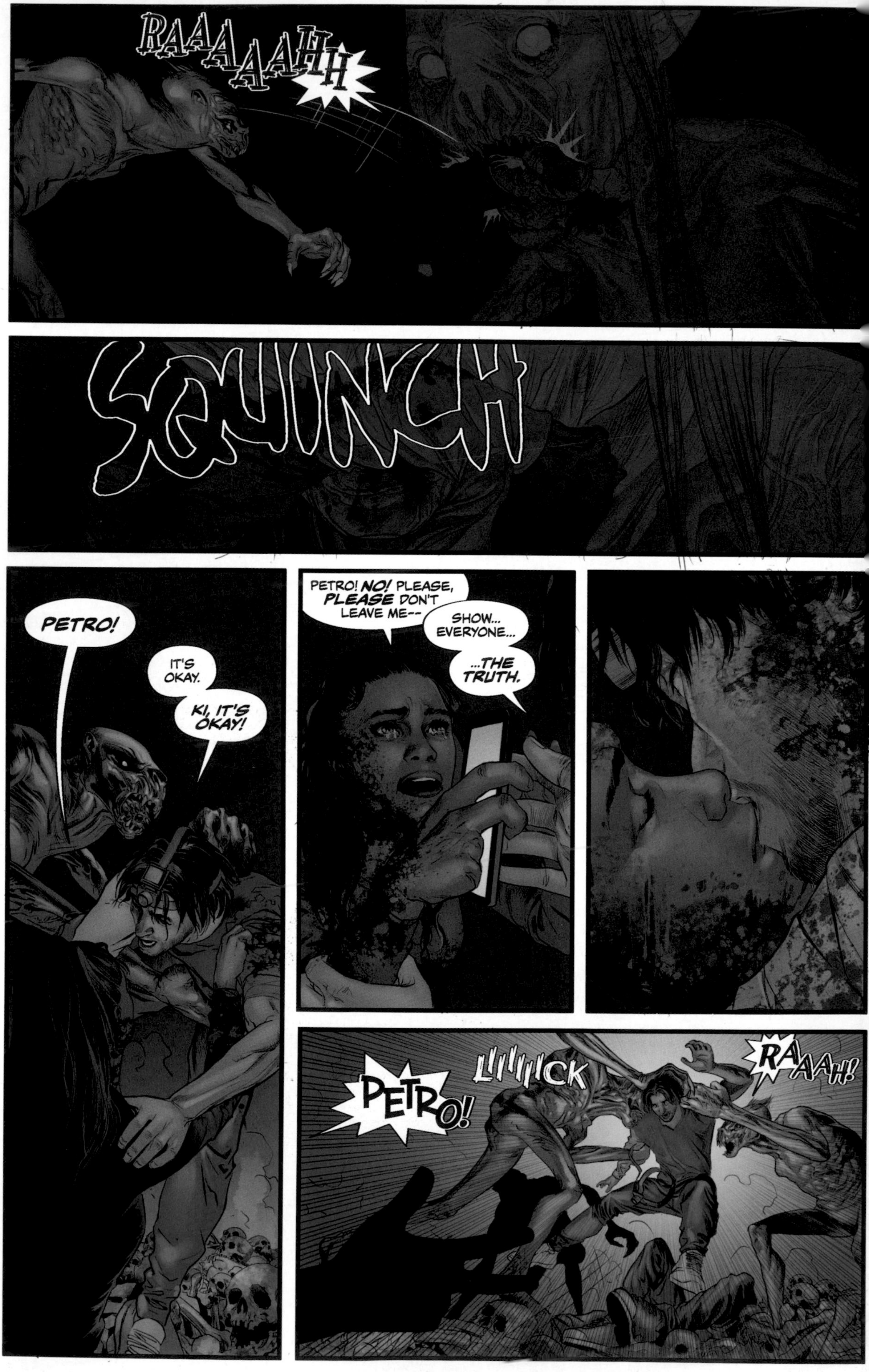
RAAAAAAHH
SQUINCH
PETRO!
IT'S OKAY.
KI, IT'S OKAY!
PETRO! NO! PLEASE, PLEASE DON'T LEAVE ME--
SHOW... EVERYONE...
...THE TRUTH.
PETRO!
LIIIIICK
RAAAH!

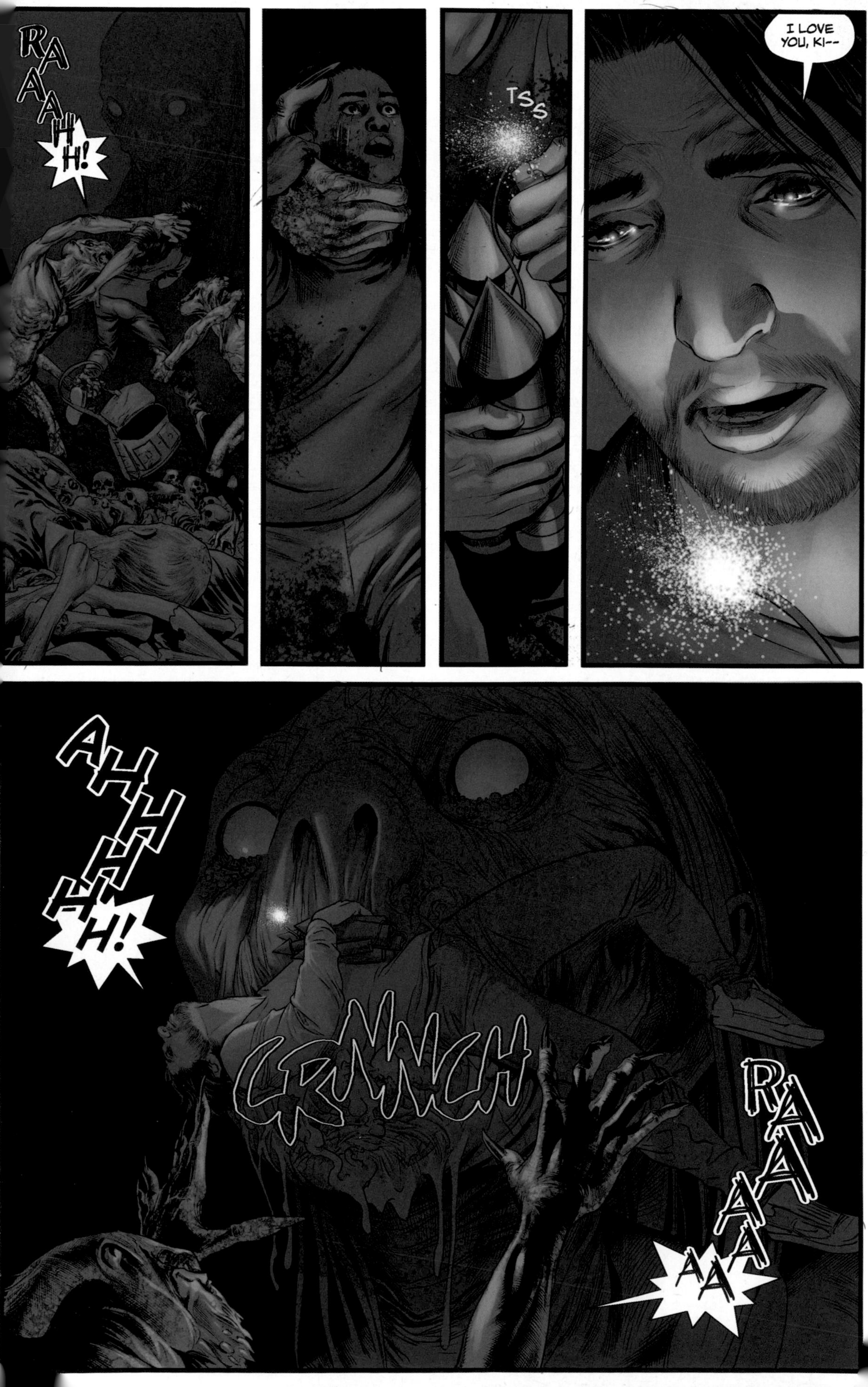
RAAAHH!
TSS
I LOVE YOU, KI--
AHHHHHH!
CRUNNCH
RAAAAAAA

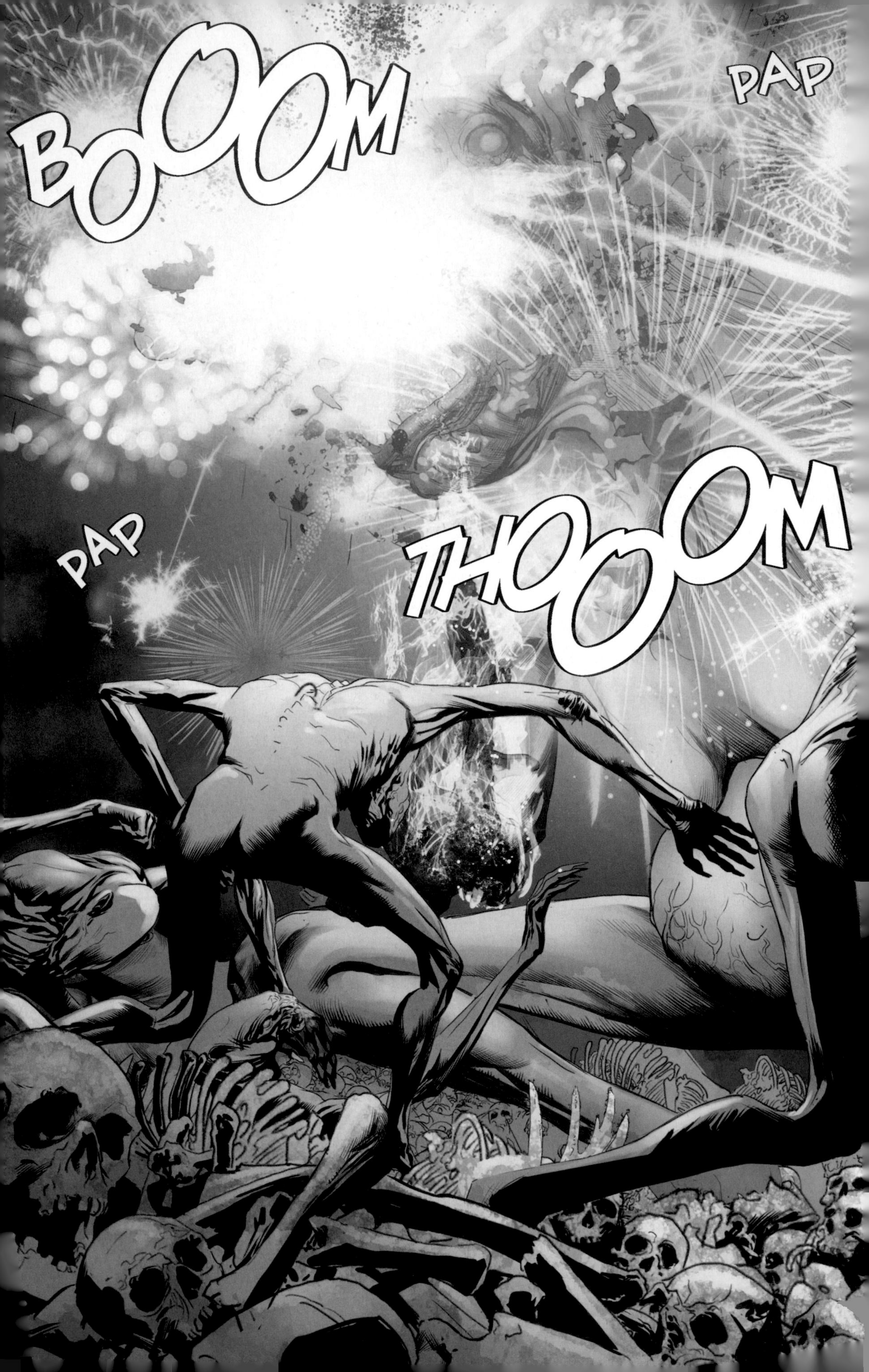
BOOOOM
PAP
PAP
THOOOOM

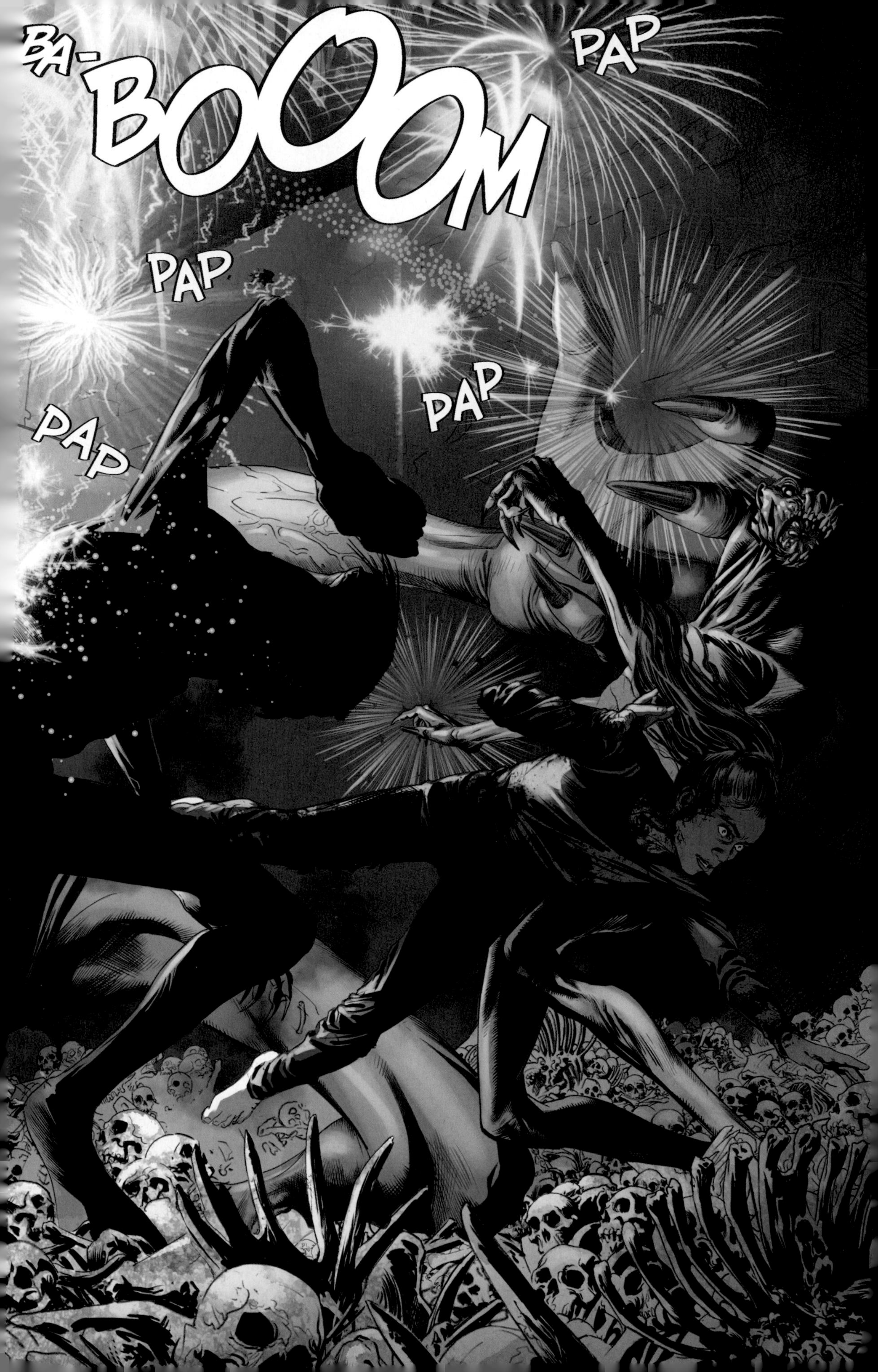
BA-BOOOOM
PAP
PAP
PAP
PAP

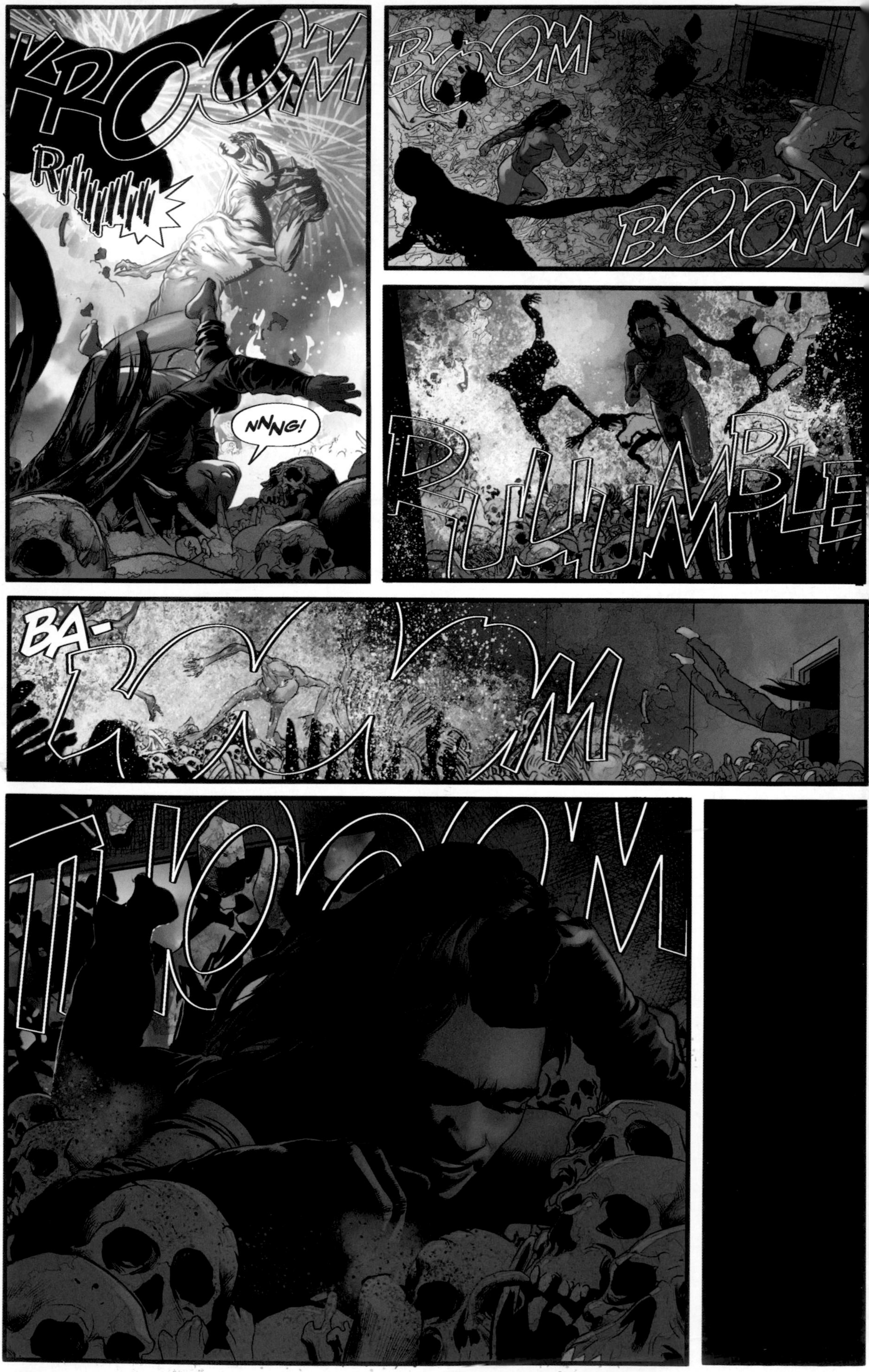
KROOM
RHHHH
NNNG!
BOOM
BOOM
RUUMBLE
BA-BOOM
THOOM

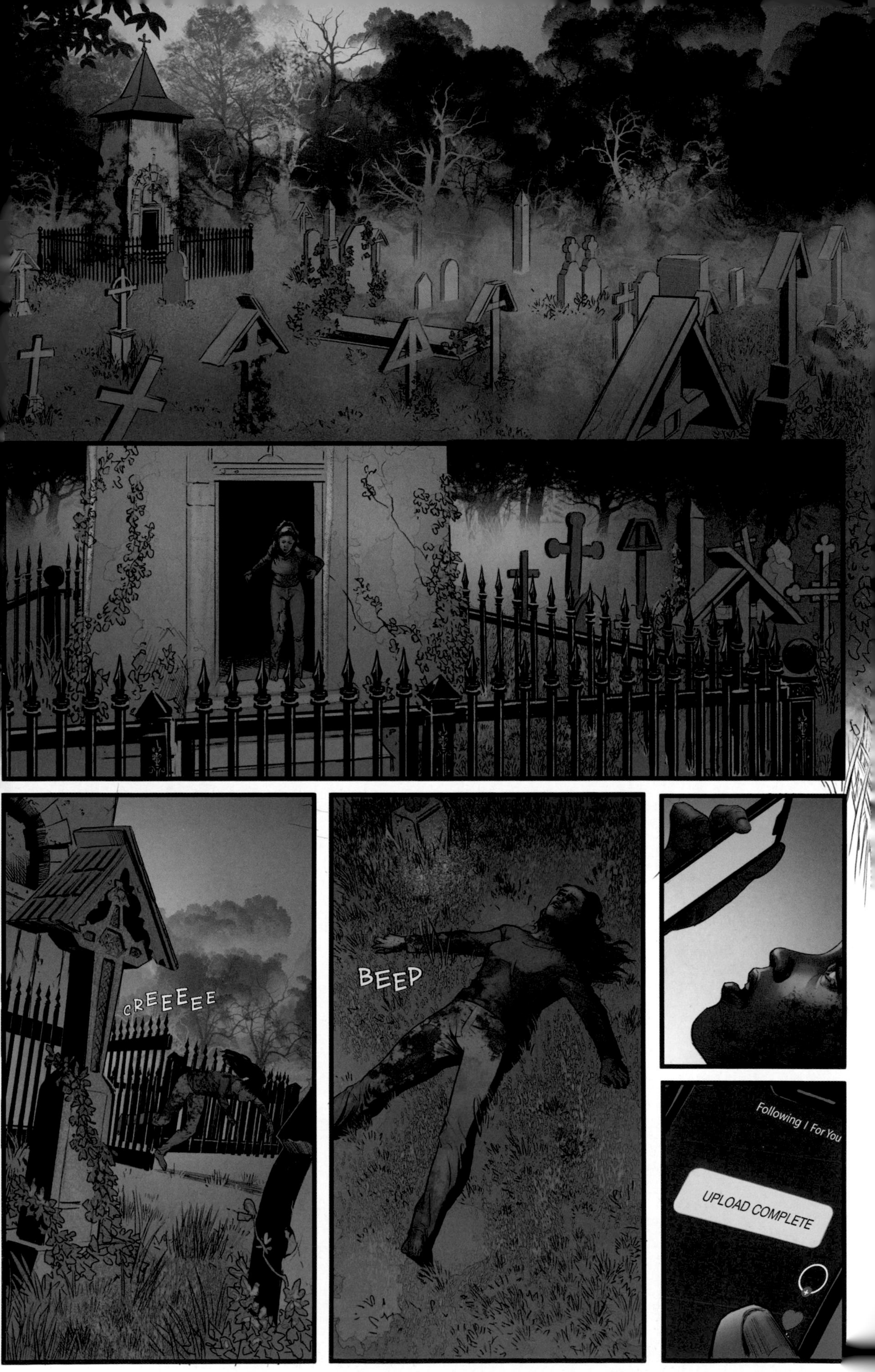
CREEEEEE
BEEP
Following | For You
UPLOAD COMPLETE

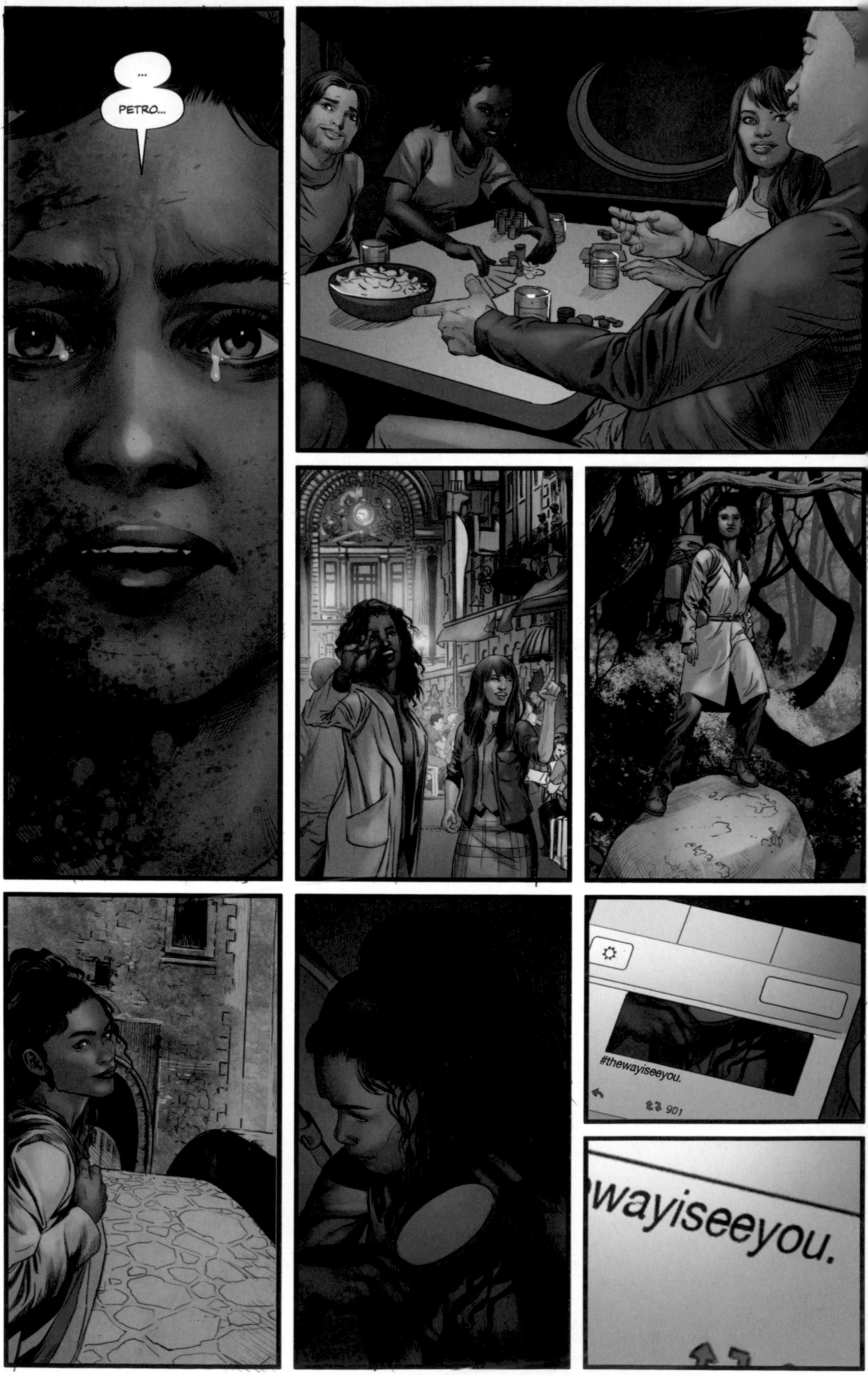
...
PETRO...
#thewayiseeyou.
901
wayiseeyou.

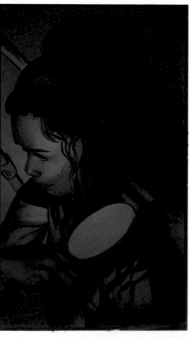

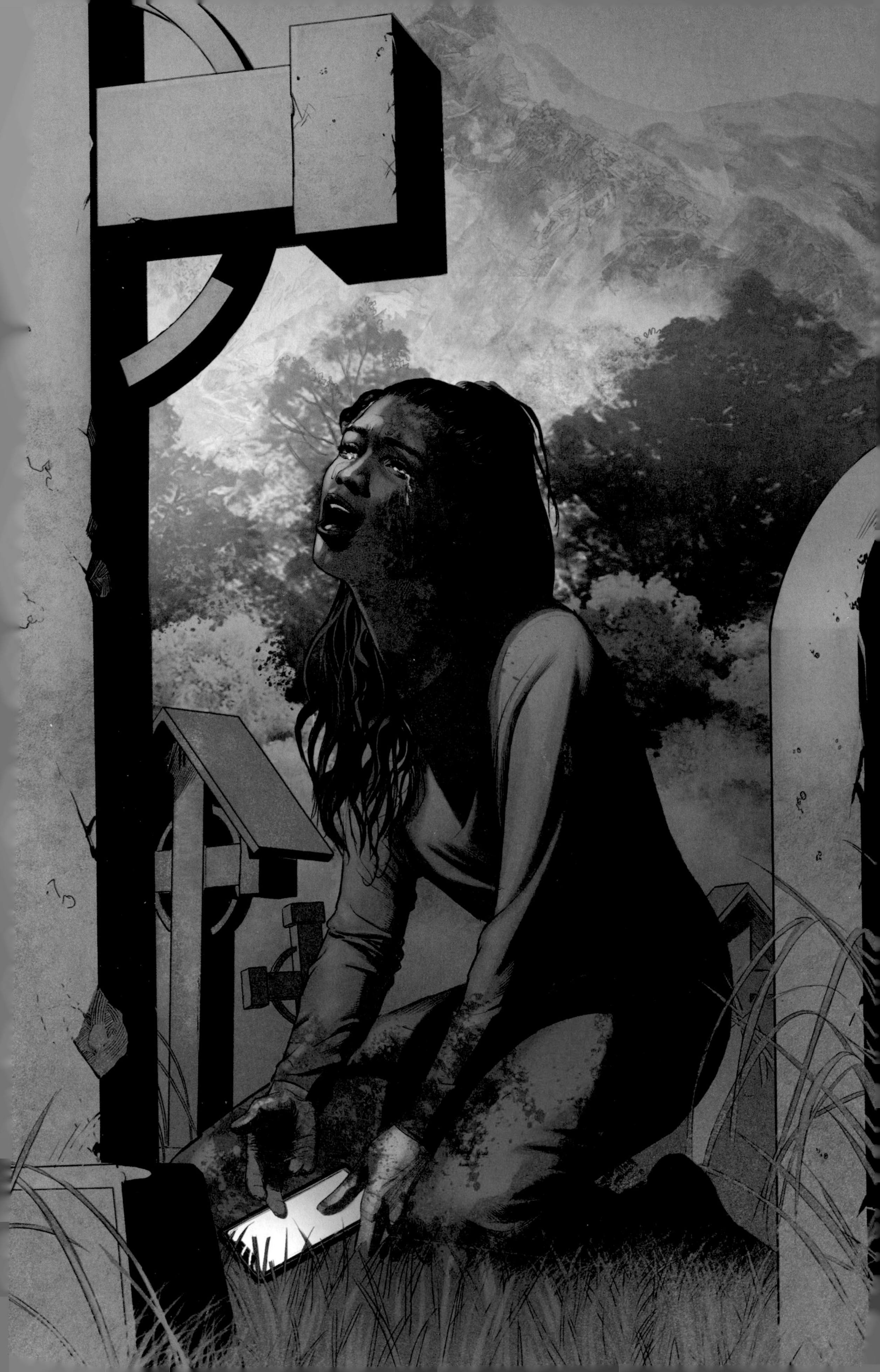

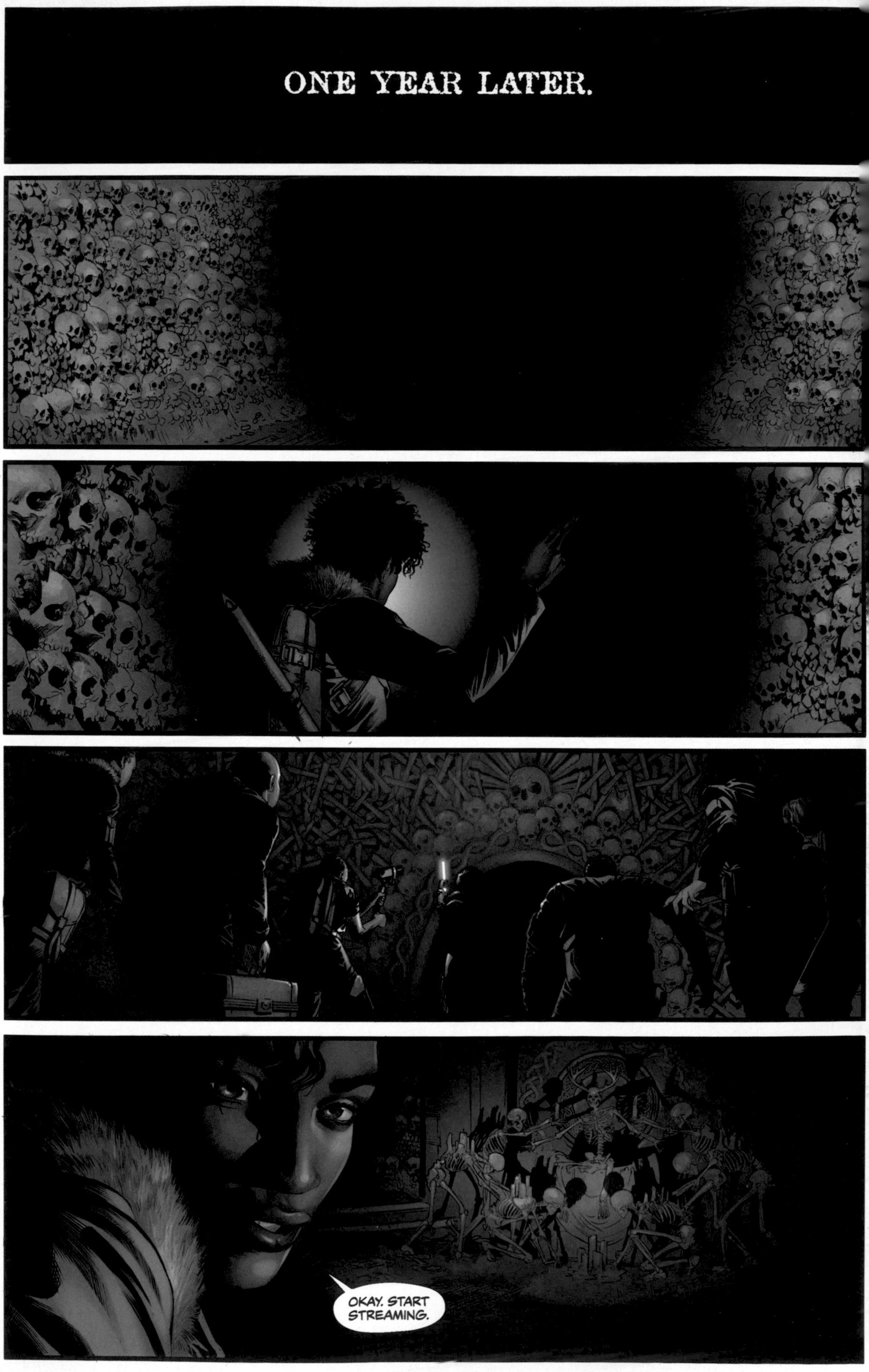
ONE YEAR LATER.
OKAY. START STREAMING.

These pages showcase the original character designs that artist Doug Wheatley did in order to lock in our characters' looks in *Creeping*.

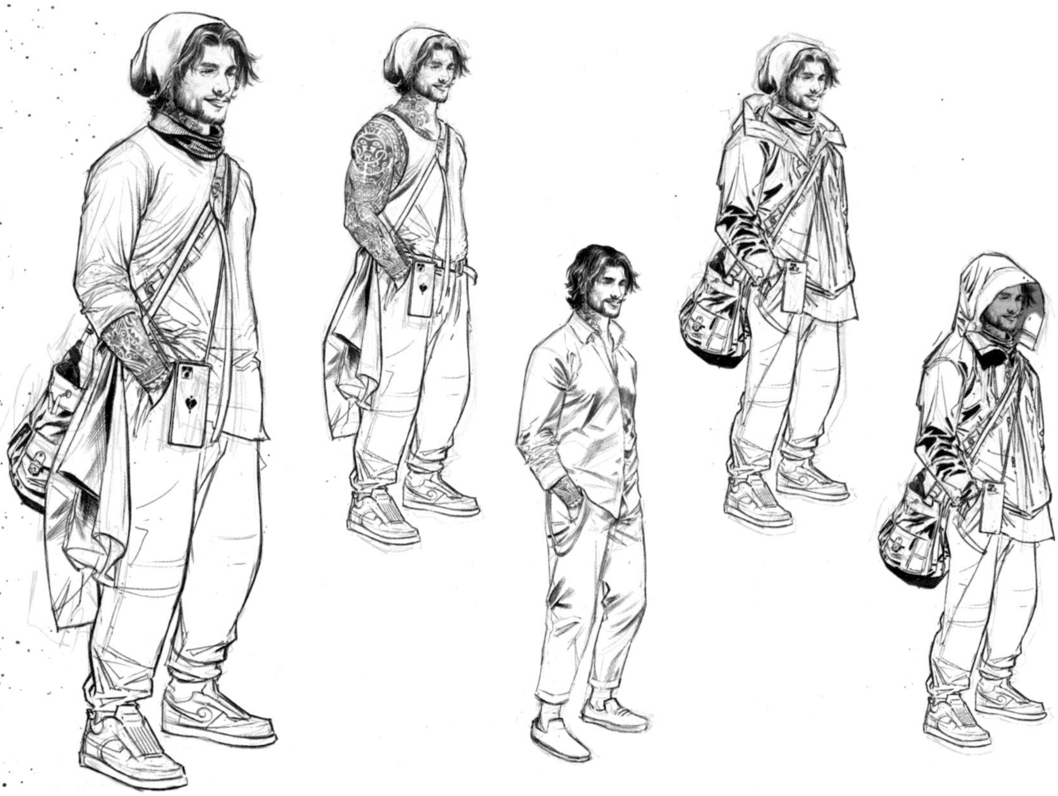

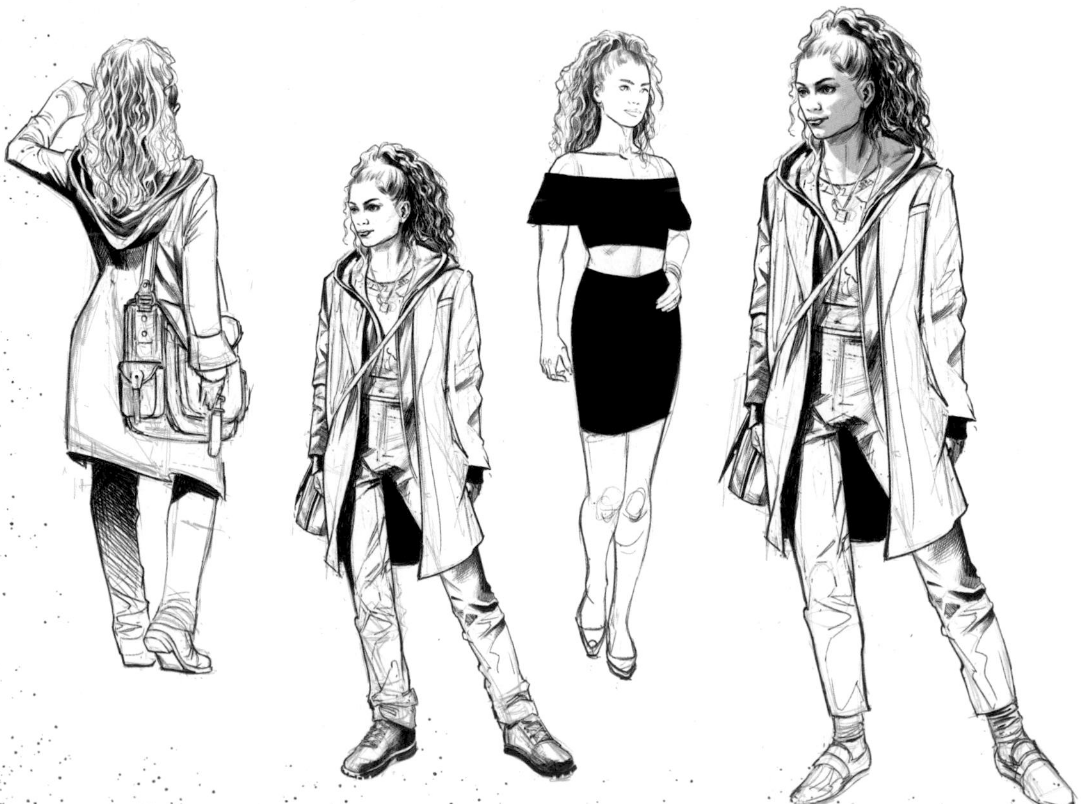

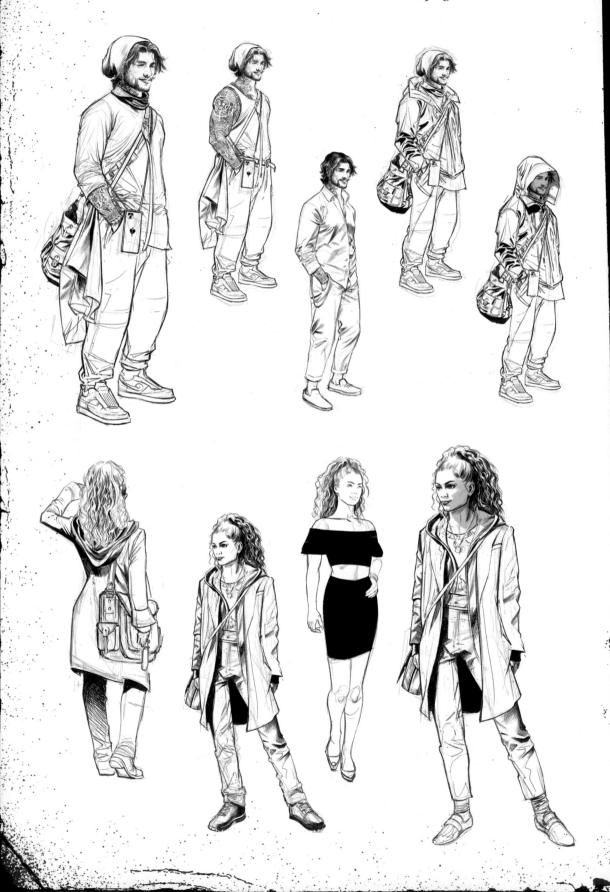

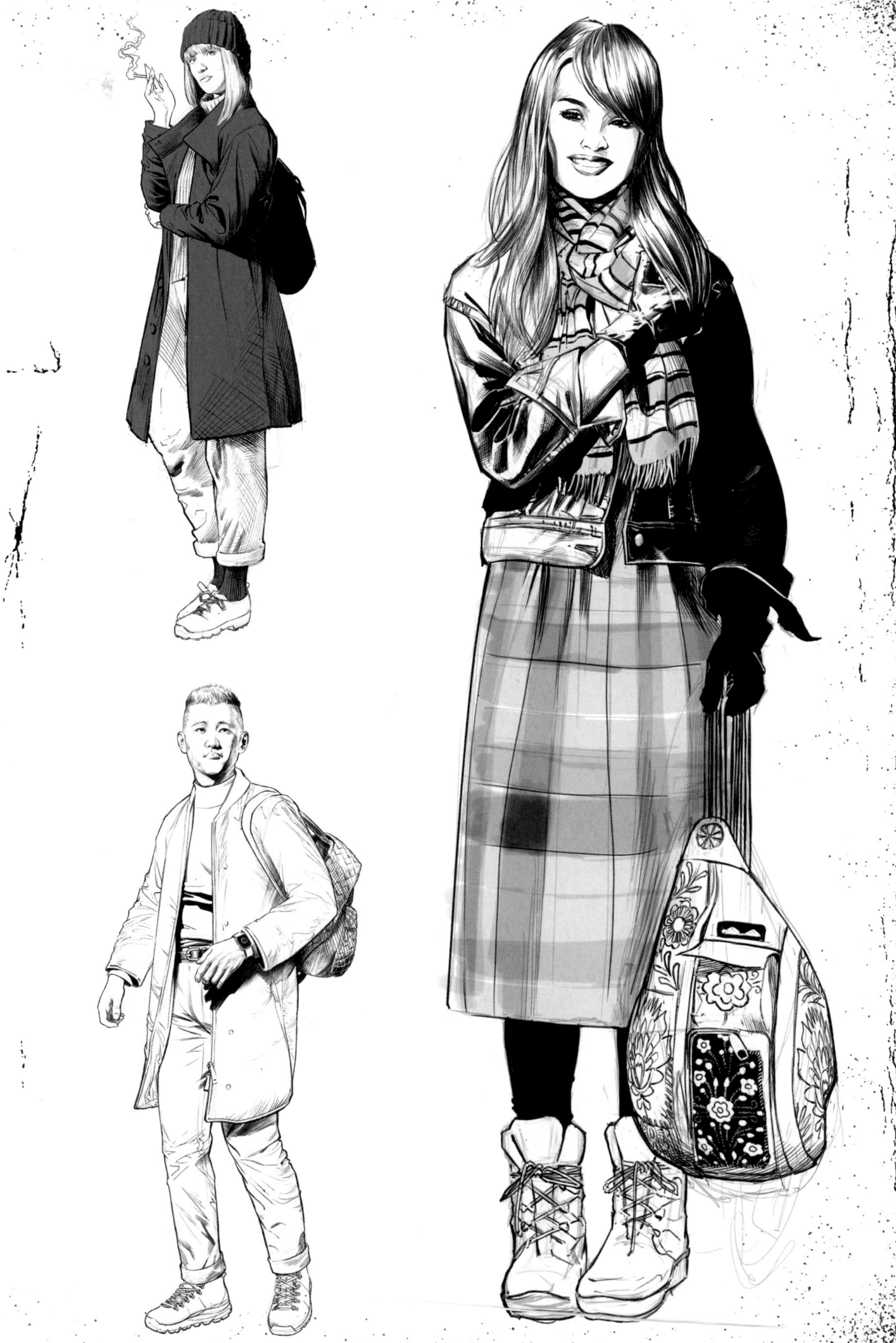

More titles from

MIKE RICHARDSON and Dark Horse . . .

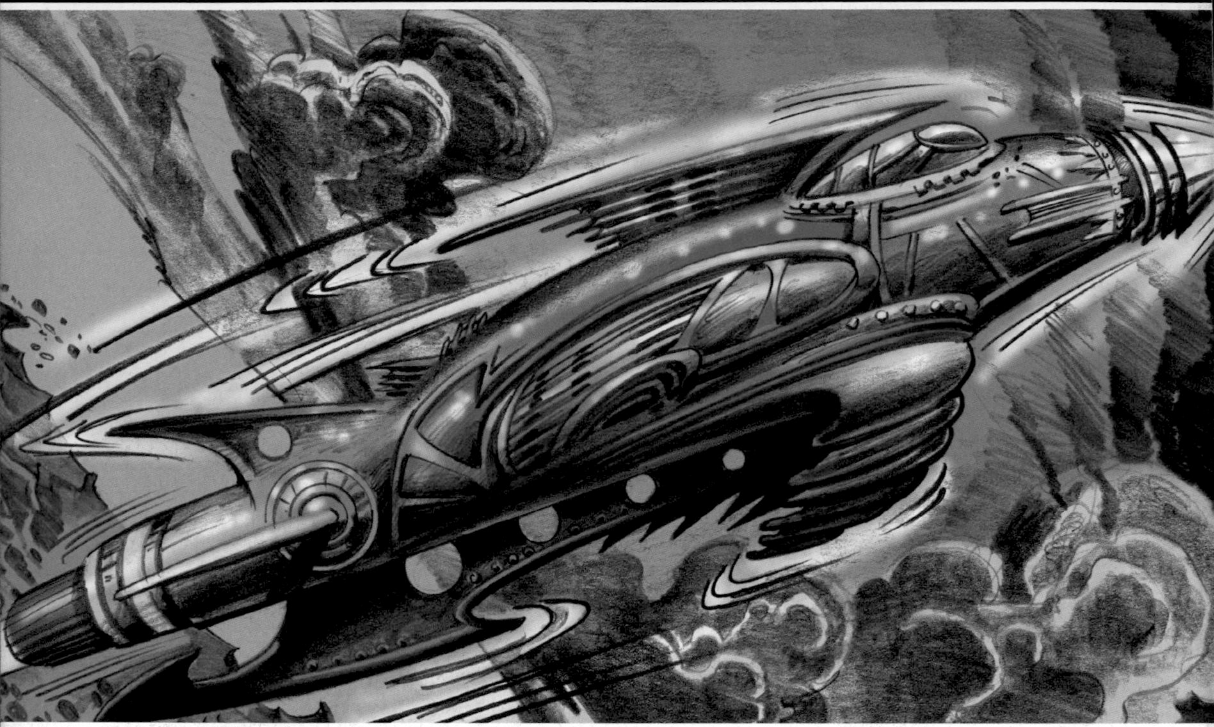

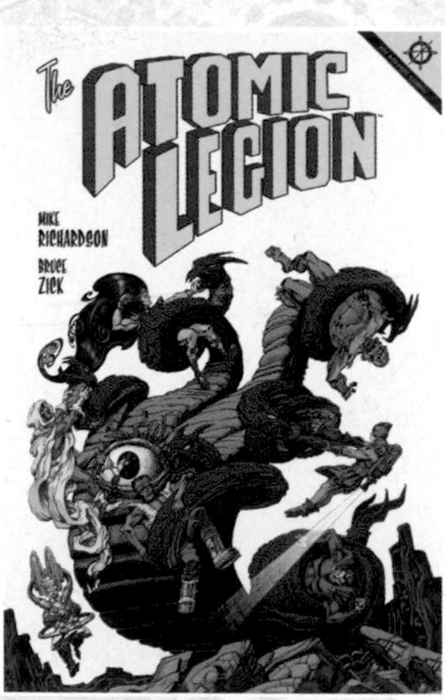

The ATOMIC LEGION
MIKE RICHARDSON
BRUCE ZICK

THE ATOMIC LEGION
With Bruce Zick
978-1-50671-782-8 | $19.99

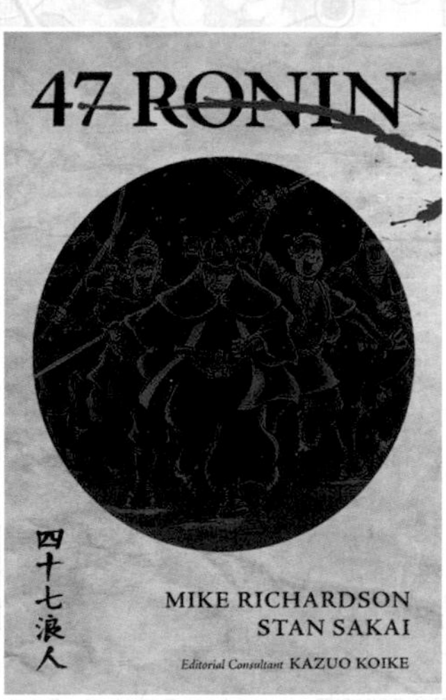

47 RONIN
四十七浪人
MIKE RICHARDSON
STAN SAKAI
Editorial Consultant KAZUO KOIKE

47 RONIN
With Stan Sakai
978-1-50671-799-9 | $19.99

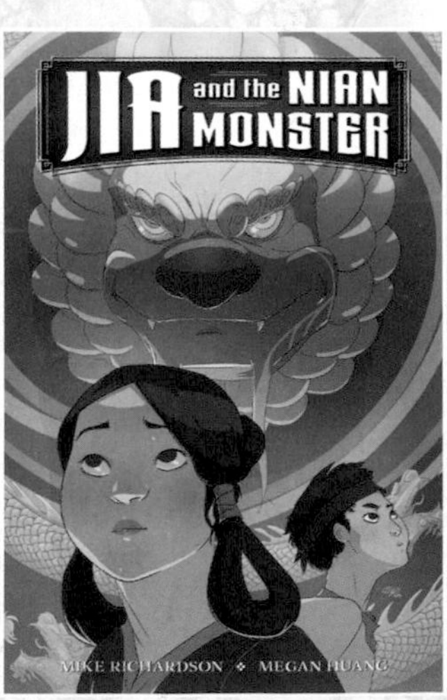

JIA and the NIAN MONSTER
MIKE RICHARDSON ◆ MEGAN HUANG

JIA AND THE NIAN MONSTER
With Megan Huang
978-1-50671-496-7 | $12.99

DARK HORSE BOOKS

AVAILABLE AT YOUR LOCAL COMICS SHOP OR BOOKSTORE!
To find a comics shop in your area, visit comicshoplocator.com.

For more information or to order direct, visit DarkHorse.com